THE CAT SITTER'S
NINE LIVES

This Large Print Book carries the
Seal of Approval of N.A.V.H.

A DIXIE HEMINGWAY MYSTERY

THE CAT SITTER'S NINE LIVES

BLAIZE AND JOHN CLEMENT

THORNDIKE PRESS

A part of Gale, Cengage Learning

GALE
CENGAGE Learning·

Farmington Hills, Mich • San Francisco • New York • Waterville, Maine
Meriden, Conn • Mason, Ohio • Chicago

GALE
CENGAGE Learning®

LIBRARY OF CONGRESS CATALOGING-IN-PUBLICATION DATA

Clement, Blaize.
  The cat sitter's nine lives / by Blaize and John Clement. — Large print edition.
    pages ; cm. — (Thorndike Press large print mystery) (A Dixie Hemingway mystery)
  ISBN 978-1-4104-7486-5 (hardcover) — ISBN 1-4104-7486-0 (hardcover)
  1. Hemingway, Dixie (Fictitious character)—Fiction. 2. Women detectives—Florida—Fiction. 3. Murder—Investigation—Fiction. 4. Large type books. I. Clement, John, 1962– II. Title.
PS3603.L463C38 2015
813'.6—dc23   2014038466

Published in 2015 by arrangement with St. Martin's Press, LLC

Printed in Mexico
1 2 3 4 5 6 7 19 18 17 16 15

For Mom

ACKNOWLEDGMENTS

As always, deepest thanks go to my superb editor, Marcia Markland, and everyone else at St. Martin's Press, including associate editor Kat Brzozowski, editorial assistant Quressa Robinson, and publicist Sarah Melnyk. Thanks also to my friends Dana Beck, Hellyn Sher, and Mike Harder for their priceless encouragement; to Detective Sergeant Chris Iorio and Lieutenant David Parisi of the Sarasota County Sheriff's Department for their expertise; to India Cooper for her extraordinary copyediting; to my agent, Al Zuckerman at Writer's House, for his guidance; to Ellen Thornwall and the real Cosmo, as well as author Elizabeth Hand and the real Mrs. Silverthorn for giving me good character names; and finally to David Urrutia, Zoe, and the rest of my family for their undying love and support.

Unable are the Loved to die
For Love is Immortality.
— Emily Dickinson

1

There are lots of good things about having a boyfriend — especially a new one. First of all, you get to do all those corny, young-love things that new couples have been doing since the dawn of time: hold hands on the beach, watch the sun set, make out like teenagers. Then there are the more practical advantages. For example, you get to mention how the trash needs to be taken out, and if you have a well-trained boyfriend, he'll take it out. You get to look in the mirror and mutter, "I look like warmed-over toast today," and he'll lavish you with compliments. If you have a *really* well trained boyfriend, you might even get a box of chocolates now and then (my own personal weakness). At the end of the day, a boyfriend is a very good thing.

But there's a downside.

Don't get me wrong, Ethan is as smart as a whip, 100 percent thoughtful, and devas-

11

tatingly, bewilderingly, *unrelentingly* hunky. But now that I have a boyfriend, I can't really sit around all afternoon eating Fritos and ice cream and watching old reruns of *Golden Girls*. Not that that's the sort of thing I do on a regular basis — at least not anymore. Ethan is under the impression that I'm the kind of girl who listens to hip music and reads the latest thought-provoking books in her spare time.

I'm not sure where he got that idea, but I have to try to live up to it as much as possible.

I'm Dixie Hemingway, no relation to you-know-who. I used to be a deputy with the Sarasota Sheriff's Department, until my whole world came crashing down around me and I quit the force, or to be accurate, the force quit me. I think the official words on my discharge report were "unfit for duty." Now I'm a professional pet sitter on Siesta Key, an eight-mile barrier island that sits just off the shore of Sarasota, Florida, in the Gulf of Mexico.

I've built a pretty good business for myself. Most of my clients are cats, but I have a few regular dogs, too, with an occasional bird or iguana, and even recently a giant tank full of priceless exotic fish. I draw the line at snakes, though. Some people think snakes make a real neat pet. Those people are crazy.

It was a little after 5:00 P.M. when I left my last client for the day and pulled my Bronco out onto Ocean Boulevard, heading south toward the center of town. My plan was to stop by Beezy's Bookstore on my way home and buy something impressive to read. Beezy's is the type of place where you can find the latest blockbuster novel right next to an old, dog-eared copy of *Gulliver's Travels,* complete with faded yellow highlighting and scribbled notes in the margins.

I was looking forward to it. I hadn't been there in years, but I was a regular customer when I was a little girl. I remember sitting in the aisle with my older brother, Michael, while our grandmother was shopping at the market across the street. I loved the feeling of being surrounded by all those dusty thoughts and dreams of writers from all over the world, all with their own story to tell. I distinctly remember the moment I realized I'd never live long enough to read every book in the world. I cried for days.

The northern end of Ocean Boulevard is mostly old houses and runs along a stretch of beach, but as you get closer to the center of town, all kinds of shops start popping up on both sides. Most people just assume the street was named for its breathtaking view of the Gulf of Mexico to the west, but in fact, the man who originally bought up all the land in this area named it after his wife, whose name just happened to be Ocean.

I was keeping an eye out for a parking spot when something in the rearview mirror caught my eye. It was an old, cherry red convertible sports car right behind me, flashing its headlights and weaving from side to side. The driver was a thin-faced man with expensive-looking sunglasses perched on top of his pale, balding head. He had that blank, set-in-stone expression that only a true . . . well, let's just say a true *jerk* can muster. He was revving his engine and drawing within inches of my back bumper, waving his hands in a frantic "Speed up!" gesture.

Now, I'm no angel. I've been known to drift outside of the traffic laws every once in a while. I even got pulled over once for going thirty miles per hour over the speed limit, which sounds bad enough except the speed limit was seventy. In my defense, I was twenty-one years old and dumb as a fruitcake, driving my own car for the first time in my life, not to mention I was the only car on the road for miles. I was midway along State Road 84, a sun-parched two-lane highway that cuts a straight horizontal swath right through the Florida Everglades. The only thing you have to worry about running into there (besides a cop with a speed gun) is the occasional alligator lumbering across the broiling asphalt.

But here we were in the middle of a beach town, not to mention in the middle of tourist season — shops and cafés on either side of the street, happy retirees on two-person bicycles ambling along on the shoulder, and kids skipping around with ice cream cones and listening to music on their iPods. I was already going about five miles per hour over the limit. There was no way I was speeding up just so some ember-head could get to his golf game two minutes earlier. I gently eased off the gas and slowed to the actual speed limit, which in town is only twenty-five.

I looked up in the mirror and saw the man smack his forehead in exasperation. His cheeks were beginning to turn a deep shade of plum. He leaned his head out over the striped lines in the road to see if he could pull around me. Normally, I'd stick to my guns and cruise along at exactly the posted limit just to teach him a lesson, but I was pretty sure he was about to make a run for it, and there was too much traffic to do it safely.

I decided to act like a grown-up — something I do every once in a while. I flicked on my turn signal and started to slow down, but before I'd even moved over to the side his tires screeched and he came peeling around my back bumper into the oncoming lane. I put my face in a perfect "You bald jackass" expression so he'd know exactly what I thought of his antics, but he didn't even give me the pleasure of shooting me a dirty look as he roared by. He just glanced at me with a blank expression on his face, all business, as if nothing were wrong.

I took a deep breath. Siesta Key is home to only about three thousand full-time residents, and thanks to our sugar-white sand and bathtub-warm waters, we have another three or four thousand part-timers on top of that, but it's a whole different story in the winter. That's when the snowbirds descend on our little paradise, and the population swells to about twenty-four thousand. While folks up north are shoveling snow and chipping ice off their windshields, we're sipping daiquiris out on the deck or watching dolphins frolic in the Gulf. On Christmas Day, you can find whole families headed down to the water to spread their presents out on beach blankets. The kids play in the surf with their new toys while Mom and Dad blissfully soak in the sun with a good book and a beer or two.

There are some snowbirds, though — like my friend here in the red convertible — who have a genuinely hard time smoothing out their feathers once they land. It's as if they haven't unpacked yet and they're dragging all their baggage around everywhere they go, full of unpaid bills, ungrateful children, looming deadlines, and mounting household chores. Not that I'm complaining. We love our snowbirds. They spend lots of money and keep us all employed and happy. Plus, they flock here from all over the world, so it gives our little town a bit of cosmopolitan cachet.

I pulled back out on the road and told myself that once ol' Baldy McGrumpypants had spent a few more days here, he'd settle down and all that pent-up anger and anxiety would melt away. He'd eventually nestle in and be just as happy and serene as the rest of us. At least, that's what I hoped.

Not more than a minute later I had a sneaky feeling something wasn't quite right. I'd been keeping an eye out for the bookstore, so I'd looked away from the road for a second, and when I looked back, coming at me like a speeding meteor was the back end of an old black Cadillac, its fin-shaped taillights glowing bright red.

I slammed on the brakes as hard as I could and heard a gut-wrenching squeal as I felt the Bronco veer slightly off kilter. I'm not completely sure, but I think at least three or four key scenes from my life flashed before my eyes as I slid to a grinding stop, just inches from the Cadillac's rear bumper.

I looked down at my hands. They were gripping the steering wheel so tightly that my knuckles had turned chalk white, and I could literally hear my heart beating in my chest. In front of the Cadillac was a pileup of at least three more cars, and in the oncoming lane farther down was a disabled landscaping truck with a red front grille and three steeple-high palm trees swaying in the breeze in the back.

I let out a sigh of relief, which turned out to be a little premature. I glanced up, and sure enough there in the rearview mirror was a bright pink Volkswagen Beetle speeding straight for the back of my car. I had just enough time to see a young woman behind the wheel, absentmindedly twirling her long blond curls in one hand and holding a cell phone to her ear with the other. As I slammed my open palm down on the horn to get her attention, the thought flashed across my mind that she could only have been operating the steering wheel with her knees. I thought to myself, *If we live through this, I'm going to kill that little bitch.*

I closed my eyes and prepared for impact, but the woman must have looked up and hit the brakes at the last moment, because I heard what sounded like a pack of howler monkeys and then when she did hit me, the Bronco lurched forward only a foot or so, bumping into the Cadillac in front of me with a loud *clank*!

I opened my eyes and looked around. Everything seemed to be in one piece. Then I looked up in the rearview mirror, primarily to see if the woman was in good enough shape for a sound beating, and all I could see was a mass of blond curls spread out over her dashboard. Without even thinking I jumped out of the car and ran back as fast as my legs would carry me.

As I approached the car I could see her through the windshield. She was wearing a black and white striped tank top and a green barrette in her hair. Her head was lying completely still on the steering wheel, and her left arm was hanging listlessly at her side. As I approached the driver's-side door, I took a deep breath and prepared myself for the worst, and just as I reached out to try the door handle she jolted her head up, eyes wide with alarm. She rolled down the window halfway, and that's when I realized she was still cradling the phone to her ear.

"I have to go," she said into the phone. "I just hit somebody."

She flicked the phone closed and dropped it down into the cup holder next to the seat and stared straight ahead. I reached out and put one hand on the hood of her car to steady myself. "Umm, are you okay?"

She looked up at the mirror in her sun visor and blinked her eyes a couple of times, like she was checking her makeup. "Yeah, I think so."

I thought to myself, *Now is the time to strangle this woman to death.* Just then she looked at me, pulled her curly locks away from her face, and said, "Are *you*?"

She was much younger than I'd thought, probably not a day older than the legal driving age, which in Florida is eighteen. Her eyes started to well with tears.

I sighed. "Yeah, I'm fine. Why don't you put that phone to good use and call 911."

She touched a finger to her lip. "You're bleeding."

"Huh?"

"Your lip is bleeding."

I looked at my reflection in the backseat window. She was right. My lower lip was bleeding, but not badly, just smudged with a bit of red, as if I'd been interrupted in the middle of putting on lipstick. "I must have bit my lip when you hit me."

Handing me a tissue, she said, "I am so sorry. I was talking on my phone and I guess I just got distracted."

"That's alright," I said, dabbing at my lip. "I used to be young and stupid, too. Just call 911. I'm gonna go up and see what happened."

But I already knew what had happened: Baldy McGrumpypants. He'd probably been weaving in and out of traffic and caused an accident. I tried to stay positive, but with so many cars and people around, it was hard not to think someone could've been hurt. As I headed up I glanced at my rear bumper to assess the damage.

My Bronco is pale yellow, like homemade lemon ice cream, so it shows even the slightest nick or speck of dirt, but there was hardly a scratch, just a couple of dime-sized dents on the chrome guard. The girl's front fender was slightly concussed, but nothing a good body shop couldn't hammer back into shape in a couple of minutes.

"Ma'am?"

I looked back at the girl, who was already on the phone with 911. She was leaning her head out the window. I hate it when teen-aged girls call me ma'am. She said, "What street is this?"

If she hadn't looked so serious I would have thought she was joking. "It's Ocean Boulevard."

She gave me a quick thumbs-up and then got back on the phone, gesticulating wildly with her hands. I could tell she was describing the accident to the emergency dispatcher.

Okay, I thought to myself, *maybe I was never* that *young and stupid,* but I had to smile. She was just a kid, and she was lucky. We both were. Except for a bloody lip and a few tears, we'd both come out smelling like roses. I had a terrible feeling not everyone up ahead had been quite so fortunate.

I reached into the Bronco and switched off the ignition. At first I thought I'd better grab my backpack in case there were any serious injuries to contend with. I keep it stocked with all kinds of supplies for pet emergencies: scissors, bandages, rubbing alcohol, cotton balls, a pocketknife, etc. Then I told myself I was probably overreacting. I tend to have a pretty healthy imagination. Plus, every once in a while my old cop training comes bubbling up to the surface and I have to remind myself that it's no longer my job to protect the public welfare.

I took the backpack anyway, slinging it over my shoulder as I dropped my car keys down in the hip pocket of my cargo shorts and headed toward the front of the pileup. There was a burly man with short-cropped black hair in a blue business suit standing next to the black Cadillac in front of me. He was holding a monogrammed handkerchief to his forehead and talking to an elderly woman who was sitting at the driver's wheel.

As I got closer I heard the man say to her, "No, I'm not a cop. I said the cops are probably on their way."

The woman wore what looked like a man's overcoat over a white dress, with a white hat sitting atop her perfectly coiffed hair, with that wiglike, hair-sprayed look they give you at the beauty shop, and her makeup looked like it had been applied with a child's hand — lips smeared beet red and powdery pink cheeks. She wore a lavender scarf wrapped tightly around her neck and tied in a bow at her throat, with white gloves stretched tautly over her hands.

I said, "Are you folks okay?"

I heard the woman mutter under her breath in a smoker's growl, *Bastard!*"

The burly man smiled at me as he pulled

the bloody handkerchief away from his brow. There was a scratch about an inch long in the middle of his forehead. He pointed at the baby blue BMW in front of the Cadillac. "That BMW's mine. I hit the car in front of me, and this nice lady hit me, but we're all fine. I can't say the same thing for those guys up there, though."

As he said "this nice lady," he rolled his eyes, but my attention was already focused up ahead, where a small crowd of people was forming around the green landscaping truck. There was a plume of white smoke rising up from its front grille, which was painted bright red.

The man said, "I just called 911. It ain't pretty."

That was when I realized — the smoke wasn't coming from the truck, and the truck's front grille wasn't red. What I was looking at was the cherry red convertible that had been tailgating me, only now it was folded around the front of the landscaping truck like a piece of shiny red wrapping foil. That bald idiot must have been trying to speed around someone again and had pulled into the northbound lane and plowed into the landscaping truck head-on. It would be a miracle if he was still alive.

I ran up as fast as I could, and sure

enough, there was Baldy, slumped over the air bag in a haze of smoke and fumes in the passenger seat, which was a good thing since the driver's side was so crumpled the whole thing barely looked like a car anymore, just a triangular mess of red metal — like a giant slice of steaming pizza. Strewn all over the ground like pieces of mushroom and bits of pepperoni were hundreds of shards of glass and little strips of black plastic.

The man's bald head was shiny with blood, but to my utter surprise his eyes were open and looking right at me. He must have somehow managed to extricate himself from the driver's seat and climb over to the passenger side, or else he hadn't been wearing a seat belt and the impact had tossed him right out of harm's way. I noted that his expensive-looking sunglasses were nowhere in sight. I tried to open the passenger door, but it was stuck, and now there was more smoke pouring out from under the dashboard and a thick, syrupy smell in the air. I could hear the familiar wail of a siren approaching not very far away, but I knew there wasn't a moment to waste.

My heart started racing like a jackhammer. I reached in and laid my hand gently on his shoulder. "Sir, my name is Dixie. I'm going to get you out of this car, okay?"

He didn't move. I wondered if he even understood what I was saying, and yet he didn't take his eyes off me.

He said, "I am not dead?"

"No, sir. No, you're not dead, but I need to get you somewhere safe."

His eyes narrowed and he smiled, almost like he'd just thought of a funny joke, and then he nodded slightly, as if considering the punchline, and said, "Safe . . ."

I wasn't sure what he could possibly think was so funny at that moment, but I hoped it was a good sign as I considered my options. Normally it's a pretty good idea to leave an accident victim completely still until paramedics arrive — moving someone with broken bones or spinal damage can cause irreparable harm — but the smoke from the car was getting heavier, and I could feel heat rising from behind the dashboard. This car was about to go up in flames, and this man needed help.

I braced myself for a fight as I hooked my arms under his shoulders. Sometimes people in accidents can go into a state of shock and resist being handled. It's like some deeply rooted, ancient survival instinct kicks in, and they'll fight tooth and nail before they'll let strangers touch them no matter how bad off they are. Luckily, Baldy

26

didn't look the least bit fazed by the idea of being moved. In fact, the expression on his face was eerily peaceful.

Just then the burly man in the blue suit appeared behind me. He pointed at the smoke and said, "Uh, lady, I think you better get away from that car."

I looked back at him and blew a strand of hair away from my face. "Ya think?"

I could hear creaking coming from deep inside the car as I tried to pull Baldy up enough to hook my right arm under his legs, but he was deadweight. I could barely lift him.

"Aw, goddammit." The burly man whipped off his jacket and slipped in next to me. "I'll get this half and you get his legs."

I shuffled over as he reached in and locked his arms around Baldy's chest, and just then there was a loud *pop* followed by an angry hiss from somewhere under the hood. I glanced over at the dashboard and gasped — there were black blisters starting to bubble up in the center. The burly man flashed me a look as if to say, "Ready?" and I nodded.

He said, "One, two, three . . ." and then in one swift motion we heaved Baldy up out of the car. He let out a low moan, and I felt a shiver go down my spine — I couldn't even imagine the pain he must have been in.

As we moved away from the car it jolted backward spastically off the grille of the truck, and then a high-pitched scream started from deep inside the engine. I heard a little voice in my head say, *It's too late,* and I had a vision of us all flying through the air in a ball of fire and glass and twisted metal.

Someone yelled "Run!" — for all I know it could have been me — and then we were racing with Baldy in our arms as fast as we could through the crowd of gawkers who were running, too, pushing their way past us. The screaming sound was getting louder and louder, and by the time we got beyond the row of cars parked along the sidewalk it sounded like a steam whistle going off inside my head. We got Baldy down on the sidewalk as fast as we could, and then without even thinking my old training kicked in. I covered his body with mine, clenched my eyes shut, and waited.

The explosion shook the entire street.

The high-pitched screaming was gone now, replaced with an eerie silence, but I wasn't about to move. I stayed huddled over Baldy's body and counted to ten. In the movies, when a car blows up, two or three

28

other cars usually blow up too just to make it extra loud and scary, but all I could hear was Baldy's labored breathing and the dying wail of the siren pulling up to the scene. I opened my eyes to find the burly man standing at Baldy's feet and looking back at the accident. The firemen were already scrambling to get their hoses off the truck, so I knew they'd put the fire out before it had a chance to spread.

The burly man squatted down and sighed. "Jesus, who the hell are you? Wonder Woman?"

For a split second, I thought of how as a little girl I would sneak down to the beach in the middle of the night and let the waves wash up over my bare feet. I pretended the sea foam was magic, and if I stood there long enough, the magic would seep up my legs into my whole body. Then I'd stretch my arms out. Once my body had soaked up enough magic, I could rise off the sand and fly through the air. I'd form a picture in my mind of where I wanted to go, and then my body would take me there. I could see through walls, so I'd hover over my school and look inside all the empty classrooms, or I'd go to the firehouse and sit on the roof to watch my father inside, playing cards and Dominoes with his fireman friends.

I slipped my backpack off. "No, I used to be a sheriff's deputy."

"Ah. That explains it." There were beads of perspiration on his forehead, and his dress shirt was wet under the arms.

I said, "You better sit down. You look like you're about to keel over."

"I probably am. You nearly got us killed!"

I looked down at Baldy's face. His eyes were closed now, and his shirt was bunched up at his neck and soaked in blood. I loosened the top buttons just in case they were restricting his breathing and then mustered up a smile for my burly accomplice. "Well, thanks for your help. I don't think I could have gotten him out of that car by myself."

He nodded. "You've got blood on your lip."

"Yeah, I know. I'll be okay."

"I mean, you should probably get that off."

I knew what he was getting at. There are all kinds of nasty blood-borne diseases, and whether or not Baldy here had any of them, I certainly didn't want his blood anywhere near my mouth.

I pulled some gauze out of my backpack. "It's okay. My car was at the back of the

30

pileup. I think I bit my lip when I got rear-ended."

He stood up and stuck his hands down in his pockets. "Oh, good. I mean, it's not good you got rear-ended, but you might want to make sure you don't get any of this guy's blood on that."

"What are you? A doctor?"

A faint look of guilt flashed across his face. He extended his hand. "Dr. Philip Dunlop."

I shook his hand. "Oh. Dixie Hemingway. Nice to meet you."

"Yeah. I guess I better go see what the driver of that truck looks like."

A crowd of people had formed around us, and as he made his way through them I heard him say, "Alright, people, give 'em some air," as if we were on some kind of TV hospital drama.

I wadded the gauze up and gently dabbed it at the blood on Baldy's head. He opened his eyes and looked around, checking out his new surroundings.

"It's okay," I said. "Help is on the way."

He looked at me and frowned, and then groaned as he lifted his head off the sidewalk to see past me into the street.

I said, "Oh, no, sir, please don't try to move."

His frown disappeared, and again a

strange smile played across his lips. I turned to see what he was looking at, but there was nothing but the row of cars stopped in the street. I could see the young girl that had rear-ended me pacing up and down the sidewalk, holding her cell phone to her ear and gesticulating wildly with her free hand, and just opposite us was the cranky old woman in the black Cadillac. She was staring at us with a look of utter disgust, as if Baldy had ruined her entire day by nearly getting himself killed.

Just then a pair of black boots stepped into my field of vision. They were almost knee height, shined to a glossy, mirrorlike finish with steel toes and thick rubber heels. I recognized them immediately. They were the same boots I'd worn every day for years — the boots of a Sarasota County sheriff's deputy.

I looked up to find Deputy Jesse Morgan staring down at me over the frames of his mirrored sunglasses, which he'd slid partly down the bridge of his sharp nose. He had broad shoulders, a buzzed military-type haircut, and a lone diamond stud in his left ear. I knew him, not from having worked for the department — he joined the force after I left — but from several other unfortunate occasions when our paths had crossed. He's about as fun as a bag of rats, but I respect him.

"Dixie," he said, his lips pursed to one side.

I looked down at my cargo shorts, which were smeared with blood. There were red splotches all over my white T-shirt, my hands were covered in blood, and there were red streaks running up and down my arms and legs. I wasn't sure what Deputy Morgan was thinking at that particular moment, but let's just say this wasn't the first time he'd found me kneeling over a listless, bloody body.

"Don't look at me," I said. "He was like this when I found him."

2

I've never been a smoker. My grandfather smoked Camels, unfiltered. Sometimes he'd have several cigarettes going at the same time. He'd be sitting on the deck after dinner, listening to the waves roll in, his cigarette precariously balanced on the edge of the hand-painted clamshell ashtray I made for him in the fourth grade. He'd get up, stretch, and go inside to grab a beer. Then he'd forget what he'd gone inside for and settle down on the couch with an ice-cold Coke, light up another cigarette, and watch the Lawrence Welk show. Then he might leave that cigarette, wander into the kitchen to talk with my grandmother while she made dinner, and light up *another* cigarette.

It drove my grandmother bonkers, and it's a wonder he didn't burn the house down, but my point is I had lots and lots of opportunities to sneak a puff now and then.

Only when I did, it felt like my throat was on fire and my lungs were about to explode right out of my chest. At school, all the cool girls gathered out behind the bleachers smoking cigarettes and talking about home-work and boys. I desperately wanted to be part of that crowd, but I just couldn't hack it.

Deputy Morgan had asked me to wait around a bit to answer a few more ques-tions about the accident since the old woman in the Cadillac and the burly doctor had both gone on their merry way the first chance they'd gotten. Except for the young girl in the car behind me and the driver of the landscaping truck, who'd surprisingly come through without a scratch, I was the only witness.

I had pulled into a parking spot so the cops could get the emergency vehicles through, and now I was sitting on the hood of the Bronco and wishing I had a cigarette. My grandfather always said they calmed his nerves, and mine felt like they'd just been through an extra spin cycle at the Laundro-mat. Two near-miss crashes was one thing, but pulling a bloody man from a ticking time bomb was a whole other ball of fish or kettle of wax or whatever it's called.

The firemen had doused Baldy's convertible immediately after the explosion, and miraculously the landscaping truck hadn't caught fire, which was a good thing for everyone involved since it would surely have exploded, too, and probably taken out half of Ocean Boulevard with it.

From my perch on the hood of the Bronco, I watched as the EMTs loaded Baldy into the ambulance while the firemen lumbered around like astronauts in their big yellow helmets and puffy protective clothing, oxygen tanks strapped to their backs.

They weren't taking any chances with Baldy's car. It took two of them to hold the hose steady while another directed the water all around its smoldering carcass, poking the hose inside all the wheel wells and under the cracks of the buckled hood, like a hygienist cleaning teeth at the dentist's office.

Even though I knew my brother, Michael, was off duty, I was still keeping an eye out for him. He's been known to go racing out of the house in the middle of the night to help his buddies kill a fire, or as Michael says, "put the wet stuff on the hot stuff." Our father was a fireman, and so was his father before him, so when Michael joined the squad just out of college, firefighting was already programmed in his genes. He's blond and blue-eyed like me, but with broad shoulders and muscled arms, kind of like those cover models on the romance magazines they sell at the grocery store.

I let out a little sigh of relief when I felt pretty confident he wasn't showing up. Michael's been taking care of me for as long as I can remember. Our father died in action, fighting a fire in an old abandoned warehouse north of the airport, and our mother was not exactly what you'd call a domestic goddess, so Michael tends to be pretty protective — you might even say overprotective. I'm sure the sight of me sitting on the hood of my car covered in blood would have sent him right over the edge.

Now that the ambulance had taken Baldy away and the fire was out, people were walking by on the sidewalk and gawking at me. I thought about how they always say the most beautiful people in the world are the ones who've experienced true tragedy and suffering. Of course, nobody was looking at me for my world-weary beauty. They were mesmerized by the sight of a bloody, blond-haired mess sitting on the hood of her car.

I looked down at my arms and legs and felt a little shock go through my body. Somehow I'd managed to block out the fact that I was smeared from head to toe with another man's blood. At that moment the only thing that kept me from having a complete nervous breakdown was the promise that as soon as I'd answered whatever questions Deputy Morgan had for me, I'd make like a homing pigeon and head straight for my shower.

I've never been to Tibet or Jerusalem or any of those other places where people go to find inner peace or the meaning of life. Hell, I've never even crossed the Florida state line. I don't need to. The shower is my own personal mecca. There's nothing like a strong, steady stream of hot water to make you feel like you're a fully enlightened deity. For now, though, some old towels and a bottle of rubbing alcohol would have to do the trick.

I slid off the hood and went around to the back and opened up the cargo door. I keep a big plastic cat carrier and two old canvas tote bags back there. One has some extra leashes, a few collars of varying sizes, a Baggie full of bacon-flavored treats, some chewed-up Frisbees, a couple of peacock feathers, and a collection of collapsible food bowls. The other has a fresh supply of clean towels, which come in handy for lining cat carriers or drying off a wet dog, and they're good for keeping fur off upholstery, too.

I don't like a messy car. In my book, your mind is only as clean as your car, so I keep the Bronco as spotless as the day we drove it off the lot. Back then, I kept the back fully stocked with paper napkins, baby wipes, goldfish crackers, and juice boxes . . . but that was a whole other life.

I pulled a bottle of rubbing alcohol out of my backpack and unscrewed the lid. Then I took one of the towels out and folded it into a square. I doused one side of it with alcohol and then, humming along to myself as if it were the most normal thing in the world, wiped the towel up and down first my right leg and then my left. I'd planned on averting my eyes so I wouldn't have to see exactly how much blood there was, but I couldn't help myself. In no time at all, the towel looked like a red tie-dyed T-shirt an aging hippie might wear to a Grateful Dead reunion concert.

I folded it over, dabbed a little more alcohol on the clean side, and then ran it up and down my hands and forearms. It looked like I'd gotten it all, but just to be on the safe side, I took another towel out of the tote bag and did the whole thing over again.

Feeling a little more civilized, if not

completely sanitized, I stuffed the stained towels down into a plastic bag, closed up the back of the car, and returned to my spot on the hood to watch the sun set over the proceedings. I could see patches of the ocean between the shops and buildings on the Gulf side of the street. It was turning a deep indigo blue, and reaching up all along the horizon were vast fields of cadmium and scarlet, all shot through with glowing slivers of white clouds, like undulating seams in the fabric of the sky.

Just when I was thinking I'd probably have to sit on the hood of my car all night long waiting for Deputy Morgan, he came peacocking across the road, his tool belt weighted down with all the accoutrements of a sworn officer of the law: flashlight, handcuffs, department-issue pistol, billy club, digital recorder. He had that smug cop-strut down to a tee. I should know. I used to have a smug cop-strut of my own.

"Fancy meeting you here," he said as he leaned his hip against the hood and pulled out his report pad.

I nodded. "Yep."

Morgan and I have a pretty long history of encounters at crime scenes, largely due to the fact that I seem to have a knack for getting myself involved in all kinds of things

I shouldn't. Granted, my job puts me in lots of places where most people would never be: alone in strangers' homes with their pets, in all kinds of neighborhoods, at all hours of the day and night. Plus, it's a small town. Naturally if anything exciting is happening, the odds of my being somewhere in the vicinity are probably higher than the average Joe's. Still, drama seems to track me down like a chump-seeking missile.

Morgan flipped his report pad open and clicked his ballpoint pen, which he somehow managed to do with an impressive amount of attitude, and cocked his head at me. "So, tell me what happened."

I told him all about Baldy (who hadn't been carrying a driver's license or any other ID, so I'd just have to go on calling him Baldy) and how he had been in a huge hurry, how he'd flashed his lights at me and then swerved into the oncoming lane, and how the next thing I knew he was wrapped around the front of that landscaping truck, and how the burly doctor had helped me pull him out before his car exploded.

"So how long would you say he was behind you before he went around?"

"Probably less than a block. It all happened pretty fast. Wherever he was going he was in a big hurry to get there."

"Well, he's lucky he didn't kill somebody. Do you remember how fast you were driving?"

"Yeah, because I had specifically slowed down to the speed limit when I realized he was tailgating me."

Morgan raised an eyebrow. "You *slowed down* to the speed limit?"

I gulped. The last thing I needed right now was a speeding ticket.

He made a note in his pad. "And just how fast were you going before you *slowed down* to the speed limit?"

At that moment, the thought flashed across my mind that if I hadn't let Baldy pass, this whole thing might have been avoided entirely. If I hadn't been so nice, he would have been stuck behind me and forced to drive the speed limit — more or less. I might have disrupted the whole chain of events, the whole time-space continuum or whatever. For some reason, that, plus the thought of getting a speeding ticket on top of everything else, made something in me go *snap.*

I jumped off the hood of the Bronco and started waving my hands around in front of Morgan's face like a conductor. "Are you kidding me? There is no way in hell you're giving me a speeding ticket! I just pulled a guy out of a burning vehicle. I'm covered in blood. I almost got blown to smithereens. You should be giving me a goddamn medal, not a stupid traffic citation!"

Morgan stared down at me for a couple of seconds and then burst out laughing. "Aww, come on, Dixie! How long have we known each other? You really think I was gonna give you a speeding ticket?"

He flipped his report pad closed with a wink and sauntered off toward his patrol car. I could hear him chuckling as he walked away, and then he called over his shoulder, "You gotta lighten up, babe. Take a vacation or something."

I could feel my cheeks burning, and for a moment I considered taking off one of my shoes and throwing it at the back of his head, but I figured I'd better not press my luck. Also, I couldn't remember ever seeing Morgan smile, much less chuckle. Either he was going soft as he got older, or he didn't take me to be the stark-raving madwoman that I just assumed everyone at the sheriff's department thought I was. It actually felt good to joke around with one of the deputies. It felt like old times, even if I was the butt of the joke.

I got in the front seat of the Bronco and sighed. Except for a catnap in the middle of

43

the day, I'd been up since five in the morning, and my head felt like it weighed a hundred pounds. The roadblocks were still up, and it didn't look like they were clearing them out anytime soon. What remained of Baldy's convertible was sitting in the middle of the road, and probably the landscape truck would have to be towed away, too. I was thinking I'd have to ask the cops to move the barricades so I could go home, but I knew they already had their hands full and I didn't want to get in their way.

Just then I looked up and saw a familiar sign on the front of one of the shops up the street. It read BEEZY'S BOOKSTORE — NEW AND USED.

"Well," I said to myself, "I've done crazier things."

I reached in the backseat and grabbed Ethan's black hoodie. It fit me like a king-sized mattress cover, but it did a nice job of concealing my bloodied clothing, and I planned on whipping into the store as quickly as possible and picking out the first book that caught my eye.

In a small town like this, you always have to consider the possibility that you'll bump into somebody you know, but if I was lucky I could be in and out in five minutes and no one would ever see what a whack-job I looked like. With one more check of my reflection in the car window, I zipped up the hoodie, smoothed my hair back, and headed off for Beezy's Bookstore.

If I'd known better, I would have gotten right back in the car. In fact, if I'd known better, I would have gotten right back in the car, calmly backed out of the parking space, shifted into gear, crashed through the police barricades, sped out of town like a bat out of hell, and never looked back.

Instead, I went shopping.

3

The front window of Beezy's Bookstore was one of those big rounded affairs that the old shops used to have, with thick iron muntins framing glass panes so old they look like they're melting. There were all kinds of books in the display, some old, some new, all artfully arranged and lit by two hanging lamps with milky glass shades. In one corner was a small terra-cotta urn with an impossibly vigorous devil's ivy spilling out in every direction. It weaved in and around all the books, climbing up both sides of the window and intertwining again across the top. In the window pane just next to the door was one of those old OPEN signs with a little clock face and movable hands.

In the other corner, the one farthest from the door, was a stack of old dictionaries about two and a half feet tall, on top of which was a fluffy coating of fur, as if the books had sprouted a thick head of orange

hair. I knew right away that hiding somewhere inside was a very lucky, very furry
tabby cat.

When I pushed the door open I heard a
little tinkling bell over my head and immediately felt a rush, as if I'd just gone
down a slide. It had to be the same bell that
was there when I was a child, because all
kinds of memories came rushing into my
head, memories of being sprawled out
under a big claw-foot table in the middle of
the store, my head resting on a stack of
books-to-read, holding whatever was my
current favorite aloft over my head, lost in
its world.

I felt like I'd stepped out of a time machine. The place was virtually unchanged
from how I remembered it. Just inside the
door to the left was an antique cash register,
sitting on top of a dark, glossy wood counter
with burled edges and brass corners. There
was an old metal-backed stool with a well-
worn cushion behind the counter, surrounded by stacks and stacks of books, old
ledgers, boxes of receipts, and paper bags
brimming over with magazines and comics.

A narrow aisle led down the middle of the
store, lined on either side with antique
bookshelves reaching almost to the ceiling
and overflowing with books of every size,

shape, and color. It had that intoxicating bookstore smell you'll never find surfing around one of those online megabook Web sites: a delicious mixture of vanilla, stale popcorn, dust, cedar, and coffee.

Immediately I felt like I was home, and then just as fast I felt a twinge of guilt for staying away so long. Mr. Beezy had probably passed away years ago, and here I hadn't even bothered to notice. I'd grown up and moved on, gone to school, joined the sheriff's department, started my own life . . . and then things got very busy and very complicated. Life does that to you sometimes.

One thing was new, though: On the ends of all the shelves were pictures, framed in glass and hung one on top of the other in a vertical row. At first I thought they were just copies or pictures torn out of a magazine, but looking closer I realized they were originals — pen-and-ink drawings — and absolutely exquisite. I leaned in to inspect one particularly nice portrait of a young woman holding a tiny kitten in her lap. She was wearing a ring with a diamond the size of a ten-cent gum ball. In the corner of the drawing was a signature: *L. Hoskins.*

I paused in the middle of the store. There, just as I remembered it, was a large, round claw-foot table. It was piled high with all kinds of books: romances, poetry, nature journals, science fiction, reference volumes, graphic novels, mysteries — every type of book imaginable — all tumbled together in a great big wonderful mess.

When I was a little girl, it never occurred to me that all those books weren't there for my own personal pleasure. That was thanks to Mr. Beezy. He never once complained to my grandmother that I needed to either buy a book or get out. He'd let me lie there on the floor for hours, only occasionally sneaking up to quietly lay down another book he'd picked out for me.

Now I had that same old feeling again, like a kid in a candy store, except I was beginning to think I was the only one there. All the lights were on, but the thought crossed my mind that maybe the shop was closed and whoever was in charge had gone home for the day and forgotten to lock up.

"Hello?" I called out. "Anybody home?"

Just beyond the last aisle was a waist-high, carved-wood railing with a swinging door that stopped about a foot above the floor, almost like the doorway to an Old West saloon. Beyond that was a small office space, with a big antique mahogany desk and a polished-brass lawyer's lamp sitting next to an ancient automatic coffeemaker. The room made an L shape to the left, and I could see part of an over-stuffed Victorian sofa jutting out from around the corner. It had dark green velvet upholstery and gold tassels hanging off its arms.

Timidly, I tried again. "Hello?"

I was beginning to think maybe I'd better leave when suddenly an orange blur shot out from under the swinging door and went streaking past my feet toward the front door. Sure enough, it was a big fat tabby with an impossibly fluffy, white-tipped tail. It slid to a stop at the register, took a couple of quick looks around, and then zipped under the front counter. That's when I heard a dull thud from the back room.

I called out louder this time, "Hello? Anyone here?"

"Yes," a creaky male voice came from the back. "Be right with you!"

I let out a sigh of relief. "No rush, I just wasn't sure you were open."

He mumbled something unintelligible as I looked at my watch. It was 6:04. I hadn't even thought to see if the shop's hours were posted in the front window, but of course it was probably closing time. On a weekday, most shopkeepers in town go home at sunset, and it was almost dark outside now.

"Never mind Cosmo!" the man called out. "He's always racing around like that."

That should be easy, I thought as I wandered down one of the aisles, tilting my head to the side so I could read the titles. Cosmo had absolutely no interest in me. I was sure by now he'd taken up his spot back on top of those furry dictionaries and settled in for a cozy nap.

I envied him. It must be nice to know exactly where your place in life is.

I heard another thump from the back and figured I'd better get a move on so I wouldn't keep the poor guy working overtime. I was thinking something fun and trashy would be good, like an epic romance, or maybe a good old-fashioned whodunit — after all, who doesn't love a good mystery? Then I remembered the whole point of buying a new book was to impress Ethan.

I rolled my eyes with disgust. There was something about having a boyfriend that had me acting like a silly schoolgirl. I reminded myself that I was a grown woman, and that here in the twenty-first century, grown women didn't go around pretending to be smarter or prettier or nicer just to hold on to a man, even if that man happens to be a pure dreamboat gift from heaven. Myself countered, if that were true, why was

I all of a sudden putting on lip gloss and mascara in the morning? Well, I snorted, certainly not because of Ethan. Myself then reminded me that my pet clients don't care what I look like. All they care about is whether I show up on time and whether I have some tasty treats in my pocket, like little cubes of cheese or carrot slices. They don't give a rat's patootie how long and luxurious my eyelashes are.

Well, that shut me up. Myself had a point.

I decided to compromise and get two books, one fun, trashy book for me, and then one literary book for show, something classic like *Anna Karenina* or *Jane Eyre* — two of my favorites when I was little. As I scanned the shelf, I realized I was in the math and science section. I pulled one of the books down and read the title out loud.

"Nonlinear Dynamical Systems and Control: A Lyapunov-Based Approach."

I giggled to myself as I imagined Ethan discovering me in a hammock with this book propped up on my chest. I flipped it open to a random spot and practiced, stumbling over the weird mathy language. "Oh, hi Ethan. Hey, did you know that if P is a unique positive-definite solution, then the zero solution is globally asymptotically stable?"

"Pardon me?"

I nearly jumped out of my shoes. An elderly man had appeared at the end of the aisle. He was wearing big, square tinted glasses, what I call "helmet" glasses, the kind that practically wrap around your entire head and cover half your face. His cheeks were ruddy and flushed, as though the walk from the back of the store had winded him. He wore a bright red beret, with long strands of gray hair hanging down both sides of his face, and he was slightly stooped over. He looked a little bit like a bridge troll in a fairy tale, or Albert Einstein if he were an aging elf in Santa's workshop.

I slapped the book shut and slid it back on the shelf. "Oh, sorry, I was just talking to myself."

He nodded, patting his breast pocket and looking around as though he'd misplaced something. His gray trousers were a couple of sizes too big, held up with yellow suspenders over a red shirt with shiny brass buttons, except that he'd forgotten a couple of buttons in the middle. Either he'd been in a hurry when he got dressed for the day or he was just a wee bit absentminded. I was pretty sure it was the latter.

He said, "Terribly sorry. I didn't hear you

come in. I was doing some cleaning up in the back, trying to move some rather heavy boxes . . . I actually thought the door was locked."

I said, "Oh, no, are you closed? Because I can always come back later. I was part of the pileup, so I figured while I was waiting for the police to clear the road I'd just slip in and grab a book or two."

He stepped back a bit, and I noticed his shoes were black leather, polished to perfection, and both untied. "The pileup?"

"Yes. Just a while ago. There was an accident right down the street from here."

"Oh my, how dreadful."

"A man in a convertible was driving like a maniac and hit a big truck head-on. I'm surprised you didn't hear the sirens."

"Sirens?"

Sometimes my mouth says things it shouldn't. Most people have a little trip switch that monitors what travels between their brains and their mouths. It filters out the moronic and tactless thoughts, rating them not suitable for general broadcast, and only lets the reasonable, appropriate thoughts through. I don't have one of those trip switches. Or if I do, it's faulty.

This poor old man was probably a little hard of hearing, which would explain why he hadn't heard me calling for him. He probably hadn't heard the bell ring when I came in either.

"Oh my," he mumbled, "I suppose my hearing isn't exactly what it used to be."

I immediately thought of my grand-mother's favorite expression, "Getting old sucks." Luckily my brain-to-mouth filter managed to stop that one in time. Instead I changed the subject. "Well, if you're closed I don't want to keep you . . ."

He nodded, but then suddenly shook his head. The idea of kicking me out seemed to utterly confuse him. "Oh, no, that's silly. It's my fault, and you're already here . . . How long were you waiting?"

"Not long at all. I used to come here all the time when I was a little girl, so I was having fun just looking around."

He had started toward the front of the store, but now he stopped. "Oh, you knew Mr. Beezy, then?"

"I did. He was always so nice to me. Is he . . . ?"

"Oh my, no, Mr. Beezy passed away years ago."

"I was afraid you were going to say that."

He nodded and looked down at the floor. I couldn't see his eyes through the big, tinted glasses, but there suddenly washed over him a profound weariness. I wasn't sure, but I got the distinct impression that he must have been very close to Mr. Beezy.

I pointed at his shirt. "You forgot a couple of buttons."

He looked down and chuckled. "Oh my! Goodness me, how embarrassing."

"No, don't be embarrassed. If it were me I'd want to be told."

He nodded with a bashful smile as he fumbled with the buttons on his shirt. "Now if you'll excuse me, I suppose I'd better lock that front door before we get any more stragglers wandering in."

"No problem," I said. "I'll take a quick look around and be right out of your way."

He shuffled off toward the front of the store. "Not to worry."

Just then, my eyes fell on a smallish cardboard box on the floor at the head of the very last aisle. Inside was a collection of about ten leather-bound books. They looked well cared for and shiny, as if they'd recently been polished with Lemon Pledge or whatever you use to freshen up leather books. One was particularly pretty. It was a deep, burnished green with gold lettering across the front cover. It read *The Furry Godmother's Guide to Pet-Friendly Gardening, by V. Tisson-Waugh.*

I picked it up out of the box. It felt solid and heavy, the way a good book should. I flipped it open and saw that it was published in 1887. The paper was crisp and creamy yellow, like onion skin, and printed with a floral, antique font. The introduction read:

Above all things, we must endeavor to attach as many persons to the land as possible, as I am convinced that gardening with an animal companion in mind will naturally take the place of many a desire that is much more difficult or impractical to gratify — desires that lie beyond reach of the average man or woman.

"Huh," I muttered to myself. "I think I'll take this one."

The old man had just locked the front door and was shuffling around to the front counter. "That didn't take very long, did it?"

I marched back up to the front of the store and slid the book across the counter with a proud grin. "Sold!"

He looked down at the book and then back at me.

I said, "I didn't see a price on it, but it's perfect. I'm a pet sitter, and my brother is a big-time gardener."

I slipped my backpack off my shoulder and plopped it down on the counter, but the old man's rosy complexion seemed to have faded a shade paler. He was just staring at me.

I said, "Uh-oh. Is it expensive?"

He picked the book up and turned it over, studying it carefully. "Well . . . to be honest with you, this one just came in, and I haven't had a chance to price it yet . . ."

I wondered how hard it could be to decide on a price for one book, but it did look rather old, and maybe he needed to do some research before he sold it. For all I knew it was a priceless antique.

I said, "I guess I could always come back in the morning . . ."

He scratched his head, and I noticed his hands were trembling slightly. "No, that would be silly. There's no point in making two trips. Why don't we say ten dollars?"

"Whew!" I said and stuck my hands down in my bag. "I was afraid you were about to tell me it was some rare, first-edition masterpiece and ask me for a thousand dollars."

He smiled. "Well, it may very well be, but you seem to be a nice young woman, and what would I do with a thousand dollars? It's more important that it find a good home."

I thought, *That, in a nutshell, is exactly what's wrong with most bookstores today.* They feel like giant, sterile farming facilities, not loving foster homes where books are tenderly cared for until they're matched with their one true owner. It was clear this eccentric old gentleman wasn't here to make a fortune. He was one of the breed of bookstore owners who are in it for the pure and unadulterated love of books, plain and simple.

As I searched through my backpack for my checkbook, I said, "Sorry, I keep so much stuff in here that it sometimes gets a little out of control."

He was scratching his head, looking around behind the counter as if he'd never been there before. "That's quite alright, my dear. I seem to be out of bags. I'll go and fetch one from the back."

On the wall behind the counter were more pen-and-ink drawings. One was of a little boy playing the violin, and there was another of a line of leafless trees along the top of a rolling hillside.

I said, "By the way, who's the artist?"

He looked up at the drawings and said meekly, "Oh my. I suppose that's me."

"So you're L. Hoskins?"

He nodded shyly. "I am."

"They're beautiful. I can't wait to come back and look more closely. The one of the young woman with the little kitten in her lap is my favorite so far."

His cheeks flushed pink as he waved his hand dismissively and headed to the back office with my book.

I decided right then and there that I'd make it a regular part of my week to stop in and pay Mr. Hoskins a visit. I felt an immediate bond with him that I couldn't quite explain. I wondered if he'd have a problem with me squirreling away under the big claw-foot table with my own private stash of books-to-read.

Meanwhile, my checkbook was nowhere to be found. I'm embarrassed to admit that I don't keep my backpack quite as neat and tidy as my car, which probably means it's a more accurate representation of what's going on inside my head. While Mr. Hoskins was in the back with my book, I took the opportunity to employ the only surefire method I know of finding anything in there: I dumped the entire contents of the main compartment out on top of the counter.

I rustled through the pile like a cat clawing through its litter box. There were my car keys, an address book, a metal tin of peppermints, a hairbrush, some biodegradable poop bags, two tubes of Burt's Bees tinted lip gloss, a Luna protein bar, my client keys that I keep on a big chatelaine, two black ballpoint pens, some foil gum wrappers, several small plastic bags of unidentified junk, and various other detritus I had accumulated since the last time I'd cleaned my backpack out, which was never.

Finally, peeking out from under a pack of tissues at the bottom of the pile was my checkbook. I held it between my teeth while I put the top of my bag up against the edge of the counter and scooped everything back in like one of those mechanical arms that clears all the pins away at the bowling alley.

I wrote the check out for ten dollars, payable to Beezy's Bookstore, and slid it across the counter next to the register. Just beyond that was a big glass bowl with what were probably chocolate-covered cherries, four or five of them, each individually wrapped in silver foil with red stripes. I had recently sworn off two of my favorite things in the world: one of them being bacon, and the other being chocolate.

Fat hips be damned, I thought to myself.

I'd barely eaten lunch, and even if dinner wasn't that far around the corner, I told myself it wouldn't kill me to have just one teeny, tiny chocolate-covered cherry. The bowl was a little out of reach, which probably meant they weren't exactly intended for customers, but I blocked that thought out.

I was just about to take one when Mr. Hoskins appeared with my book. He had already wrapped it in a crisp paper bag, tied with a piece of twine in a neat bow.

A little sheepishly I said, "You caught me red-handed. I was just about to sneak one of your candies."

He smiled. "No need to sneak, my dear. If you knew me better, you'd know I eat every chocolate in that bowl before I close up for the day, so you'd only be doing me a favor. I'm taking a trip soon, so they'll just go to waste otherwise."

I hesitated. "Well, this is probably too much information, but I have a new boyfriend, so I've sworn off sugar and fat."

"Ah," Mr. Hoskins said with a twinkle in his eye. "Just one can't hurt."

I couldn't have agreed more, except choosing just one was sheer agony. My fingers hovered over the bowl as if my life were in the balance. I settled on one in the middle and cupped it in my hand as if it were a precious, fragile treasure — which of course it was.

I said, "I've never admitted this to anyone,

but I have a weakness for chocolate. If I could get away with it I'd eat it every meal."

"Well," he said as he handed me the book and opened the door, "not to worry. We all have our weaknesses. I hope you'll enjoy both your chocolate and your book in equal measure."

He gave me a little wave and a nod as the door closed behind me. I checked out the stack of dictionaries in the corner of the window display, fully expecting to see Cosmo lounging over the top of it, but he wasn't there. He probably had lots of secret hiding places all over the shop.

Luckily, the barricades were gone now and cars were moving slowly through the street, but there were still flashing lights up where the accident had happened. The cherry red convertible was gone, but now there was a big flatbed tow truck maneuvering into position in front of the landscaping truck, and the three towering palm trees had been moved onto the sidewalk. They looked like alien visitors from another planet sitting there in their giant burlap-balled bases.

As I made my way down the sidewalk, despite everything that had happened in the past couple of hours, I felt good. Maybe it was the rush of adrenaline from being in a car crash, or from pulling a man from a burning car, or the delicious, soul-satisfying chocolate-covered cherry melting in my mouth, but I think more than anything it was returning to a place where I'd been so happy as a child, when I didn't have a care in the world and life was simple. Before things went all haywire.

I practically skipped to the Bronco, which probably looked a little odd to the emergency crews, but I didn't care. I took off Ethan's black hoodie and tossed it in the back and then carefully laid my new purchase, all crisp and new in its paper wrapping and twine bow, down on the passenger seat next to me.

Looking at it, I felt a small part of my heart open up. It was that feeling I'd had as a child whenever I got a new book. I couldn't wait to get home and crack it open. A jolt of excitement went through me as I imagined the moment I'd get to step into its secret world.

Little did I know then . . . I already had.

4

As I passed all the hotels and bungalows along Siesta Key Beach, I started thinking that maybe I'd misinterpreted the little surge of excitement I'd felt at the prospect of diving into a new book. It must have just been a little post-tramautic adrenaline, because my whole body was starting to tighten up and my neck was tingling. By the time I reached Midnight Pass Road, my shoulders felt as if they were each holding up a ten-pound bag of sugar.

Great, I thought. *Whiplash.*

I'd probably jolted my neck when the pink VW bonked into my rear bumper, and then carrying Baldy around probably hadn't helped matters any. All the more reason to take a good long hot shower as soon as I got home. I stepped on the gas. After my performance with Deputy Morgan I figured I was temporarily immune to speeding tickets.

All the way down Midnight Pass I couldn't stop thinking about Baldy — how he had looked up at me with that strange smile on his face and said, "Safe." Just the fact that he had to ask me if he was even alive kind of broke my heart. At that point he must have thought he'd died and gone to heaven, and I'm sure all those pain-blocking endorphins coursing through his bloodstream felt pretty darn heavenly.

I wondered if maybe he hadn't recognized me from before when he sped past. Maybe he was smiling at the irony of it all. Maybe it was his way of saying, "You're right, I *am* a jackass. Sorry for the trouble."

I pulled into the curving lane that leads down to the place I've called home for about as long as I can remember. The sound the crushed shell made as the wheels rolled over it actually made my shoulders relax a bit. I hear that sound every single day. It means home to me, just as much as the sound of the waves lapping up on the beach down below the house. My headlights lit up the tangle of pines, mossy oaks, sea grapes, and palms on either side of the lane, and after a couple of twists and turns, I pulled into the courtyard.

Most of the houses along this stretch of the key are sprawling, multimillion-dollar mansions filled with movie idols and star athletes, but ours came right out of the Sears, Roebuck catalog. My grandparents picked it while they were still newlyweds and dreamed of finding the right spot to build one day. Then, a couple of years after my mother was born, my grandfather was in Florida on business, and a co-worker took him on a tour of Siesta Key. When he returned home, he presented my grandmother with a brand-new deed to a piece of land on the edge of the Gulf. She nearly divorced him, but he persuaded her to come down and have a look herself. They stood on the future spot of their dream home and watched the sky turn gold as the sun settled into the ocean. My grandmother always said that buying this land was the smartest decision she ever made, and my grandfather would nod at me and wink.

It's a simple, two-story frame house with white siding, weathered a milky gray from years in the sun and salty air. After my grandparents passed away, my brother moved in with his partner, Paco, and our cat, Ella Fitzgerald. I live above the four-slot carport next to the house in the apartment our grandfather built for relatives to stay in when they visited from up north.

It has a balcony with a hammock and a

little glass-topped breakfast table, and French doors that open into a small living space with a sofa and a big, comfy armchair. A breakfast bar divides the living area from the kitchen, and then there's a short hallway that goes back to my bedroom. There's a bathroom on one side of the hall and an alcove with a washer and dryer on the other, and I have a big walk-in closet with room for a desk, which is where I take care of all my pet-sitting business. It's small, but it suits me fine.

Today, the house and the apartment aren't worth a hill of coconuts, but the land they're sitting on . . . well, that's a whole other story. We could all retire and travel like queens all over the world on the money we'd get for it. We'll never sell, though. It's practically a member of the family now.

As I rolled past the courtyard, I noticed Michael and Paco were out on the deck laying fish and sliced vegetables on the grill. I was happy to see them — not every girl gets to come home to a couple of shirtless hunks making her a gourmet dinner, but also, our schedules don't always line up so great. Michael works twenty-four/forty-eight at the firehouse, which means he's at the station one full day and then off for two days. Paco is an agent with the Special Investigative

Bureau, which means his schedule, not to mention his job, is a complete mystery to all of us. He's sometimes gone for days on end, working undercover.

I pulled into the carport to find Ella Fitzgerald perched on the hood of Paco's pickup. She was licking one white paw and daintily drawing it over her left ear. When she saw me, she stretched herself into a scary Halloween cat and let out a little *nik-nik* sound to signal that she would very much appreciate it if I would be so kind as to come over and give her a couple of scritches behind the ears.

Ella is a pure calico-Persian mix, with alternating patches of red, black, and white fur. She was a gift to me, but it didn't take her long to figure out that all the good stuff is in Michael's kitchen — in addition to being a first-class fireman, he's a world-class cook — so she spends most of her time there. I still think of her as mine, though. I learned a long time ago that just because you love something doesn't mean you get to keep it forever.

I shut off the ignition and planned my course of action. If I played my cards right, I could slip past the boys, hide my bloody clothes, take a quick shower, and get back down for dinner in a cat's pounce. Not that

I get some sort of thrill sneaking around behind their backs, but I didn't think it would do Michael any good to see me looking like a bit player from *Dawn of the Living Dead.* He has enough on his plate as it is, and being my older brother hasn't exactly been a tiptoe through the tulips, so whenever I can I try to spare him the bloody details, so to speak. Although the thought did cross my mind that he'd be pretty proud to find out I'd practically saved a man's life.

I put Ethan's hoodie back on and watched Michael and Paco at the grill, waiting for the right moment to make my move. Just then, they both went back inside to get something from the kitchen, and I took a deep breath. My heart quickened, and I felt like James Bond or George Smiley, as if I needed to synchronize my watch or whisper into my sleeve, "We're goin' in!"

I heaved my stiff body out of the Bronco and closed the door as quietly as possible, then gave Ella a quick rub on her head as I went by. She could tell my heart wasn't really in it, though. "Sorry, Miss Ella," I whispered. "I'll make it up to you later."

I tried to take the stairs two at a time, but my neck was so sore I could barely handle them one at a time, so instead I took little baby steps, slowly so I wouldn't make any noise, and just as I was halfway up, Michael came out with a big bowl of mixed greens. I pressed myself against the side of the railing and froze as he set the bowl down on the big teak table our grandfather made. Then, as slowly as possible, I slithered sideways up the steps, keeping my back flat against the wall.

I've always thought that if my pet-sitting business didn't work out, I'd convince Paco to get me a job at the Special Investigative Bureau. I'd make a good spy. *Even injured, I'm nimble as a cat and sneaky as a snake,* I thought to myself.

Michael said, "Dinner in five, Dixie."

I sighed. Well, maybe not.

"Okay, great," I said as I trudged up the rest of the stairs. "I just have to take a quick shower, and then I'll be right down."

"What? A shower? Didn't you already take a shower this morning?"

"Yes, Michael, I did, and now I'm going to take another one. I'm covered in cat hair."

He walked over to the edge of the deck and cocked his head to one side, as if he were inspecting a steer at market. "Are you okay?"

I paused at the top of the stairs. "Yep. I'm fine."

"Um, isn't that hoodie a little big for you?"

71

I turned around and put my hands on my hips. "What is this? Twenty questions?"

"Whoa." He put his hands in the air like a bank teller in a holdup. "Okay, grumpy. Five minutes till dinner." He shook his head as he headed back to the grill.

I put my keys in the door and breathed a sigh of relief. That was close. I congratulated myself on my spy skills. Of course, I'd eventually tell him what happened, but after what I'd already been through that day, the last thing I felt like listening to was a lecture about the dangers of getting near a smoking car or pulling semiconscious strangers from accidents. At that point, all I cared about was stripping out of those bloody clothes and getting in a nice hot shower.

I swung the door open, and there was Ethan, grinning, his arms stretched out for a hug.

"Hey there, gorgeous."

Now, I may or may not have mentioned that Ethan is about the most handsome man I've ever laid eyes on. Women generally swoon in his presence. I don't mean metaphorically. I mean actual swooning. As in eye-rolling, knee-weakening swooning. Chests heave, bodices rip — you know the type. Basically, he's *smokin' hot.*

"No," I said, pulling the hoodie tighter. "I

can't hug you, I'm covered in hair."

He stepped in front of me. "What? I don't care about a little cat hair, come here."

"No, seriously, Ethan, I'm a mess."

He was wearing jeans and a faded pink V-neck T-shirt, but that's all I saw at first. I was trying not to look at him. When I'm around Ethan, I tend to lose my concentration if I'm not careful. There are a number of things about him that can be a little distracting: his beautiful light brown eyes, his thick lashes, his curly locks of long black hair, his broad shoulders, his muscled arms, the soft hair on his chest . . . I could go on.

"Hey," he interrupted. "Is that my hoodie?"

"Yeah, sorry. I got a little cold, so I put it on."

"Umm, it's like eighty degrees outside."

"Yeah, I know that, but . . ." I cast about in my head for a good excuse, but all I could come up with was a plaintive "I like how I look in it . . . ?"

He raised one eyebrow. "Yeah. You're like a hot shoplifter."

I shrugged and flashed him a sweetly disarming grin, but he wasn't buying it.

"Dixie, what's going on? And what happened to your lip?"

I sighed. "Alright, but you asked for it."

I put my backpack down and said, "Now, I'm totally fine, but . . ." I unzipped the hoodie and slid it off my shoulders.

Ethan's jaw fell open. "Holy . . . Dixie, what the hell happened to you?"

"I was in an accident, but really, I'm fine."

His face went pale as he looked at the bloodstains on my clothing, and for a second I thought he was about to swoon himself.

I put my hand on his chest just in case he tipped over. "No, no, no. The blood's not mine!"

He stood there, nodding for a couple of seconds and taking it all in. Then he said, "Yeah. I need to sit down."

I led him over to the couch, and he stretched out on his back and crossed his arms over his chest.

"Okay," he said, looking up at the ceiling. "Go ahead."

I knelt down at the edge of the couch and smiled sheepishly. "You okay?"

He nodded vigorously. "Oh sure. Yeah, I'm great. Go on."

I told him everything that had happened. All about the accident, how Baldy had been tailgating me, how after I'd let him pass he had hit a truck head-on, about the pileup and how I'd been rear-ended by a girl who was talking on her cell phone and only braked at the last minute.

His eyes were closed, but I went on anyway. "And now, except for a stiff neck and a little cut on my lip, I'm really, totally fine."

He turned and looked at me. "Good story. Now get to the part where you pulled the bloody guy out of his car."

"Oh right, yeah. So then I pulled the bloody guy out of his car."

He waved one hand in the air nonchalantly. "And hence the blood."

"Ethan, I didn't have a choice. There was smoke pouring out of it. If I hadn't gotten him out before it exploded, there's no way he would've survived."

He stared at the ceiling. "Exploded."

"Oh. Yeah, his car exploded. Well, 'exploded' seems a little dramatic. It blew up."

He shook his head and started laughing quietly to himself.

"Ethan, seriously, there was nobody else there to help him. What was I supposed to do?"

He turned and looked at me. "I know. You're amazing."

I held up my hand for a high five. "Finally! This is what I've been trying to tell everybody!"

He shook his head. "No, seriously. That took guts. How bad is your neck? Maybe we should get it looked at."

"Oh please, don't be such a drama queen. I'm fine."

He sat up slowly. "Are you sure?"

"Yes, I'm sure. It's nothing an aspirin and a hot shower can't fix. And look, can we please not tell Michael and Paco? I don't want them to make a big deal out of it."

He put his hands on my knees. "Okay. Sure, if that's what you want. I'll give you one of my patented neck massages later."

I sighed. "Okay, good. I mean, I'll tell them later. I just don't want Michael to freak out."

He nodded, and that was it. No lecture, no hand-wringing, no "next time this" or "next time that." Just a little dramatic light-headedness and then he simply listened. I've said it before, and I'll say it again: I like a man who knows how to listen.

I like a man that knows how to listen *a lot.*

"So here's the plan," I said. "I managed to sneak upstairs without them getting a good look at me. So now you go down and tell them I had a phone call or something. Meanwhile I'll hide the evidence, take a hot shower, and be right down like nothing ever happened."

He stood up, "Okay, let's reconnoiter downstairs. Ten-four, Agent 99, over and out."

He saluted and then stuck his hand out for a handshake. I swatted it away. "Very funny."

As soon as he was gone I was out of my clothes and in the shower in less than ten seconds. I'm a champion shower-taker. I can stand there until all the hot water runs out and my fingertips look like little wrinkled babies' butts, or I can be in and out in under three minutes, as efficient as a pit crew at the Indy 500. This time, I didn't exactly empty the hot water tank, but I let the water run over my neck and shoulders long enough for a few muscles to relax back to their normal spots.

I toweled off quickly and slipped on my nicest pair of long slacks, which is what you wear to lounge around in when your work uniform is shorts and a T-shirt, and then a pale yellow linen blouse with little blue cornflowers embroidered on the cuffs that I bought at an Indian shop downtown years ago. I wear it whenever I want to feel extra clean and carefree, which is exactly how you want to feel after you've spent a few hours covered in somebody else's blood.

On my way out, I paused in the kitchen.

There was an envelope in the basket at the end of the counter where we put the mail. For a second, I just stared at it. My eyes were working fine, but my brain was having a little trouble processing the name in the return address.

It read *J. P. Guidry.*

5

The view from my balcony was almost enough to make me shed tears of joy. There were tiki torches surrounding the deck, giving the entire courtyard a flickering golden glow, and the big table in the middle looked like a photo shoot for one of those fancy food magazines. At one end was an old tin bucket, its sides sweating in the warm air, filled with ice and two bottles of white wine attended by four chilled wineglasses, all glittering with the reflected light from the torches. At the other end of the table was a big bowl of elkhorn lettuce, arugula, endive, and Swiss chard, tossed with big shaves of Parmesan, sliced red onion, and black olives — not the yucky canned type but the nice ones from the Italian market. In the center, practically glowing in all its glory, was a platter full of fresh grilled fish.

I knew right away that Paco must have been in charge of the meal. Michael is the true chef in the family, but every once in a while one of us steps in to give him a break. If it's my turn, I order takeout — I'm not much of a cook — but when Paco takes over, it's a special treat.

Paco is the kind of man who women dream about turning straight. He's of Greek American descent, but with his dark good looks and facility with languages he could pass for almost any nationality in the world. I can barely master my own native tongue, but Paco speaks at least six fluently, and he's always learning more. He's been studying Korean for two years now, usually at the end of the day when everybody else is watching TV or playing Sudoku or staring at the wall. That kind of dedication comes in handy when you're an undercover agent. His family name is Pakodopoulos, but that's a mouthful for most people, so we call him Paco for short.

His parents immigrated to the States before he was born, but his mother taught him all the recipes she remembered from her own mother's Mediterranean kitchen. Tonight he'd made striped bass, filleted and sprinkled with lemon juice, freshly ground cayenne, and coarse sea salt, then grilled to utter perfection on a quilt of fennel, tops and all. White fish tends to dry out on the grill, but as the fennel steams, the moisture rises up through the fish, keeping it moist and lending a note of anise and celery, while the charred, feathery greens curl up around the fish and give it smokiness. Paco served it on a bed of wilted kale with couscous and roasted pine nuts, sprinkled with ground peppercorns and paper-thin slices of lemon.

If I ever meet Paco's mother, I'll get down on my hands and knees and kiss her feet.

As I joined them at the table, Michael handed me a glass of wine. "Hank called from the firehouse and asked if I could be on call tonight. He said there was a bad accident on Ocean. Some guy in a convertible got hit by a garbage truck head-on."

Before I could stop myself I said, "A landscaping truck."

"Huh? How'd you know that?"

I winced and glanced at Ethan for help. "Um, yeah, I drove by there on my way home from work."

At the same time, Ethan said, "Yeah, it was on the news."

I grabbed my fork and shoved a big bite of salad in my mouth while Ethan reached for his wine.

Michael shrugged. "Oh. I guess Hank got it wrong. Anyway, he said it was pretty bad.

81

Two people had to pull the guy out of his car."

I tried not to choke on my salad. "Wow, that's impressive."

"Yeah, he said the car was on fire, so this blond girl and another guy literally picked the dude up and carried him to safety."

"Huh," I said.

"And then the dude's car exploded."

Ethan was looking down at his plate, moving his couscous around with his fork. "I guess they probably saved that guy's life." He looked up and flashed me a sly smile.

Michael nodded. "Oh yeah, definitely. Luckily the guys were right on it. They got everything hosed down before it could spread anywhere. Hank said the blonde was cute but a little broad in the beam."

I paused. "Huh?"

Michael held his plate out over the table, and Paco put some salad on it. "You know, broad in the beam — isn't that what Grandma used to say? I think he meant she had a big butt."

I put my fork down and calmly took a sip of wine.

"He said she was kind of cute, but with a huge big fat butt, and she was wearing a white T-shirt and cargo shorts. Oh, and she drove a pale yellow Ford Bronco."

I looked Michael levelly in the eyes. A big, mischievous grin spread across his face. I said, "I am going to come over there and personally beat you up."

Paco burst out laughing, and Michael raised his hands in mock surprise. "What did I say?"

I turned to Ethan. "You traitor. You told them!"

"I swear I didn't say a word!"

Michael said, "Dixie, did you think the guys down at the firehouse wouldn't recognize you?"

I said, "Look, I was going to tell you. I just didn't think you'd want to see me all messed up."

"What do you mean, all messed up?"

"Michael, the guy was in a head-on collision. There was a little blood involved."

He frowned. "Oh, I didn't even think of that."

"Right."

"Okay, I get it. Yeah, I would not have enjoyed that. Thanks for sparing me."

"You're welcome. And for the record, the truck didn't hit him. He hit the truck. I was coming down Ocean from my last client, I was on my way to the bookstore, and he was tailgating and weaving in and out of the road. So I pulled over and let him go by."

Paco said, "That was mature of you. Nothing annoys me more. People don't understand you shouldn't be closer than one car length for every ten miles per hour you're traveling. And they're not just putting you in danger, they're putting themselves and everybody else in danger, too."

I said, "I know, but this guy was in a hurry. I don't think safety was very high on his priority list at that point."

Ethan said, "Was he local?"

I shook my head. "I don't know, but I doubt it. By the time I got to him he was barely conscious, and he didn't have any ID. They put him in the ambulance, and that's the last I saw of him."

Paco sighed. "I wonder if he made it."

We all sat there in silence for a few moments. I didn't want to say, but suddenly the way Baldy had looked up at me when he was lying there on the sidewalk made me less than hopeful about his chances — that serene smile on his face, almost as if he were at peace . . .

Michael was peering at me across the table. "Wait a minute. What happened to your lip?"

I said, "Oh, it's fine. I bit it when the girl rear-ended me."

He put his elbows on the table and cradled

his head in his hands. "Oh my God. What girl?"

I sighed. "Oops. Yeah, I forgot that part. The head-on caused a pile-up. I slammed on the brakes to avoid hitting the car in front of me, but the girl driving behind was on her phone, so she was a little slow on the uptake. But Michael, she barely tapped me. I mean, the Bronco only flew forward like maybe a foot."

He let out a little groan.

"And my neck is kind of sore . . ."

He groaned again and said, "Let's just change the subject."

I nodded vigorously. "Okay, okay. Let's change the subject."

I looked at Paco and Ethan, but they weren't any help, so in my most cheerful voice I said, "Oh, while I was waiting for the street to open back up I found a really cool book at the bookstore. You're gonna love it."

Still cradling his head in his hands, Michael peered at me through his fingers. "You pulled a bloody man out of a burning car and then went to the bookstore?"

"Well, it was right there, so . . ."

Paco said, "Umm, didn't they wonder about the bloodstains all over your clothes?"

Ethan raised a finger in the air. "Yeah,

that's where I come in."

I said, "Ethan had left one of his old hoodies in the back —"

Ethan interrupted. "Well, it wasn't *that* old —"

"So I covered up with that before I went in."

Ella Fitzgerald was curled up on one of the chaise lounges watching us intently. I swiveled around toward her and said, "Oh, and Ella, the man that owns the bookstore has a very handsome orange tabby named Cosmo. Maybe you'll meet him one day."

I always like to include Ella in the conversation. She hopped off the chaise and came padding over to the table. I'd prefer to think she was fascinated with my line of conversation and the prospect of making a new friend, but I think she was more interested in the grilled fish than anything else. She hopped up on her appointed chair and said, *"Thrrrip?"*

Michael said, "You're not telling me Mr. Beezy is still there, are you?"

I shook my head. "No, he passed away years ago."

"That's too bad. I remember that old guy. He was cool."

"Michael, you wouldn't believe it — the store looks exactly the same as it did thirty years ago."

Ethan reached over and gave Ella a couple of scratches under her chin. "It's looked the same forever. That whole section of the street does. It's all still owned by the same family that originally built it."

Paco said, "You mean the Silverthorns?"

Ethan nodded. "Believe it or not. I know because my grandfather did some work for the Silverthorn family, and we still handle all the business permits and rental agreements for those shops along there."

I'd never known any of the Silverthorns personally, but I had grown up hearing the name, and I certainly knew the Silverthorn Mansion. It was one of the last remnants of old Siesta Key, when wealthy land barons had bought up most of the beachfront property and built summer homes here.

The Silverthorn Mansion was at the bottom of the Key, at the end of a long, narrow strip of sandy soil that now forms the southern part of Midnight Pass. The story is that it had originally stood in the center of a vast country estate in England, and that Mrs. Silverthorn, heir to her family's vast railroad empire, had it dismantled, shipped across the Atlantic, and put back together like a jigsaw puzzle. It was a surprise for her new husband, a third cousin from a not so wealthy limb of the family tree whose last name was also Silverthorn, which of course only served to make the whole Silverthorn family all the more exotic and mysterious.

By the time I came around, the mansion had already become a landmark for us kids. The railroad industry had taken a dive, and the family's fortune had been divided among its heirs and then divided again, so the Silverthorns barely had enough money to keep the mansion from crumbling down around them. Most of us believed it was haunted, and the fact that it had fallen into such disrepair strengthened that notion. We made up stories about missing children locked away inside to scare each other, and at least once a year one of us would declare that we planned to sneak in that very night and explore every inch of it. Of course, we never did.

I remembered playing along the beach down below the house, in the days when we were free to roam around the island without having to worry about crossing onto private beaches. There was rarely more than one light on in the entire place, and we always said it was because they could only afford one lightbulb.

Ethan said, "I probably shouldn't say, but it's actually a huge tragedy. Just about every

penny they make from their rental proper-
ties goes to pay their land taxes, and Mrs.
Silverthorn refuses to sell off any of it. She's
pretty eccentric. People call her the 'cat
lady.' I've heard that mansion is filled with
hundreds of cats. And all our business is
either through the mail or over the phone.
If I need something signed, I have to mail it
to her. She won't let anybody on the property."

Just then Ella perked up and said, *"Mrrrap!"*
She was probably reminding us that fish is
a well-known favorite among many feline
species, but she knows not to push it. If she
sits quietly, paws off the table, she can stay
in her seat and watch. If she's really good,
there might be a reward in her bowl later.

I was just about to tell Michael more
about the gardening book when I heard my
cell phone ringing upstairs. I'd left the
French doors to my apartment open, and I
could hear its familiar ring mixed with the
chorus of crickets that had risen up since
we'd started eating.

Michael raised an eyebrow as he refilled
my wineglass. "Don't you dare."

We all sat and ignored the ringing, even
Ella. I'd like to say that we have an unspoken
rule about not answering phone calls during dinner, but since my cell phone is

constantly ringing with new jobs or traveling clients calling to see how their pets are doing, the rule has to be spoken just about every time we sit down at the table. It's mostly because of Michael that we still follow it, a remnant of one of the few domestic rules our mother established. I pretend to be against it, but I'm really not. It helps keep dinnertime sacred and reminds us that family, no matter what shape it takes, always comes first.

Later that evening, I was sitting in bed with Ethan. He was leaning back on a couple of fluffy pillows, and I was leaning back on his chest. He was gently massaging my neck with one hand while flipping through one of the manly, outdoorsy-type magazines he subscribes to with the other. This one was *Backpacker Magazine.* As far as I'm concerned, it's a miracle they can even fill one issue, but apparently he gets them every month.

I'd always just had one bedside table and lamp, but now I'd added another one on the side closest to the door. That was Ethan's side. I need to sleep nearest the wall — don't ask why. I wasn't sure if he was spending the night yet, and probably he wasn't sure either. Our cohabitation schedule was still evolving. We were at that tricky point in a relationship where it feels dangerous to spell things out clearly, where doing or saying anything to acknowledge the fact that you're spending every free minute together might somehow jinx it.

For the time being, things just kind of happened on their own. Sometimes Ethan would stay the night with me, and sometimes he'd go home, especially if he needed to be at work early. He's an attorney. His practice is in the same sand-softened stucco building his grandfather's practice was in, which is just a ten-minute walk from his apartment near the center of town.

I had just unwrapped my new book and was about to open it up when Ethan said, "So . . ." and then fell silent.

I waited, but it didn't seem like there was more. I said, "So . . . what?"

His eyes still on the magazine, he said, "So . . . J. P. Guidry. What did his letter say?"

I'd almost forgotten. The letter. I suddenly felt a wave of sleepiness wash over me. "Yeah . . . I didn't open it yet."

He was quiet for a moment and then said, "Okay."

"It's probably nothing . . ."

"Mmm-hmm."

Then I must have fallen asleep, because the next thing I knew it was five-thirty in the morning, my radio alarm was going off, and Ethan was nowhere to be seen.

6

J. P. Guidry.

Just seeing his name on that envelope had made my heart stumble. There was a time, and not in the very distant past, when just the thought of Guidry would have sent tiny vibrations of pleasure through my entire body, but so much had happened since then that now . . . Well, I had no idea what it made me feel . . . except confused.

I opened up my French doors and inhaled the cool, briny air, letting it fill my lungs completely. It was still way before sunrise. There was just a hint of light breaking above the horizon on the bay side, but the moon was so bright the whole beach looked as if it were lit with hidden blue floodlights. The birds were still sleeping, so the only thing I could hear was the sad sound the waves made as they lapped up on the shore down below. I leaned against the railing and looked out over the courtyard.

The story of how Guidry and I met is not exactly the most romantic tale ever told. To make a long story short, I found a dead man in a client's house, lying facedown in a cat's water bowl, and Guidry was the lead homicide detective for the sheriff's department. At the time, the last thing I was looking for was a relationship but, of course, it hadn't hurt one bit that Guidry was tall, dark, and handsome.

But more than that, he was unlike any man I'd ever known. Quiet. Complex. A mystery, really. Eventually somehow I managed to let my guard down, and we had an on-again, off-again relationship longer than any two normal people ought to have without choosing either ON or OFF. Then he was offered a job with the police department in his hometown of New Orleans, which is really where his heart was, and I couldn't very well argue with him, since my heart was here in Siesta Key.

He moved to New Orleans. I stayed here. And that was that.

Except now there was this damn letter. Why was I so afraid to open it? The only thing I could come up with was that, with Guidry at a safe distance, I could finally admit to myself that I'd been in love with him. For me, that's saying something. Not that I'm some kind of cold-hearted spinster, but I've learned the hard way that love can be ugly. Unrestrained, my heart is as strong and fierce as a wild animal, so I've gotten really good at building a wall around it, reinforced with nonstop work and general sassiness, which works just as good as coiled razor-ribbon wrapped around concrete. That way, everybody's safe.

I looked down at the beach. There was one lone seagull by the water. She was clutching something in her beak, probably a clam, and hammering it against one of the rocks that jut out at the water's edge. It was making a *tap-tap-tap* sound, almost like the drummer in a rock band setting the tempo for a new song.

Well, I thought, *that letter's not opening itself.*

I stood up and was about to go inside when I saw a dark shape moving around in Michael and Paco's kitchen. A light was on, which is unusual — normally I'm the only one up that early — and the first thing I thought was *burglar.*

I froze. The kitchen door opened slowly, and for a second I felt a scream forming at the bottom of my throat.

Out stepped Ethan, holding a cup of coffee in one hand and balancing a silver tray with the other. He tiptoed across the deck and made his way up the stairs.

"What the hell are you doing?"

He let out a little yelp. "Damn, woman, you scared me!"

I said, "You scared me first! I thought you were robbing us. What are you doing sneaking around at this hour?"

He held out the tray. There was a round tortilla basket overturned on top of one of Michael's blue dinner plates, with a folded napkin, silverware, and a tiny glass of fresh-squeezed orange juice.

He grinned. "I made you breakfast."

"Huh?"

"Well, not really. It's more like I raided Michael and Paco's kitchen. But I put everything on the tray myself. Well, actually Michael did that. But I held the tray."

I folded my arms across my chest. "Since when do you serve me breakfast on a silver platter?"

He smiled. "Since you became a local hero and pulled a guy out of a burning vehicle with your own bare hands."

"Wow," I said. "I have no words. Just wow."

I sat down at the little breakfast table on my deck, and Ethan slid the tray in front of me. He was starting to lift the basket off the plate when I stopped him.

"Wait a minute. Is that letter under this basket?"

All innocent, he said, "What letter?"

"You know exactly what letter."

He smiled. "I thought about it, but no."

"I promise I'll open it today. It's not a big deal."

"If it's not a big deal, why didn't you open it last night?"

I shrugged innocently. "I guess I forgot it was even there."

He lifted the basket to reveal a bowl of freshly cut fruit. Mango, kiwi, and strawberries sprinkled with pomegranate seeds and topped with a dollop of crème fraîche. Next to that was a scrumptious-looking buttered scone.

He sat down and said, "Fresh out of the oven. Paco's up early today."

It hadn't taken Ethan long to pick up on the subtleties of the secret language that Michael and I have developed over the years for talking about Paco. Working as an agent with the Special Investigative Bureau means Paco rubs elbows with all sorts of interesting characters — mobsters, narcotics dealers, counterfeiters, animal smugglers — so whenever he's away on a job, both Michael and I walk on eggshells, trying to pretend everything's just as normal as can be, as if Paco's gone out on an errand and will be back safe and sound any minute.

The fact that they were up and about this early could only mean one thing — Paco was starting a new assignment today. "Fresh out of the oven" meant Michael was in the kitchen, nervously trying to distract himself.

"Oh my gosh," I said, biting into the scone. "This is the best breakfast ever."

He folded his arms over his chest and smiled. "And how's your neck?"

My mouth was full of scone, so I managed an "Mmmph!" and gave him a thumbs-up.

"Okay, good," he said, pushing his chair back from the table. "Then my work is done."

"Wait a minute! Where are you going?"

He stood up and disappeared inside, calling over his shoulder, "Sorry, babe! I've got a meeting in Tampa with a new client."

Just then my cell phone rang from the bedroom, and Ethan called out, "Somebody's calling you."

The only people in the world that could possibly be calling at this hour were Michael, Paco, and Ethan, so I decided I'd just enjoy my breakfast and check my voice mail later. Except, if it was a client with an emergency, like a lost cat or . . .

"Hey, can you see who it is?"

There was a pause, and then he said, "Sara somebody."

I couldn't think of any clients named Sara. The only Sara I knew was a girl who worked the hot dog stand at the pavilion on Siesta Key Beach, and I wasn't even sure she knew my name. "Sara Somebody" was probably a new client. I figured I'd check my voice mail after breakfast and call back at a more godly hour.

Just as I was digging into my fresh fruit, Ethan came back out on the porch in a crisp white dress shirt with a dark gray jacket. He leaned against the railing and draped a pale, silvery-blue tie around his neck.

"Hey, I've been meaning to ask you . . ." There was a forced nonchalance to his voice that immediately made me a bit nervous.

"Whaffat?" I said, my mouth full of mango and kiwi.

"So . . . what's the EPT for?"

I swallowed, "The huh?"

I knew exactly what he had said, but for some reason I needed a little time to think. He crossed the skinny end of his tie over the fat end and looped it around into a bow. "The early pregnancy test that's in your medicine cabinet."

"Oh!" I wiped my mouth with a napkin. "Um . . . I bought that."

He nodded slightly, gazing off into the distance as he slipped the tie's long end through the bow and pulled it into a tight knot. "Okay . . ."

It took me a couple of seconds to figure out what he was getting at. The vague note of a question in his voice finally tipped me off. I said, "Oh my gosh! You didn't think . . ."

He shrugged, "Well, I was kind of wondering."

"No! It's not for me. It's for a girl I know — the daughter of a client. It's a long story, but basically she thought she was pregnant. It turns out she wasn't, but I figured she should probably have a way of knowing if it ever happens again. Hopefully she'll never need it."

He nodded and straightened his jacket. "Okay. It just got me thinking."

I put an impossibly large heaping spoonful of fruit in my mouth. I was about to ask what it was he was thinking, but I wasn't sure I wanted to know the answer.

He leaned over and kissed me, and I immediately got a little dizzy-headed. Ethan's kisses have the ability to make me feel like I've had a couple of fine Belgian chocolates, or a shot of very expensive, smooth whiskey.

He whispered, "Your lip looks better."

I smiled drunkenly. "Thanks."

Usually I'm not all that attracted to business types — I'm more of a jeans and T-shirt kind of girl — but the more time I spent with Ethan, the more I realized I was turning into a suit and tie kind of girl. As Ethan went down the stairs and crossed the courtyard to his car I thought to myself, *There goes one sexy, suit-wearing hunk of hotness.* Of course, if Ethan walked around in a burlap sack and a shoe box on his head, I'd probably turn into a burlap sack and shoe box kind of girl in two seconds flat.

My first stop almost every morning is Tom Hale's condo on Midnight Pass Road. Tom is an accountant. He works out of his home since traveling back and forth to an office is a little difficult for him, to say the least. Ten years ago, he was in one of those sprawling home improvement stores shopping for doorknobs when a wall display collapsed on top of him and crushed his spine. He never walked again. Sometimes I think if that had happened to me I wouldn't have the strength to go on, but Tom is one of the most cheerful people I've ever known. He does my taxes and deals with everything else money-related in my life, and in exchange I go over twice a day and walk his retired greyhound racing dog, Billy Elliot.

I'm pretty sure that most greyhounds who spend their entire lives on a racetrack, work grueling hours, and are treated like slave mules would prefer to lounge around on a velvet pillow in their old age and never see a racetrack again. Not Billy Elliot. Twice a day, we go down to the big circular parking lot outside Tom's building, and Billy races around like his glory days aren't yet behind him. He's one of the lucky ones. Greyhound racing is not for the faint of heart. Broken toes, bone fractures, torn ligaments, and crippling arthritis are par for the course. Most retired greyhounds Billy's age can't walk fifty feet without having to stop and take a rest.

Usually I jog along panting like a fool with Billy trotting next to me pretending we're going at a respectable pace. It's only when I let him off the leash to run a few laps on his own that his true colors shine through. He zips around the parking lot like greased lightning. Then we admire ourselves in the mirror as we ride back up in the elevator, both of us spent and happy and panting like . . . well, like a couple of dogs.

Tom was still in his office working when

we came in, so I didn't want to interrupt him. I patted Billy on the head and told him I'd stop by for another round in the afternoon. He gave me a kiss on the nose, blinked twice, and then trotted down the hall to take his place on the dog bed under Tom's desk. I felt a little smile play across my lips. There's nothing like a dog at your feet or a cat in your lap to right the wrongs that the world has dealt you.

Riding back down in the elevator, I remembered with a little shock that not only had I forgotten to see who'd called me during breakfast, I'd also forgotten to check for messages after dinner the night before. I immediately blamed Ethan. If he hadn't so rudely made me breakfast I would have remembered. I have a very well honed routine I follow in the morning, but Ethan had thrown a wrench in the works — a very nice wrench, but still it had me all discombobulated.

I pulled out my cell phone to check my messages, but the display just read *Two missed calls.* I figured maybe Sara Somebody had called again, or perhaps it was a wrong number. Either way, I thought, if it was important they'd call back.

Next on the schedule was Timmy Anthem. Timmy is the coach for our local high school's hockey team, the Seagulls. You'd think hockey wouldn't be a big deal in a semitropical beach town. The only time you see ice on the ground around here is if somebody drops a sno-cone in the beach parking lot, but Timmy Anthem is kind of a hockey legend.

He grew up in a small town in Canada, where apparently kids learn how to ice-skate while they're still in diapers, and he was the star player in his high school. Nobody really knew how good he was, though, not even his own family, until he won a full scholarship to play hockey in college and led his team to the national championships not once but twice. He still holds one of the top records for most goals scored in a single game.

Venturing into Timmy's apartment is always the same. As soon as I pull my keys out, there comes from deep inside the apartment a string of loud, ferocious-sounding barks. Then there's a pause, and by the time I've turned the lock and am about to open the door, the barking is closer and louder, only now it's a little muffled.

I braced myself and opened the door. Zoë came running toward me at breakneck speed, her barks muffled by the fleece pull-toy in her mouth, and slid to a perfect sit right at my feet. Zoë is a pit bull, or sometimes Timmy calls her an American Staffordshire terrier. She's all white except for a few spots splashed across her tummy and a field of black and brown on her rump, which is how she got her nickname: Brindlebutt.

Depending on who you talk to, pit bulls and Staffordshire terriers are exactly the same thing. Either that or they're two totally different, totally unrelated breeds. I still don't know which is which. All I know is that Zoë is about the sweetest dog I've ever laid eyes on.

She swung the pull-toy around seductively and then looked up at me with big brown expectant eyes.

I said, "Oh my goodness, what a big scary pit bull!"

She flicked the pull-toy on the floor in front of me, her wagging tail beating like a metronome on the tile, and nosed it up onto my feet.

"I know, honey," I said, "but we just have to wait a little while longer."

About five months earlier, Zoë had torn a ligament in her left hind leg. Surgery was the only solution, after which she was on strict orders from the vet to stay off her paws as much as possible. That meant no walks, no running, no playing, no jumping — basically no fun — for eight long, miserable weeks. For a dog like Zoë, it must have felt like she'd gone to prison, but she soldiered through it like the good little trouper she's always been. Now that her leg was healing up, she was allowed a little more activity and longer walks, but tug-of-war was definitely not on the menu.

I knelt down and gave her a big hug, and she returned the favor by licking my neck.

I said, "We're gonna have a good time anyway, don't you worry."

She grabbed her pull-toy and trotted along beside me through the apartment to the back door, which leads out to a small pool inside a screened lanai. I grabbed her leash, and we went through the lanai to the running trail that runs along behind the apartments. After a good long walk, we headed back to the pool for our favorite part of the day.

Pit bulls, at least the ones I've known, are not exactly champion swimmers. In fact, the first time I met Zoë, she got so excited that she jumped in the pool and promptly sank like a rock. Timmy had to jump in fully clothed and fish her out. As he made his way to the steps with Zoë cradled in his arms like a baby, he said, "Zoë, you can't swim!" She had given him an exasperated look and sighed, like a kid whose dad won't let her have any fun.

After Zoë's surgery, the muscles in her hind legs began to wither away from inactivity, and I was worried she'd never get back to normal if she didn't get some kind of exercise in. So Timmy and I put our heads together and came up with the perfect solution. It took some time and patience, as well as a floaty vest, but eventually I had Zoë doing laps in the pool. At first she'd just thrash around like a maniac, but once she realized the vest kept her afloat when I let go of her, she would happily motor around the pool like a brindle-butted tugboat.

I sat down on a chaise lounge at the edge of the pool, and as soon as Zoë saw me slide my bag over she started barking excitedly and swimming in circles. I pulled a couple of tennis balls out and tossed them in the pool. She immediately paddled after them, letting out an excited *yip* to let me know she'd take it from there.

Her goal is to get ahold of both balls at the same time, which even for her big maw is a tall order, so she's busy for at least twenty minutes, sometimes longer. Eventually she'll climb out of the pool, thoroughly spent, and loll around in the sun panting happily. It's a good solid workout.

I stretched out on the chaise. When a dog's happy and well exercised, there's not much more to do than check the water bowl. Cats, however, are a whole different story. They have a flair for mischief rarely matched in the canine world. A cat can have all sorts of side projects in progress — toilet paper sculptures, potted plant demolition, trash can spelunking — so I consider it part of my job to do a thorough check of the house and right any feline wrongs I find, but with Zoë splashing around in the pool, I figured I could afford to take a break.

I pulled my new book out of my backpack and slipped it out of its crisp wrapping. I knew it was crazy, but I just couldn't get over how beautiful it was. The cover was a deep forest green, its edges burnished darker by generations of curious readers, the embossed print gleaming like gold, which for all I knew it actually was.

I smiled with anticipation as I opened it up to the title page: *The Furry Godmother's Guide to Pet-Friendly Gardening, by V. Tisson-Waugh.* The paper was a creamy white, and opposite the title page was a colorful, intricately drawn illustration of a long-tailed Maine Coon cat, perched proudly atop an overturned fruit basket set in the midst of a garden of flowering plants, all aflutter with bumblebees and butterflies.

There was an introduction by the editor, which invited the reader to enjoy the book as it was written, slowly and with loving appreciation for all things living, and not, as it said, "with one's heel pressed firmly at the horse's flank." I ran my finger down the table of contents. The chapters all had Latin titles, which I assumed were all different plants, but they sounded more like fatal diseases you might get from a swamp mosquito, like *Nepeta cataria* and *Dactylis glomerata.*

The very bottom of the index page had been torn out, probably by some mischievous nineteenth-century cat, so I leafed to the back of the book to see how it ended.

"Huh," I said.

Now I knew why somebody might have been willing to part with such a beautiful book. There was a section missing in the back, probably not more than twenty pages. All that remained of them were some ragged strips of cream-colored paper clinging to the inside of the spine and a few dangling threads here and there. For a second I thought, *No wonder it was so cheap,* but I had a feeling Mr. Hoskins hadn't even noticed it.

By now, Zoë had pulled herself out of the pool and was stretched out on her back on the warm concrete, paws in the air and snoring loudly. I snapped the book shut and slipped it down in my backpack.

"Okay, Brindlebutt! Let's move it inside."

She hopped up and trotted over while I pulled out one of the striped beach towels Timmy keeps in a basket by the back door. As I dried her off, I could feel the long, thick bands of muscle in her hind legs. I congratulated her on the progress she was making. She wagged her tail and grinned all the way to the living room, where she took her place on the couch while I clicked on the TV with the remote and tuned to the Learning Channel. I personally wouldn't allow any dog of mine to watch one single episode of *Toddlers & Tiaras,* but if that's what Zoë likes, who am I to judge?

I left her with a kiss on the top of her velvety head and a promise I'd be back in a few hours for another swim. I figured I had just enough time to swing by the bookstore on the way to my last morning client. Not that I had any intention of returning my new book, but I figured Mr. Hoskins might want to know about the missing section, and he'd probably want to check the other books it came with just in case they'd been mangled, too.

Now when I think about that moment, I wonder how things might have been different if I'd just stayed there in Timmy's apartment with Zoë for the rest of the morning. If I'd known what I was about to walk into, I would have sat right down on the couch next to her and watched a whole *Toddlers & Tiaras* marathon — every single episode of every single season.

But no.

That's not what I did.

7

I have a morning routine that I've worked out over the years, and I stick to it with an almost military dedication. I roll out of bed, stumble into the bathroom, splash cold water on my face, and pull my hair back into a tight ponytail. Then I pad into the closet and paw through the shelves for my standard uniform: khaki cargo shorts, white sleeveless tee, and a fresh pair of white tennis shoes. Anybody who knows me knows I can't stand old, smelly shoes, so I keep a steady supply of brand-new Keds lined up on the rack in my closet. As soon as one of them gets even the slightest bit ragged, out they go, right to the Salvation Army.

I'm out the door and on the road by the time the sun's coming up, and when my morning rounds are done, usually around nine or so, I head straight over to the Village Diner, where I have the same exact breakfast every single day. Then it's home for a shower and a nap, and then on to my afternoon rounds, and then dinner and then bed. It's the same every day, seven days a week.

In other words, I don't like surprises.

Then again, as I cruised down Ocean Boulevard on my way to the bookstore, whistling happily along like one of Snow White's seven dwarves, I had to admit: Breakfast on a silver platter was a nice change, especially when it was served by a beautiful man. I chuckled at myself for still thinking about it, but I couldn't stop. Even though I felt like my schedule was still a little out of whack, it had put me in a good mood, not to mention the fact that my neck felt worlds better.

I wondered how I could convince Ethan to make sure that both nightly massages and breakfast service became standard additions to my daily routine.

I was looking forward to seeing Mr. Hoskins again. I had instantly liked him, as befuddled as he was, and I think I was kind of hoping that maybe we'd become friends. He was a little more disheveled than I remembered Mr. Beezy being, but there was definitely something similar about them. Of course, I couldn't hope to re-create the bond I'd felt with Mr. Beezy, but it certainly couldn't hurt to try. I think those bonds we form as children are almost impossible to find again, especially after we grow up and see the world for what it really is.

I pulled the Bronco into a spot just in front of Amber Jack's, a local hangout with an open-air patio and a little stage in the corner for live music. During the day it's deserted save for a few sparrows and snowy egrets foraging around under the tables for bits of french fries or burger buns from the night before, but in the evening it's PTB — the Place to Be. In fact, they even have a live webcam so people can check out the crowd from the comfort of their own home anywhere in the world. The beer is cheap and the music is good, and it's the kind of establishment where tourists can rub elbows with us locals and pretend they live in paradise all year long, too.

I grabbed my book and had just opened the car door when my cell phone rang. One look at the caller ID and I laughed out loud. It read SARA MEM HO.

I was pretty sure this was the same "Sara Somebody" who had already called a couple of times, but I knew right away it wasn't the Sara who works the hot dog stand down at the beach pavilion, and it wasn't a new client either. Sara Mem Ho was caller ID shorthand for Sarasota Memorial Hospital.

I'd been friends with a girl in high school named Christine Ho, but I'd certainly never heard of anybody named Mem. I grinned thinking about how I'd tease Ethan about it later, except then I remembered with a jolt that my friend Cora had recently had a little heart trouble, and my first thought was that she was back in the hospital.

Hoping with all my might that I was wrong, I flipped it open and said, "Hello?"

A young woman said in a rushed half-whisper, "Hi. You don't know me, and I shouldn't be doing this, but I just thought you should know."

I said, "Who is this?"

"I'm a night nurse at Sarasota Memorial Hospital. We're not supposed to get involved in our patients' private affairs, but . . ."

I took a deep breath and braced myself for bad news. "Okay. What happened?"

"He's been asking for you."

I frowned. "Huh?"

"Mr. Vladek. He made me promise not to call you, but then he asks for you in his sleep."

She was talking so quietly I wasn't even sure I'd heard her right. "Mr. Vladek?"

"Yes, Anton Vladek."

I let out a sigh of relief. "Oh my gosh. I

think you have the wrong number. I don't know anyone named Vladek."

There was a quick intake of breath and then silence.

I said, "Hello?"

She blurted, "Oh my God, I'm so sorry. I have the wrong number. Please don't tell anyone I called you."

I started to ask her who the heck I would tell, but then the line went dead. I sat there staring at the phone for a second and wondering what in the world that could have been about. Anton Vladek sounded exactly like the kind of person I'd get a mysterious call from if I was an international spy. For a second I fantasized about hitting redial, disguising my voice, and asking the mystery nurse to deliver a top secret, coded message to Anton Vladek: *The microfilm is in a black valise at the front desk of the Russian embassy, and the eagle flies at midnight.*

Instead, I slipped the phone down in my pocket and grabbed my new book. The last thing I needed right now was more drama in my life. Anton Vladek would just have to carry out whatever international spy-ring undercover sting operation he was working on without me.

As I came around the front of the Bronco and stepped up on the sidewalk, I saw a little crowd up the street in front of Beezy's Bookstore. The first thing that came to mind was that they were having some kind of sale, or maybe a book signing. There are lots of writers around here, so often you'll see somebody with a table set up, signing their new book at the library or the farmer's market downtown. But then I realized they were all wearing the same thing: spruce green trousers, black boots, and short-sleeved, green polo shirts.

I stopped dead in my tracks. There were about six sheriff's deputies in all, standing in a circle behind a line of yellow-and-black police tape. There were two department cruisers parked across the street, and two policemen were stringing more tape around the two shops on either side of the book-store. They'd also cordoned off the parking spaces directly in front of the shop, which were vacant except for a dusty maroon minivan parked right in front. On the side of the van was a black circle of lettering that read BEEZY'S BOOKSTORE, and inside the circle was an image of an open book.

The door to the bookshop swung open, and two policemen stepped out, followed by a tall woman with sorrel hair and pale, freckled skin. She wore a knee-length skirt the color of a baked potato, with a gray blouse and dull black mules. I recognized her immediately.

Samantha McKenzie. When Guidry had moved to New Orleans, it was McKenzie who'd taken over as lead homicide detective for the Sarasota County Sheriff's Department. I had met her a couple of times before. She wasn't much older than me, but I always felt like a little child in her presence, and I must have looked like a fool standing there with my arms dangling at my sides and my mouth hanging wide open. When she saw me, our eyes locked for a second. She had a look on her face that I had seen before — intense alertness and concentration, but with a vague, resolute sadness.

She stepped forward and held out her hand. "Ah, Miss Hemingway, we were just talking about you."

8

I was standing just inside the bookstore, next to the old burnished-wood counter with the antique cash register on top. It was eerily quiet except for the low hum of the air conditioner built into the wall over the front door. The shop looked the same as it had the night before, except now all the lights in the back of the store were off. The light over the register was on, as were the two hanging glass lamps in the display window, but there was no sign of Cosmo anywhere.

I had the urge to call out for Mr. Hoskins to let him know we were here, but of course that would have been crazy. Somewhere in the back of my mind I must have known what was going on, but there seemed to be a part of me that just wouldn't allow it. My eyes scanned the pen-and-ink drawings arranged on the wall behind the register, as if I might find some sort of answer in their innocent scenery. In one, a comely woman with long dark hair falling off her shoulders peered down at me with wise, comforting eyes.

I glanced into the back of the store, but since the only light was coming from the front, it was too dark to see anything clearly.

I turned to Detective McKenzie and said, "What's happening?"

She cleared her throat, and I felt the inside of my palms start to sweat. "We got a call this morning from the man that delivers the newspapers every day. Normally when he gets here the shop's not open for business yet, so he knocks on the door to let Mr. Hoskins know he's here and then leaves his stack of papers on the sidewalk."

She pointed outside, and there on the sidewalk next to the door was a stack of newspapers wrapped in white nylon twine.

"He said usually by the time he's back in his delivery van, Mr. Hoskins has come to the door and they exchange a wave or a 'good morning.' But this time Mr. Hoskins didn't come to the door. So he got out and went back to look through the door window. The lights were on inside, but the door was unlocked. That's when he realized something was wrong."

I looked around the shop. It didn't seem

like there'd been a burglary or a fight or anything like that, so I still couldn't quite fathom what McKenzie was doing here. At that point, I'm not even sure I understood why the whole place was surrounded with police tape. To me, it was obvious what had happened. Last night, I'd shown up at closing time and interrupted Mr. Hoskins's normal routine. He'd simply forgotten to lock up before he went home.

I said, "Mr. Hoskins seemed a little absentminded. Maybe . . ." but the expression on McKenzie's face stopped me. She shook her head slowly and glanced over my shoulder at something on the countertop behind me.

I didn't want to, but I turned and looked. Right away, I knew why she'd been talking about me when I arrived. The check I'd made out to Beezy's Bookstore the night before was still lying next to the bowl of chocolates beyond the cash register. She'd seen my name on the check and was probably about to call me. My check wasn't what McKenzie was looking at, though.

There, in a diagonal line across the countertop, was a row of red splotches, each about the size of a quarter and spaced a few inches apart. My stomach tightened into a fist as I realized — it was blood.

McKenzie said, "The cash register is empty, and just before you arrived, Mr. Hoskins's daughter called the station. The doorman in his apartment building said he never came home last night."

My legs were beginning to feel like jelly. I looked at her and said, "I was just here. I was here last night before he closed up."

She nodded at the check. "Yes, I figured as much."

I looked down at the book in my hand, and then my eyes followed the central corridor to the round claw-foot table in the center of the store, but it was too dark to see anything farther back.

I said, "Is he . . . is he back there?"

McKenzie shook her head slowly. "No. We don't know where he is. I was hoping you might be able to help with that."

I hugged myself and sighed with relief. Just then, one of the deputies waiting outside tapped on the door and pushed it open slightly.

"Ma'am," he said, "there's something out here you should see."

She turned to me. "Dixie, would you mind waiting a bit?"

I nodded mutely and then just stood there in a daze. I think I was still trying to process exactly what was going on.

She smiled slightly and said, "Um, outside, if you don't mind?"

I reached for the door, but she slid in front of me. "Let me get that for you."

She nodded at the deputy, and he pushed the door open. I noticed he was wearing blue latex gloves. I looked down at McKenzie's hands and realized she was, too. It was only then that it dawned on me that this wasn't just Beezy's Bookstore anymore. It wasn't just a place to come and explore, to lie on the carpet with my head resting on a stack of books and forget about the world outside. It was a crime scene, and everything inside was potential evidence.

The deputy led McKenzie past the big display window to the edge of the building and lifted up the police tape for her. Before she went under, she turned back and said, "Dixie, I know you're busy, so I won't be long, but I do have a few more questions for you."

I nodded. Even though she hadn't asked me any questions yet, I knew I'd already answered some. Guidry had taught me that you can sometimes learn more from watching a person's first reaction to a crime scene than you can from a hundred hours of interrogation. I was sure McKenzie had taken note of my every move, what my eyes had

123

lingered on inside the store, how my breathing had changed, where I put my hands, what my first words had been.

I was standing with my back to the street, but I could see the reflection of two of the deputies in the display window as they inspected Mr. Hoskins's van. Another one of the deputies was across the street with a woman in a white apron, probably someone from the market. I figured they were interviewing every shop owner on the street to find out if anyone had seen anything suspicious.

I looked at the stack of dictionaries in the far corner of the display, half hoping Cosmo would be there, snoozing away safe and sound in his favorite spot. If he was there, I'd know this whole thing was just one big misunderstanding, that there was an explanation for everything and that Mr. Hoskins was totally fine. If he was there, I'd know I hadn't stepped right into another big pile of crazy.

Of course, he wasn't there.

9

I'd probably only been standing in front of Beezy's Bookstore for a few minutes, but it felt like an eternity. I was beginning to wonder if McKenzie was planning on leaving me there to stare into the display window all day long, but she finally appeared in front of the butcher shop a few doors down, accompanied by the deputy who had interrupted us earlier. For some reason I fished my cell phone out of my pocket and flipped it open, pretending to study something very important on it, like a text message from Prince Charles or a phone call from the state lottery board.

I don't know why, but there was something about Detective McKenzie that always made me a tad nervous. Well, more than just a tad. She was thin-boned and plain, but I could tell by the way people treated her that she was a power to be reckoned with. I pictured her brain like the interior of an intricately designed clock, with all its cogs and wheels spinning full speed, sending off little sparks and bits of metal. She walked behind me, putting her latex gloves back on, and as I made one last check of the blank screen on my phone, she opened the door to the bookstore and the little bell over the door rang again.

She said, "Shall we?"

There was an eerie silence inside the store, like the silence inside a shell after its owner has abandoned it. Like a silence you can hear.

McKenzie said, "Sorry for the wait. I just had a very interesting conversation with the butcher."

"No problem." I nodded absentmindedly. "I do have a few more pets I need to check on this morning, but they can wait."

"I'd just like you to take a look around and tell me if anything seems different."

"Different?"

"From the way you remember it. Just anything you notice, no matter how small."

She walked around behind the counter and flicked on several light switches. Now I could see all the way to the back of the store, and everything seemed the same. I could even see the box on the floor at the very last aisle where I'd found my gardening book.

I said, "I don't notice anything."

"And what time did you say you were here?"

I realized I hadn't ever told her a time, but I let it go. "It was exactly 6:04. I know because I remember looking at my watch. Mr. Hoskins was just closing when I arrived."

"Did you see anyone else in the store?"

"No. In fact, he locked the door right after I came in."

She flipped through a couple of pages on her silver clipboard and then pulled a ballpoint pen from one of the pockets on the front of her skirt.

I said, "Detective McKenzie, do you think Mr. Hoskins . . ." but my voice trailed off.

She shook her head, "I can't say for certain, but it doesn't look good. We have an unlocked shop, we have a missing shopkeeper, we have blood across the shop's front counter, and we have a person smeared with blood leaving the scene. So were you shopping for any one book in particular?"

My eyes widened. "A person smeared with blood?"

McKenzie nodded, "Yes. Leaving the scene. It was last night after most of the

127

shops were closed. The butcher was locking up when he saw a woman leave the bookstore and get in her car. She took off her jacket, and he noticed her clothes underneath were stained with blood. Normally I wouldn't be so quick to believe someone could identify bloody clothing in low light from a distance of thirty feet or so. But a butcher . . ."

"That was me."

"I'm sorry?"

"I said, that was me."

She nodded nonchalantly. "Yes, I explained to the butcher about the car accident, but he wasn't convinced. He didn't think anybody who'd just dragged a body away from a head-on collision would be crazy enough to go shopping right afterward."

I could feel my ears turning red. I'd only had a handful of conversations with McKenzie in the past, but they generally left me feeling like I'd been tossed out of a roller coaster.

I said, "The whole reason I was in the neighborhood was to buy a book, and I've been coming here since I was little. And they had the road blocked off so I couldn't go anywhere. I figured while I was waiting I'd run in and get a book. I put the jacket on over my clothes so I wouldn't freak anybody out."

She pulled a strand of thin, mouse-colored hair away from her face and tucked it behind her ear. "Seems fairly reasonable, although you may have a harder time convincing the butcher. And did you notice anything unusual about Mr. Hoskins at the time?"

I tried to think, which wasn't easy around this woman. "Well, he seemed a little eccentric, and he was out of breath."

She raised an eyebrow. "Out of breath?"

"His face was kind of flushed, and he was breathing heavy. He said he'd been moving boxes around in the back. I think maybe he'd gotten a delivery of books, because he said the one I bought had just come in."

"And why do you say he seemed eccentric?"

"Well, maybe that's not the right word. Just a little absentminded maybe, and the way he was dressed. Kind of rumpled, shoes untied, and he was wearing big wraparound sunglasses."

She nodded. "He'd had an appointment with his ophthalmologist earlier in the day. His daughter said they had dilated his pupils, so the glasses would have been to protect his eyes. Do you remember what else he was wearing?"

"He had suspenders on because his pants were too big, and they were yellow. And a red beret. His pants were brown, or maybe gray, and his shirt was red. I remember it was a button-down shirt because the buttons were shiny brass and he'd missed a couple."

"Anything else?"

"No, just the big sunglasses, and he wasn't at the register when I came in. I had to call him a couple of times before he heard me."

"Oh? Where was he?"

"In the back, but that's because he was closed. Or at least he thought he was. He said he should have locked the door but he'd forgotten."

She made a note in her clipboard. "And how about the cat?"

"There's a stack of dictionaries in the window. I noticed when I came in it had orange fur on top of it, so I knew there was a cat here somewhere."

"Did you actually see a cat?"

I sighed. I figured he'd probably have hidden somewhere. It hadn't even occurred to me that the cat might have been missing, too, but I could tell that's where she was going. "Just for a split second. I was beginning to think something was wrong, and then the cat came running out of the back office. Mr. Hoskins called him Cosmo."

"Did you notice if Cosmo was hurt?"

"Hurt?"

She tipped her chin at the counter. I looked closer at the red splotches and felt a shudder go down my spine. The red splotches were cat prints. Either Cosmo was bleeding or . . .

McKenzie said, "I'm assuming you would have noticed if the cat was hurt."

I nodded. "I didn't get a real good look. He ran by like a flash, but cats don't usually race around like that if they're hurt. They're more likely to find a place to hide and hunker down."

"Where did he run to?"

I pointed to the space under the front counter. "He came from the back and disappeared right under there. I didn't see him again."

"Okay. When you say you thought something was wrong, what did you mean by that?"

"Well, like I said, when I first came in there was nobody at the register. I called out a couple of times, but nobody answered. I was beginning to think maybe the place was empty, but I was about halfway through the store when I heard something in the back, and that's when Cosmo came running out."

McKenzie was staring at me, almost as if she were boring a hole straight into my brain, and I suddenly realized one of the reasons I got so nervous around her was that she never looked me straight in the eye. Instead, she seemed to focus on a point somewhere in the middle of my forehead.

I tried to keep my train of thought. "So . . . then I called out a little louder and Mr. Hoskins heard me that time. He said, 'Be right with you.' "

She nodded. The strand of hair that she'd brushed away had fallen back and was hanging across her face, but she didn't seem to notice.

"And Mr. Hoskins, was he racing around the store like a flash as well?"

"Huh?"

She pursed her lips together, looked up at the ceiling for a split second, and then looked back down at the middle of my forehead. "You said you didn't see anyone in the store when you came in, and then you said Mr. Hoskins locked the door right after you came in, and then you said you were midway through the store when Mr. Hoskins called out from the back office. I'm just trying to come up with a reasonable explanation as to how he pulled that off, and your account makes perfect sense if both Mr. Hoskins and his cat were racing around the store like flashes."

This woman was either an utter bat-case or a complete genius, or more likely a combination of the two, but either way I felt like my head was about to explode. Plus, I was starting to get a little tired of being spoken to like a fourth grader.

I took a deep breath. "Okay. No, I guess I misspoke. Mr. Hoskins was not racing around the store like a flash. He locked the door *after* he came out from the back."

She nodded curtly and made another note in her clipboard. "Did he seem nervous or upset?"

"I don't think so, maybe a little absent-minded, and his hands were trembling, but I hadn't ever met him before, so I don't know if his hands always tremble or not."

She studied me for a second and took a deep breath, but I stopped her just in time. I knew exactly what she was about to say. I had just told her I'd been coming here since I was a child, but now I was saying I'd never met Mr. Hoskins.

I held up my hand. "Hold on there, Sherlock. The answer to your question is this: I spent a lot of time here when I was little, but then I didn't come back for years. In the meantime, the original owner passed away and Mr. Hoskins took over the store. Yesterday was the first time I'd been back since then."

The corners of her lips rose in a faint smile as she looked over her notes.

I sighed. "Sorry. I guess I'm just feeling a little overwhelmed."

She closed her clipboard. "It's alright, I know how you feel. I was up all night on another case. I haven't been home in twenty-four hours. I barely remember what my daughter looks . . ." She stopped herself and her cheeks flushed red.

I said, "I'm a little worried about the cat, too. I'm wondering if maybe he got out of the store at some point."

She finally brushed the strands of hair that had been hanging in her face away again and said, "I rather hope he did."

I didn't quite know what to make of that, but it made me wonder if there was something else she wasn't telling me. My mind felt like it had turned to mush, and I suddenly had an overwhelming desire for sleep. I half considered excusing myself and lying down in my spot under the big claw-foot table, but I didn't think McKenzie would take too kindly to that.

She led me to the door. "I have a lab unit on the way, so we'll know soon enough whether the blood on the counter is human or feline, but until then, if you think of anything else, anything at all, please give me a call right away."

She handed me her card, which wasn't really necessary. I already had her number in my phone, but I took it anyway. Out on the sidewalk, I looked once again at the stack of dictionaries. Thinking about Mr. Hoskins and Cosmo, that something bad could have happened to them, unleashed all sorts of emotions in me. I was afraid I was about to break down into a sobbing mess right there on the sidewalk, but I held myself together. I had a feeling 99 percent of the deputies in the sheriff's department already thought I was a certified basket case. I didn't want to make it any worse.

McKenzie snapped off her latex gloves and took one of my hands in hers. At first I thought she'd noticed something was wrong. I was expecting her to give me a sympathetic smile and ask if I was okay, but instead she just shook my hand firmly and said, "Oh, I almost forgot. Why are you here?"

"Huh?"

"Why are you here?"

I was thinking I could easily have asked her the same thing. Mr. Hoskins couldn't have been missing more than twelve hours or so, and a track of bloody paw prints across a countertop hardly seemed reason enough to launch a full-scale murder investigation, but then again, it was entirely possible McKenzie did know something I didn't know. In fact, I had a feeling she knew a *lot* of things I didn't know.

I showed her my book and flipped it open to the back. "It's the one I bought from Mr. Hoskins last night. It's missing a whole section in the end. I just stopped by to tell him."

She said, "Hmm," and then seemed to get lost in her own thoughts. "Well, call me if anything comes to mind."

"Detective McKenzie, I'm worried about those chocolates."

"What about them?"

"Well, they're toxic to cats."

She nodded. "I understand. I'll remove them myself before we leave today."

For a second I wondered what she planned on doing with them. Surely she wouldn't just throw them away . . . I toyed with the idea of offering to "remove" them myself, but then a mobile forensics unit pulled up and I snapped back to my senses. Sometimes I really do wonder if I shouldn't join the local chapter of Chocoholics Anonymous.

McKenzie signaled for two of the deputies to follow her back in the bookstore and then held out her hand. "Let me know if you remember anything else?"

I nodded and then watched her disappear into the bookstore as the lab techs opened up the side door to the truck and unpacked their gear.

When I was a deputy, which hadn't been that long ago in the grand scheme of things, a mobile forensics unit had consisted of a couple of oversized tackle boxes, but in the past year an anonymous donor had given the department almost half a million dollars. That was enough to buy a new state-of-the-art mobile crime truck, complete with sophisticated evidence collection systems, lab chemicals, computers, and satellite Internet, not to mention two full-time lab technicians to drive it around.

I would have liked to see the inside of it, but I figured those techs had better things to do than give me a private tour. As I made my way back to the Bronco, a van pulled up. I imagined it was probably a photographer, called in to take pictures of every inch of the bookstore. A photographer is standard procedure at any crime scene. No matter what happened afterward — even if the entire place burned to the ground — there'd always be a detailed photographic record of exactly how everything looked at the scene of the crime. That way they wouldn't have to rely on anybody's memory to re-create it.

Which was good, because I planned on forgetting the whole thing as quickly as possible.

10

According to *Cosmopolitan* magazine, I am a woman in the prime of her life — physically, sexually, and mentally. Physically, I'd say my daily jogs with Billy Elliot keep me in relatively good health. Sexually, well, that's in progress; I'll report back later. Mentally? Well, for argument's sake let's just say yes.

Still, I misplace things all the time. I lose my car keys at least once a month. I've found them at the bottom of my dirty clothes hamper, I've found them in the washing machine, and more than once I've found them in the freezer, tossed in next to the ice cream and the frozen corn. Sometimes my mind just starts wandering and I forget what I'm doing.

Mr. Hoskins may have been a lot of things, but he was clearly not a man in the prime of his life. It seemed perfectly reasonable to me that he could easily have misplaced his keys somewhere. In fact, I distinctly remembered him patting his pockets and looking around as if he'd lost something, and that would explain why the door was left unlocked overnight.

It was simple. He couldn't find his keys and it was the end of the day, he was tired, and he wanted to go home — who would rob a bookstore anyway? It's not like they're known for having lots of cash on hand, especially not in this day and age when anybody with half a brain and an Internet connection can sit around in their underwear all day and buy every book their little heart desires with just the click of a key. So Mr. Hoskins probably decided the store was perfectly fine and he'd just look for his keys in the morning, but to be on the safe side, he had emptied out the register and taken the cash with him. It all made perfect sense.

Except none of that explained the bloody prints on the counter, not to mention the fact that he hadn't come home the night before . . . and he *had* seemed a little nervous . . .

I shook my head. There was nothing I could do about it, and it wasn't my business anyway. I had already let myself get mixed up in plenty of things I shouldn't in the past, and with Ethan, my life was already busy enough. I didn't need any more things to distract me.

By the time I pulled into the covered carport at Julie Caldwell's condo, I'd made up my mind. Whatever had happened in that bookstore after I left the night before had absolutely nothing to do with me. Yes, Detective McKenzie was a little odd, and yes, she made me feel like a child on the first day of kindergarten, but she was also about the smartest person I'd ever met, and if anyone could figure out what had happened to Mr. Hoskins, it was her.

Not to mention the fact that I was no longer with the sheriff's department. For some reason I had to remind myself of that little fact every time I turned around. I had a whole new career, and I had just embarked on a whole new life with a smart, handsome man who didn't know it yet but was about to start serving me breakfast on a regular basis.

I shut off the ignition and gave myself a little nod in the rearview mirror, as if to say, *Good for you.* It's unlike me to just let things go, but I can recognize a good decision when I make one, and forgetting about Mr. Hoskins and whatever had happened in that bookstore was one of the best decisions I'd made in a very long time.

Then a little voice in the back of my head said, *Yeah yeah yeah, but what about the cat?*

I ignored it and grabbed my backpack.

Julie Caldwell is a cosmetologist. Originally I thought that meant she could tell me what my moon-sign says about my love life, but turns out I was wrong. Her specialty is hair color. Her clients, mostly doyennes of old Sarasota or young movie stars, pay up to eight hundred dollars for a single appointment. She's got four chairs in her salon, and they're usually all booked months in advance.

She gave me highlights once for free as a birthday present. As I sat in one of the chairs in her salon while she moved from client to client, I did the math:

4 appointments an hour × 8 hours a day

=

Julie is filthy rich

If I'd known I could have been a millionaire just by coloring people's hair, I'd have gone to beauty school myself.

Julie had called me up the week before to ask if I could take care of her "cat" while she was in Miami for a few days. I say "cat" with quotation marks because Esmerelda is in no way an ordinary house kitty. She has a deep tawny coat splashed all over with chocolate brown spots, long graceful legs that ripple with lean muscle, and big cupped ears perched on top of her head like two furry satellite dishes. She clocks in on the scale at a whopping (for a cat at least) twenty-six pounds, and from the tip of her nose to the end of her tail, she's four and a half feet of pure feline awesomeness.

Esmerelda is what is known in the cat world as a Savannah — a cross between a regular domestic house cat and a wild cat from Africa called a serval. Servals hunt at night, dining on everything from mice and crickets to frogs and fish, but they've been known to take down bigger animals, too, even the occasional deer, The first time I met Esmerelda, I took one look into her deep, yellow eyes and saw the wisdom of generations of proud, free-roaming cats. I got the distinct impression that she took one look at me and saw dinner. She had that same sparkle in her eyes I have when you slide a plate of bacon in front of me.

For walks, she wears a soft leather harness. It's pink, studded up and down with little rhinestones, and probably costs more than my entire wardrobe. Julie says she chose it for several reasons. First, Julie wears a lot of rhinestones herself. She's kind of flashy that way, and pink is her favorite color. In fact, over the years it's become her trademark. Every time I see her, she's dyed her hair a new color, but it's always a variation of the same thing — *pink*. Second, people tend to get a little alarmed when they see her walking down the street with Esmerelda. They usually think she's some crazy person who's busted a small leopard out of the zoo, but once they see the matching pink outfits and all the rhinestones — not to mention Julie's pink hair — they just assume she's with the circus.

Almost a hundred years ago, the Ringling Brothers made Sarasota their hometown, so there are all kinds of clown schools and circus performers in the area. It's completely normal to see clowns in full makeup in the drive-through at the bank or on line at the coffee shop, so stands to reason you might see a circus handler with an exotic animal or two every once in a while.

Esmerelda greeted me at the door and let me know she was happy to see me by fluffing her big tail out like a feather duster and butting her head into my ankles. It can take an hour just to walk her around the block, mainly because everybody that goes by wants to stop and meet her, but also because her favorite thing is to crouch low in the grass and watch the birds and squirrels play in the trees. If you let her she'll stay there for hours, still as a statue, watching with complete and utter rapture. I always imagine she's tapped into some deep ancestral memory, which makes me smile, but it also makes me a little sad. She'll never get to run free in an African savannah, even though that's where half her genes are telling her she belongs.

On our way back in from the walk, I stopped and checked Julie's mailbox. It was all junk mail, but it made me think of Guidry's letter. I still hadn't opened it, and I was beginning to wonder if I shouldn't just toss it in the trash.

While Esmerelda ate her breakfast, I did a thorough check of the condo, and I wondered if my fear didn't have something to do with Ethan. The last time I'd spoken with Guidry, he'd said that he had met someone, so I'd felt free to move on with my life. Did I really think there was something in that letter that could threaten what I had with Ethan? In the master bedroom, I paused in front of the big window and looked out at the ocean. There were two massive rain clouds looming on the horizon like lumbering giants rising out of the sea.

After Esmerelda was done eating, I washed

her bowl out with soap and hot water and left it to dry on a wooden dish rack next to the sink. Julie keeps a collection of toys in the junk drawer next to the refrigerator, so while Esmerelda sat nearby and watched with rapt attention, I opened the drawer and went over the choices of the day.

"Well, of course, we always have this little stuffed mouse . . ."

I held it out for Esmerelda, and she nudged it gently with the tip of her nose.

"Or there's this catnip-stuffed ball . . ."

She wrinkled up her nose and backed away a step.

"Okay, definitely not that one. There's always this old standby . . ."

I held my hand out and showed her a purple Wiffle ball with holes all around it the diameter of a Magic Marker. She said, *"Rowwwk!"* and swiped one big paw at it.

"Alright then, we have a winner!"

I cut a couple of slices of cheddar cheese into little strips and pushed them through the holes in the Wiffle ball. Then I gave Esmerelda a squeeze and told her to be a good girl and that I'd be back in a little while. As I went out the door, she was happily chasing the Wiffle ball around the living room, not unlike a lion chasing an antelope around the African savannah.

By the time I made it back down to the south end of the Key and was pulling into my driveway, those giant clouds had moved inland and let loose with a very respectable downpour. People say our little island is semitropical, but sometimes it feels like a full-on jungle, especially when the rain comes down like a banshee, or in the summer when only us hard-core residents hang around for the stifling heat and humidity and most of the snowbirds fly back to their homes up north.

One thing we can always count on, though, is the occasional thunderstorm to come in and cool things off. It usually only lasts long enough to give everything a good rinsing, and then before you know it the sun bursts forth again, all the birds sing in praise of fresh, clean water, and all the leaves shimmer and sparkle in the sunlight like diamonds.

The carport was empty, which meant I'd been right. Michael was at work, and Paco had started a new assignment. I streaked across the courtyard and up the stairs as fast as I could, but by the time I got inside I was soaked to the bone. I didn't care, though. The rain felt good, and it helped me forget about Guidry and Mr. Hoskins and everything else that had happened.

I stood in the shower and turned the water on full force. For a few blissful moments, I just hung there like a coat on a clothesline, and my mind went blank as the hot water streamed down my back. Once I was sufficiently renewed, I toweled off, padded down the hall to my bedroom, and collapsed stark naked on the bed. I barely had the energy to pull the comforter up around me, but the cool air from the AC felt good gently moving over my body. It wasn't long before I heard a familiar *meep meep.*

Ella Fitzgerald hopped up on the bed and pressed her nose to my cheek, purring like a miniature jackhammer. I scooped her up in my arms, and she curled up against me. I had barely closed my eyes when Mr. Hoskins's kindly face floated into view. I thought to myself, *Where in the world have you gone off to?*

It's ridiculous, I know, but every once in a while I get it in my head that I have ESP. My great-aunt Bess always said she knew exactly when a thunderstorm was headed our way, and sometimes she was even right, so I've always fantasized that if I just try hard enough I can tap into my own inner psychic.

Once I had a pretty good image of Mr. Hoskins's face, which wasn't that easy with those big wraparound sunglasses, I tried to imagine where he was, if there was anything familiar nearby, like a street sign or maybe a building, or anything that might help identify his location. It took a little while, but slowly, his surroundings actually started taking shape. I could even see something behind him, a brick wall, or maybe a bookshelf, and then he was standing next to something metal, gold or brass, and it had little round buttons on it with . . .

Never mind. It was just the dumb cash register at the front of the bookstore. Clearly I hadn't inherited my great-aunt Bess's special powers. I told myself I'd just have to try harder next time and pulled Ella a little closer. Within seconds we were both sound asleep.

I dreamed I was walking down a dark, narrow alley, lined on either side with dusty, abandoned shops. I didn't know where I was, but it felt exotic and foreign. I wore a tight black dress under a white trench coat, and I was carrying a white sequined evening bag. My hair was pitch-black and straight, with thick bangs that stopped just above my eyebrows. I ran my fingers through it and realized with a start that I was wearing a wig.

My instincts told me I was being followed,

and I knew it was important that I look like nothing was wrong, so even though it was completely dark I walked straight ahead with my chin up, as if I'd walked this narrow alley a hundred times.

I paused in front of a particularly sinister-looking shop with a big picture window in front, lit all around with rows of naked light-bulbs painted a garish red. They cast a pool of red light on the street in front of the shop, and it was only then that I realized it was paved with old cobblestones.

As I stood there I heard footsteps echoing through the alley and coming closer. As calmly as possible, I opened my evening bag and pulled out a tiny silver pistol, which I held concealed under the sleeve of my trench coat. The footsteps grew louder but then paused. Now there was a man in a bowler hat and a dark three-piece suit standing next to me. He had a name tag on his lapel with ANTON written on it, and he was holding a white sequined evening bag just like mine. I couldn't quite see his face, but I noticed his fingernails were painted pitch-black. He smiled pleasantly and then nodded at the picture window.

Behind the glass was a little stage, about four feet wide. At the back of the stage was a tiny door. It swung open, and out crawled a hairy old man dressed in a frilly red two-piece bikini. He gave a little bow and then set an old cassette deck down on the floor. When he pressed the play button, a slow, scratchy jazz tune began.

I kept my face perfectly blank, as if gray-haired cross-dressing octogenarians were a dime a dozen, and Anton said, "Do you know what time the next train leaves for Budapest?"

I held up a long ivory cigarette holder, on the tip of which was a business card, rolled into a little tube to look like a cigarette. "There are no more trains today, sir. Do you have a light?"

The old man in the window started dancing seductively, or at least as seductively as an old hairy man can manage. He was swaying his hips from side to side, but as we talked he held up a giant megaphone to his ear and leaned toward us, straining to hear our conversation.

Anton held a silver cigarette lighter up to the tip of the business card and said, "I believe you'll find everything is in order."

He held out his evening bag, and I held out mine. We exchanged them, nodded politely, and then walked away in opposite directions. As I continued on I opened the bag up and slipped my pistol inside, thankful I hadn't been forced to use it, and then casually took a few long drags on my calling-card cigarette, which gradually turned to ashes and fell away. When I was almost at the end of the alley, the old man in the red bikini ran out into the street and shook his fist at me.

He shouted, "Never mind the thunder!"

Just then a stupendous clap of thunder tore across the entire sky, and I woke with a start. I was shivering like a wet dog, and Ella was standing on my chest, her ears alert and her whiskers all aquiver. I told her it was only a storm, but she hopped off the bed and scampered down the hall to see for herself.

I sat up on the edge of the bed and said out loud, "Really?"

Sometimes I wonder what the hell my brain thinks it's doing. Most people get to dream about normal things — like flying, or finding buried treasure, or realizing too late that they've worn their pajamas to school — but no, not me. I get to dream about hairy old men in skimpy red bikinis.

They say a dream is just your subconscious trying to tell you a story. If that's true, I wish my subconscious would just keep its dumb stories to its subconscious self.

11

Just about every day of my life, rain or shine, hell or high water, dog fight or fur ball, I stop in at the Village Diner to have breakfast. It's just up the street from Donkey Joe's Pizza, which happens to have the best pizza in the world, so you might find me on this block two, three, or — I'm ashamed to admit — four times a day. The diner faces the corner, so it's bright and airy, with big windows and a good view of the street on two sides and a row of booths covered in soft teal pleather along the wall. Opposite the booths is a long stainless steel counter and a row of bar stools with round seats that spin in place.

As soon as I walked through the door, Judy snatched a mug from under the bar and filled it to the top with piping-hot coffee. Then she slid it in front of me as I sat down in my regular booth in the back, and we gave each other a little nod. Judy is long-limbed and angular, with pale skin that burns easily and a sprinkling of mocha freckles over the bridge of her nose. Her hazel eyes look out on the world with quiet resolve, like someone who's still holding on to her dreams in spite of the odds.

Tanisha winked at me from her little window in the kitchen, which meant she'd already started on my breakfast. Tanisha is what they call big-boned, practically as wide as she is tall, with a bigger-than-life personality to match. She's one of my favorite people in the world, not just because the down-home southern food that comes out of her kitchen is delicious enough to make a grown woman weep (it has happened) but also because she's taught me so much over the years. No matter how bad things get — and Tanisha has had her share of rough times — she always has a happy face for the world.

You might not know it from watching us, but with the exception of Michael and Paco, Judy and Tanisha are my closest friends, which is kind of funny when you consider we hardly ever see each other outside the four walls of this diner. We tell each other everything there is to tell. I know the whole story of all the men Judy's ever been with, as well as the whole story of all the men who ever broke her heart — because it's the same story — and I know all about Tanisha's kids and why she refuses to speak to her mother, and they both know all about Ethan and Guidry and everything else that's ever happened to me.

I took a sip of coffee as Judy slid into my booth to rest her legs for a second.

She winked and said, "What's shakin', pretty mama?"

"Believe me, you don't want to know."

"Oh, honey, I'm a waitress in a diner in a beach town. I'm all-knowing."

I smiled. "So I guess you heard about the head-on collision."

She nodded. "Yep."

"And you know it was me that pulled the guy —"

She waved her fingers like she was shooing away a fly. "Oh please. You're a hero. Yesterday's news. Yawn."

"And you know about the old man at the bookstore?"

"Yeah." Her face fell and she shook her head. "And I'm just sick about it. I stop in there every morning for a paper, and he's just the sweetest old man. He always wears that red beret, with those yellow suspenders and that red shirt with gold buttons, kind of makes me think of Santa Claus. When I saw all those cops outside his shop I nearly had a heart attack."

I said, "Judy, you haven't see his cat, have you?"

"That old tabby? Don't tell me it's gone missing too?"

I nodded. "Yeah. They can't find it."

"Oh no." She leaned back and laid her head on the back of the booth. "Well, maybe that old man took him wherever he wandered off to."

I realized she didn't know anything about the bloody paw prints on the counter, or the fact that they'd called in a homicide unit to investigate the scene. Detective McKenzie was probably keeping that under wraps. Sometimes, the less the general public knows about the details of a case, the easier it is to pin down the true culprits.

Just then Tanisha put a plate up in her window and rang the bell to signal my order was ready. Judy eyed me suspiciously. "Wait a minute. Where'd you hear that old man's cat was missing?"

I shrugged. "Oh, you know. Just around."

She folded her arms over her chest and studied me. "Just around, my ass. What are you not telling me?"

I pointed at the kitchen window. "I'm telling you my breakfast is getting cold."

156

She said, "Huh," and rushed off to pick it up. She's fast, though. In the blink of an eye she was back, holding my plate aloft with one hand.

"Tell me now, or the breakfast goes in the trash."

"Oh please, you don't scare me. Tanisha would beat you to a pulp."

She raised an eyebrow. "I'll take my chances."

I sighed. "Okay, but I don't want you blabbing it all over town."

She sat down and slid my plate in front of me. It was the same exact breakfast I have every day: two eggs over easy with extra-crispy potatoes and one hot biscuit and, sadly, no bacon. For a second I considered wolfing it all down and keeping my secrets to myself, but I knew Judy would never let me get away with it.

"I do not blab," she sniffed. "I *share*. But I promise I won't say a word to anybody."

Lowering my voice a little, I said, "Well, I'm probably the last person that saw Mr. Hoskins in the bookstore. I was there the night he went missing."

She put one elbow on the table and dropped her forehead down in the palm of her hand. "Oh, Dixie, not again."

"Yep," I said, as I took a bite of Tanisha's

world-class biscuit. As soon as it touched my lips, a warm, fuzzy feeling flooded over me. It didn't quite make up for all the crap I'd been through in the last day or so, but it came damn near close to it.

Judy said, "What were you doing in a bookstore? You don't read."

I chose to ignore that statement for now. "After the collision the sheriff's department had the whole street blocked off while they were moving the cars. I couldn't get out until they were done, so while I was waiting I went in to look for a book to buy."

"Did you tell the cops?"

"Believe me, I didn't have to. I had paid for my book with a check, and it was still sitting there on the counter, so they already knew I'd been there."

She shook her head. "Dixie, I just don't know how you do it. I swear to God you can sniff out trouble better than a hound dog in heat."

I slathered my biscuit with more butter and took a bite. "I know."

"Did you notice anything weird? I mean, did he seem okay?"

"Yeah, he seemed totally fine." I was slightly dizzy from how scrumptious the biscuit was, but I forged ahead. "He was a little flustered, I guess, but it was after closing, so I'm sure he was ready to go home. Other than that I didn't notice a thing."

"Well, I'm sure they'll find him. He probably took that cat and went off on a senior citizens cruise and forgot to tell anybody."

I dropped my fork and slapped my mouth with both hands. "Oh, no."

Judy's eyes grew two times bigger. "What?"

I said, "Oh, Judy, I'm a complete idiot."

"Again, yesterday's news. What's the matter?"

"You just reminded me of something Mr. Hoskins said. It was right when I was leaving. He had this bowl of chocolates, and he offered me one and said he was going on a trip. I totally forgot until now."

"Ha! Well, there you go. I was right. He took that cat and went on a trip. Case closed."

"I better call and tell her."

"Who?"

"McKenzie."

"Who's McKenzie?"

"Uh, the detective on the case."

She frowned. "Where have I heard that name before?"

I shrugged. "No idea."

I finished up my breakfast as quickly as possible, which when you think about it is a sin of the first order, because Tanisha's breakfasts are like gifts sent down from heaven and should be savored for the small works of wonder that they are, but I wanted to let McKenzie know what I'd remembered as soon as possible, and there was no way I could tell her in front of Judy. Even though she's my best girlfriend in the world, Judy can spread news like grease on a griddle, and I didn't want to do anything that might compromise the investigation.

I snuck out to the car and dialed McKenzie's number and tried to steel myself for whatever mind games she had in store for me. I didn't get much of a chance. She answered on the first ring.

"McKenzie here."

I said, "Detective, it's Dixie Hemingway."

"Oh, good, I was just about to call you. I'm wondering if you might come down to the station tomorrow. There's something I want to show you."

I paused. I hadn't quite prepared for that. The last time I'd walked into the sheriff's department was for a hastily arranged meeting with Sergeant Woodrow Owens, who'd been my commanding officer when I was a deputy. I'd gone in with my department-issued 9 mm SIG SAUER handgun secured in its holster, and when I left, it was on

Owens's desk along with my gold, five-pointed deputy's badge. I wasn't sure I could deal with going back in there now.

I said, "Sure. When?"

"How's tomorrow at noon?"

That seemed like a horrible time. I said, "That works."

She said, "Good, see you then," and hung up.

I stared at my phone for a couple of seconds and then pressed the redial button.

"McKenzie here."

I said, "Yeah, you know, I actually had a reason for calling you."

"Oh, Dixie, I apologize. Things are a little crazy these days, and I've got a lot on my plate."

I said, "That's alright. I know exactly how you feel."

"What can I do for you?"

"I just remembered something Mr. Hoskins said to me. I don't know why I didn't think of it before, and maybe it's nothing, but just when I was leaving he mentioned he was going on a trip."

There was a pause. "That's definitely something I'd want to know. Tell me exactly what he said."

"He had taken my book to the back of the store to wrap it up, and when he came back he caught me ogling that bowl of chocolates next to the register, so he offered me one and then he said, 'I'm taking a trip soon.' "

"When he said 'soon,' did you get the impression that he meant right away?"

"I don't know. Not really . . . but maybe. Like I said, he had just handed me my book, and I knew I'd kept him past closing time, so I didn't want to keep him any longer making small talk about where he was going or anything like that."

"What else?"

Something in my voice must have told her there was more on my mind.

I said, "I keep thinking about how when Mr. Hoskins came out from the back of the store, he was patting his pockets and looking all around. He seemed a little distracted. I know it wouldn't explain the blood on the counter, but are you sure it's not possible he left the shop unlocked because he couldn't find his keys?"

"Dixie, at this point, anything's possible, except we can assume that he had opened the store with his keys that morning, and if he'd misplaced them, it would stand to reason that they would have turned up when we searched the store for evidence — and they didn't."

I said, "Okay . . ."

"Anything else?"

I sighed. I could swear she had a hidden camera aimed directly at my personal thoughts.

"I know it's none of my business, but . . ."

"Dixie, I've learned from experience that just because a case isn't your business doesn't necessarily mean you can't shed a little light on it."

I'm embarrassed to admit it, but I felt my cheeks blush. I had helped McKenzie with another case not long ago, and it felt good to know she hadn't forgotten. I said, "Why exactly is it . . . a *case*?"

I knew she'd know right away what I meant. When I had arrived on the scene, they'd only just discovered Mr. Hoskins hadn't come home the night before. McKenzie had said Mr. Hoskins's daughter had called right before I arrived. So why would they send the lead homicide detective and a retinue of deputies to investigate some bloody paw prints and an unlocked bookstore?

She sighed. "You may remember I mentioned I hadn't gotten much sleep. A call came in at the station about midnight. A man was driving home from a party and saw someone dumping what may or may not have been a body off the Sunshine Skyway Bridge."

My heart sank. "Oh, no."

"Originally I was more or less certain it wasn't related, but until we know for sure I have to follow every possible lead, no matter how far-fetched it may seem. Unfortunately, in this case, it's looking less and less insignificant."

I could tell by the sound of her voice that she was dead serious. The idea that someone could have killed Mr. Hoskins and dumped him off a bridge into the ocean left me speechless. It just didn't seem possible. He was such a sweet man, I couldn't imagine there could be anybody who would ever want to hurt him.

"Dixie, one more thing. When you left the bookshop that night, did you open the door yourself, or did Mr. Hoskins open it for you?"

I tried to re-create that moment when he had handed me the book and we were saying our good-byes. "I'm not positive, but I think I opened it myself. Why?"

"There were no fingerprints on the doorknob, or anywhere else in the store, for that matter, which is unusual. It means after you left the bookstore, someone took the time to wipe down every door handle as well as every other surface a print might have been left on."

I remembered pushing the door open. "Even the outside?"

"Yes, your prints were on the outside handle, but that's all we can identify. Dixie, I'd like you to do something for me. Before we meet tomorrow, I'd like you to find a quiet place somewhere. I want you to sit down and go over every moment in your head, everything that happened in that store, from the moment you went in to the moment you left."

I thought I'd told her everything I could think of, but I knew what she meant. The mind is an incredible instrument. It can record the finest of details, even things you're not even aware you've noticed. It can store them away, never to be seen again, like the contents of a long-forgotten safe deposit box. In an investigation like this, even the most seemingly insignificant detail could have a great impact on figuring out what had happened. I promised her I'd sit down and try to remember every moment, but I still had one more question.

"Has there been any sign of Cosmo?"

She sighed. "You mean the cat? No, but I promise I'll let you know immediately if there is."

I rang off and dropped the phone down in

165

the side pocket of my cargo shorts. Not two seconds went by before it started ringing again. As I reached back down in my pocket I muttered under my breath, "Damn you, Michael Hemingway."

When I had handed in my gun and my badge, I'd also handed in my cell phone. For at least a year after, possibly longer, I'd done everything in my power to avoid replacing it. Michael finally won with the argument that if he was ever hurt fighting a fire, there'd be no way to reach me except with a message on the answering machine in my walk-in closet. By then, word of mouth had spread about my pet-sitting business and I was out on calls all day instead of lying on my couch in a catatonic lump 24/7, so I'd finally caved in and gotten the cheapest cell phone I could find.

Now it was my master, and I its slave.

I figured McKenzie had probably thought of another question for me, but I was wrong. It was Sara Mem Ho again. For some reason, possibly the idea of meeting with McKenzie at her office tomorrow or maybe because I'm not a big fan of hospitals in general, seeing Sara Mem Ho on my caller ID made my blood boil. I was about to scream into the receiver, "You have the wrong number. *Do not call me again!*"

I didn't get the chance.

"This is Vera Campbell at the Sarasota Memorial Hospital. I'm calling about your husband."

I felt something lurch forward in my throat, and then an electric jolt traveled all the way down to my feet and my fingers started to tingle.

I said, "What?"

"He's stable now, but he's on a lot of pain meds, so I'm not sure he even knows what happened to him, but he's been calling out for you in his sleep. I'm sorry to intrude, but every time we offer to contact you he forbids it, but he seems very upset, and since he's your husband —"

I stopped her. "My husband is dead."

"Excuse me?"

I hadn't actually meant to say that out loud; it just came pouring out of my mouth. Five years ago. Five years, four months, and seven days ago, my husband, Todd, and my daughter, Christy, were killed. An old man plowed into them in the parking lot at the local grocery store, and they both died instantly. Todd was a sheriff's deputy, too. His thirty-first birthday was two months away. Christy was three.

It's safer to say it fast like that. If I let myself pause during any of the words, I'll get sucked down into the black spaces between them, and then it's hard to find my way back. For days, months, or even years — I don't actually know — I lost myself. I barely ate. I barely slept. I just breathed.

I'd lie in my bed until Michael would come and tell me to take a shower. Then he'd sit at the table and watch me put one spoonful of soup in my mouth, and then another, as if he were nursing a baby bird back to life. Except I hadn't fallen out of my nest. My nest was gone.

In other words, I was a complete wreck.

I'm okay now, except there's an alternate universe where Todd is getting older, too, and Christy just started second grade. We still live in the same house off Cape Leyte Drive that Todd's parents helped us buy, and that ugly palm tree that jutted out over the yard finally fell on the lanai, and we're probably about to cave in and get Christy that kitten she's been whining about since the dawn of time. It's a sick way of living . . . but it's the only way I know how.

My mind snapped back and I could hear the nurse's voice through the telephone. I took a deep breath and tried to listen.

"I'm not sure I understand."

I said, "I'm sorry. I meant to say I don't

have a husband. You have the wrong number."

"You're not Mrs. Vladim?"

"No. I'm not. Someone already called me about this before."

"Oh, my goodness. I am so sorry. The police must have given us the wrong number. There's a man here who was in a terrible automobile accident two days ago, and he's been asking for someone named Dixie. I just assumed . . ."

I suddenly felt like I'd just been hit in the head with a two-by-four. Somehow I had the presence of mind to say, "Wait a minute."

"Ma'am?"

"This Mr. Vladim . . . is he bald?"

There was a pause, but it didn't matter. I already knew the answer.

She said, "Why, yes. Yes, he is."

12

I don't like hospitals. They give me the creeps, in much the same way that zoos give me the creeps. If I ruled the world, there'd be no zoos, there'd just be this thing called the Internet. If people wanted to see what a lion looked like, they could get on the Internet and call up as many pictures and videos of lions as their little hearts desired. That way, the lions and tigers and hippos and all the other animals in the zoo could live happily ever after in their own natural habitats.

Don't get me wrong. When I was little, I loved zoos with a passion. I still remember visiting the monkey house and being completely enchanted with how real it all looked with the monkeys swinging through their fake trees and vines overhead. Afterward, though, my mother had asked how I'd feel if somebody came and snatched me out of my house, put me in a concrete cell fixed up to look like my bedroom, and tossed in a peanut butter and jelly sandwich and some apple juice every once in a while.

Well, I knew the answer right away. I'd feel sad. In my heart, I knew that's how all those animals felt, too. Now zoos give me an empty feeling in the pit of my stomach. Plus, there's something about making money off the misfortune of living, breathing creatures that just makes me a little queasy.

I was thinking about that as I signed in with the guard at the front desk of Sarasota Memorial. Other than in a display case at the zoo, the hospital was about the last place on earth I felt like being — but when a man is lying in bed clinging to life and asking for you, wife or not, you have to go.

The guard handed me a little sticker with a blue border and my name written on it in blue ink and instructed me to wear it at all times inside the hospital. Instead of putting it on my chest the way people usually do, I stuck it on my hip. The guard gave me a look like he thought that was a little odd, but whenever I see a woman with a name tag on her chest, it always makes me think she's named one of her breasts. If you ask me, *that's* odd.

Even though I was technically visiting a guy who'd almost gotten me killed, it didn't seem right to show up empty-handed, so I bought a little bouquet of slightly wilted daisies in the gift shop for twenty-one dollars. Then I made my way through all the stairs and wings and elevators of the hospital, feeling a little like a lab rat in a maze.

Meanwhile I'd figured out why Baldy was asking for me. When I'd first gotten to his car, when he was sitting there in the passenger seat covered in blood, the first thing I said to him was "My name is Dixie." I remember he looked me right in the eye. There's no telling what must have been going through his head at that moment. He'd just hit a two-ton truck head-on, he'd taken a massive bonk on the head, and then suddenly there I am out of nowhere. With all that white smoke pouring from under the car, he must have thought I was some kind of angel sent down to escort him to the Pearly Gates.

My name just got stuck in his head, that's all. He wouldn't talk, and he didn't have any ID, and when they heard him asking for me, somebody, probably Deputy Morgan, had given the EMTs my number. He probably thought Baldy wanted to thank me for saving him.

Now, as to why the whole hospital staff seemed to think I was Baldy's wife, I had no clue, but one thing I did know, I kind of liked the idea that somebody thought I was an angel on earth. It was too bad I'd have to disabuse him of that notion.

When I finally made it to Mr. Vladim's room, the door was closed. I smoothed my hair back and was just about to knock when the door pulled open and a nurse stepped out. She was about five feet tall and just as wide, with a blue nurse's smock printed all over with different-colored giraffes and crispy curls of blond hair piled on top of her head. She looked happy to see me.

"Are you Dixie?"

"Yes, are you the one that called me?"

"No, but thank God you're here."

She pulled the door closed and continued in a stage whisper, "Now, he's doing much better, but don't be alarmed. He's on a pretty good cocktail of pain meds right now, so he may not know who you are at first."

I shook my head. "I'm not —"

"We haven't been able to get anything out of him except his name. He won't talk to anybody, just asks for you over and over again. I'll let the supervisor know you've arrived. He's got a lot of questions for you."

Before I could say anything more she took my arm and pushed into the room. It was dark except for a small lamp on a rolling

173

table next to a raised hospital bed. There were curtains behind the bed to divide the room in two, but they were partially open, and I could see the other bed on the far side was vacant.

Baldy, or I guess I should say Mr. Vladim, was lying on his back, propped up on two square pillows with his eyes closed and his mouth slightly open. I'd only seen him covered in blood, but now that he was cleaned up I could tell he was in his mid- to late thirties. His face was long and thin, with high pronounced cheekbones, sparse blond eyebrows, and a long patrician nose that lent him an air of gravity. I winced a little when I saw the number of IV tubes and drip lines tangled all around him. There was one coming from his nose and another from his mouth, both held in place with strips of white surgical tape. Other tubes were taped to both his arms, all leading to a collection of clear, liquid-filled plastic bags hanging on hooks behind him.

In a loud, singsong voice normally reserved for five-year-olds, the nurse said, "Mr. Vladim? Your wife is here. Do you want to say hello?"

I raised one finger in the air, like a professor about to make a very important point, but I could barely get a word in edgewise with this woman.

"I was just about to give him his bath, but perhaps you'd rather do it?"

I shrieked, *"No!"*

She nearly jumped out of her nursing shoes.

"I'm sorry, I didn't mean to shout, but —"

"Oh, I understand. This is difficult for you."

"No, you don't understand. I'm not his wife."

Without missing a beat she nodded and took the daisies from me. "Oh, what beautiful flowers. I'll put them in a vase and leave you two alone." She paused at the door. "So you don't want to give him his bath?"

I sighed. "No. I do not."

I could tell she was full of questions, but she'd probably decided it was none of her business. She nodded politely and closed the door behind her.

I stepped up to the bed, but there were so many cords and lines everywhere I was afraid to get too close for fear I'd knock one of them loose. A white sheet was pulled up almost to Mr. Vladim's shoulders, but I could see that underneath it his entire chest was wrapped in gauze and tape. The skin on his neck was bruised, and his face had a sallow, porcine cast to it. A bulging bandage covered his left ear, but there was nothing on the rest of his head, which surprised me considering how bloody he'd been at the accident. I figured he was lucky he wasn't in a full body cast.

He murmured something that I'm pretty sure was my name, and then his eyelids started to flutter a bit. I was trying to think of something to say, or some way to gently wake him up, when suddenly his eyes shot open and he looked around the room.

"Hi, Mr. Vladim. How are you feeling?"

He just stared at me, his narrow eyes dilating slightly.

"I'm Dixie. Do you remember me?"

He managed a smile. His lips were dry and crusted around the edges. "Dixie."

I said, "How are you doing? Do you remember who I am?"

He nodded slowly. "You are wife."

"Um, no . . ." I said, a little hesitantly.

His eyes widened, and he turned his head toward me. "Yes. You are wife."

Well, at least now I knew why everyone thought I was his wife. "No, I helped you after the accident. I'm one of the people that helped you out of your car."

He shook his head. "Is good."

I couldn't quite place his accent, not that

I'm good at that sort of thing, but it sounded Eastern European, perhaps Russian. He looked me up and down, like a high-class modeling agent appraising a prospective client. "Is good. You are hot wife."

"No, I'm sorry, Mr. Vladim, I am definitely not your wife."

He frowned. "You safe me. You are mistress?"

Wow. I hoped that nurse was right about the drugs, because otherwise this poor guy had suffered some very serious brain trauma.

"No, I'm not your mistress either. You don't know me. You were in an accident on Ocean Boulevard. You crashed into a truck, and I helped you until the ambulance came. You never met me before."

He closed his eyes. "I do good thing. I am boss now. You will see. I am good now."

A small tear formed in the corner of his eye and made its way slowly down his cheek. I patted his hand gently and said, "Okay, Mr. Vladim, I think I should go."

"You stay."

"No, I'll come back and see you again. You need your rest now."

His eyes still closed, he said, "You have . . ."

It was the drugs talking. His mouth fell

open slightly, and his breathing grew a little deeper. I tiptoed to the door, and just before it closed behind me, he mumbled something in his sleep.

He said, "Don't eat."

I stood in the hallway outside his door and sighed. There was no telling what drug-induced dreams were playing in his head. I hoped for his sake they didn't include a hairy old man dancing around half naked with a megaphone.

Making my way back through the maze of stairwells and halls to the main lobby, I wondered if he would even remember I had been there. Next to the gift shop was a sad-sack food bar with foam bowls of crusted Jell-O and soggy sandwiches embalmed in tight plastic wrap. *Damn right, Baldy,* I thought to myself. *Don't eat.*

I was just about to go through the big glass revolving doors to the outside world when one of the hospital supervisors stopped me, a big man in a tan business suit and a wide yellow tie. He was full of questions, but I'm afraid I wasn't much help. When I told him I wasn't Mr. Vladim's wife and didn't know a thing about him, his shoulders fell in a slump. I got the distinct impression he was mostly worried about who would be paying for all that top-notch

178

treatment Baldy was getting.

At Tom Hale's, I took Billy Elliot out for his second spin of the day, and he dragged me around the parking lot as if it were the first time he'd been out in years. It felt good. Just getting my lungs pumping with oxygen helped clear the smog that had banked up in my head. When we got back, Billy went bounding down the hall and Tom called me from the back office. He'd been badgering me to sign some papers for days, but I lied and said I was in a hurry and would have to sign them later.

I was tired. It had been a long day. Maybe I was fighting off a cold. Or maybe I was thinking about Todd and Christy. I just wanted to get home.

I rushed through my afternoon calls and purposely took the long way around the village so I wouldn't drive by the bookstore. By now they'd probably pulled out and taken down the police tape, but I still didn't want to see it.

When I got home, I dropped my keys on the bar in the kitchen, pointedly ignoring the letter from Guidry still sitting in its little basket, and wandered into my walk-in closet. I sat at the desk for a while and went through some of the bills that were piling up, and that kept my mind busy for about half an hour. Then I put a load of laundry in the washer. As it gurgled and churned away, I sat down on the couch and stared at the wall.

I toyed with the idea of calling Michael at the fire station, but I knew he'd be busy and probably wouldn't feel like listening to his little sister complain about her day. Then I wondered where Paco was, but there was no way to know and I certainly couldn't call him, so I got up and dragged myself back into the office and laid my hand on the desk phone.

Ethan.

I could call Ethan. If anybody could make me feel better it was him, except I knew as soon as he found out what kind of mood I was in he'd race right over, and I think I wanted to be alone.

Just then the phone rang, and I nearly jumped out of my skin. Usually when I'm in a funk, there's no way I'll answer the phone, but to my utter horror I realized I'd grabbed the receiver as I jumped away. It was cradled in my right hand, and a woman's voice was saying, "Helloooo?"

I put the phone to my ear. "Yes, sorry, Dixie Hemingway, how can I help you?"

She cleared her throat. "9500 Blind Pass Road, please."

It was an older woman, with a note to her voice that was either British or rich.

I said, "Excuse me?"

"Hello? Who is this?"

I frowned. "This is Dixie Hemingway. Who is this?"

"Are you or are you not a cat sitter?"

"Um. Yes, I'm a cat sitter. How can I help you?"

"Very good. I need you to come to 9500 Blind Pass Road immediately. And I can assure you you'll be handsomely paid."

I blinked. "Ma'am, I'm so sorry, but it's a little late. Can it wait until tomorrow?"

There was a slight pause and then an exasperated sigh. "A little late, indeed. Well I suppose there's bugger all you can do about it tonight anyway. Tomorrow morning then, seven sharp."

I said, "Oh, no. I can't possibly meet you that early. I have appointments all morning."

She clucked. "Pity. Then we'll meet for tea at two. Does that suit your complicated schedule?"

"Um, yes, that works, but . . . I'm sorry, I didn't catch your name?"

"Yes. 9500 Blind Pass Road. I'll be waiting."

She hung up. I stood there staring at the

receiver and shaking my head. Sometimes I think if they put my life in a movie no one would believe it for a second.

I wandered back into the living room, where I resumed my position on the couch and stared at the wall a little more. Normally a call like that would get my wheels spinning and I'd spend hours concocting all kinds of fancy, complicated scenarios in my head about who it was and why she was so mysterious, but I was pooped. My brain couldn't take any more thinking.

After a while I dragged myself into the kitchen, zapped a Party Time Deluxe frozen pizza in the microwave, and carried it out to the hammock on the deck. It tasted like warm, salty cardboard, but with the consistency of a wad of used chewing gum. I didn't mind, though. Michael and Paco have served me so many gourmet meals. A cheap frozen pizza every once in a while just reminds me how lucky I am.

I fell asleep in the hammock, gently swaying from side to side and listening to the crickets and the droning rhythm of the waves rolling in down below. I had established only one rule for the night: No old men in bikinis.

13

The next morning after I slithered out of bed, I stood bleary-eyed in front of the mirror and told myself that my little pity party had come to an end and that it was time to get a move on. If I'd had bootstraps, I would have pulled myself up by them, but instead I splashed cold water on my face, pulled on some clothes, and was out the door before sunrise.

The air was cool and still, and as I crunched across the driveway, a giant brown pelican sitting on the hood of the Bronco opened one eye and watched me sullenly. He held his ground even when I started the engine, but as soon as I put the car in reverse, he unfolded his giant wings and lumbered off into the darkness.

I was the only car on the road all the way to the village, and Ocean Boulevard was completely deserted except for a few snowy egrets dozing atop the lampposts outside

Amber Jack's, their long tail feathers gently flapping in the cool breeze off the Gulf. I pulled into a spot in front of the butcher shop and cut the headlights.

Now, I thought to myself, *where would I be if I was a cat?*

I'd been telling myself that Judy was probably right, that Mr. Hoskins was probably fine. He'd probably just decided to take a short vacation, maybe a little road trip, and he had probably taken Cosmo with him. He'd just forgotten to tell his daughter, and his doorman . . . but I knew it wasn't true. None of that explained those bloody splotches on the countertop.

Something had happened in that store after I left, and I felt a need to find out what it was, to help in some way. I admit it seems crazy, but I think somewhere, deep down inside, I knew what I was doing. I was taking all those feelings I'd had as a little girl for Mr. Beezy and transferring them right over to Mr. Hoskins. Somehow, when I went back inside that store, something inside me changed. It was as if a hidden part of me had opened up and long-forgotten images and feelings had come spilling out — feelings I hadn't had in a very long time.

The only problem was that, although Mr. Hoskins was a very sweet old man, I'd only just met him, and except for the fact that we shared a love for chocolate, I didn't know a damn thing about him. All I knew was that he'd taken over the store when Mr. Beezy was gone, he was an artist, and he was a little bit eccentric, so it was completely foolish to think I had some deep bond with him, or that I could help find him, especially with Detective McKenzie and her entire team working on it. They didn't need my help.

But Cosmo? Well, that was another story.

I like to think that I treat my pet-sitting business with the same professionalism that I brought to being a sheriff's deputy. I keep myself on a strict schedule, I'm never late, and for every animal that's ever been in my care, I have notes on their favorite toys, their favorite treats, and their favorite hiding places, as well as phone numbers to call if there's an emergency. I treat all my clients, both animal and human, with respect and dignity, and I expect them to treat me the same.

I'm proud of my job. I help people just as much now as I ever did working for the sheriff's department, and unlike most officers of the law, not to mention most criminals, I have my adrenaline addiction completely under control. Sort of.

I had decided that Mr. Hoskins had hired me to find his cat.

Okay. I'll admit, it wasn't the most professional decision, but I'd thought about it overnight and finally worked it all out. First, under normal circumstances, I would have met with Mr. Hoskins beforehand, which I kind of did. Then he would have introduced me to his cat, which he kind of did. Then he would have explained that he was going on a trip, which he kind of did, and then finally, after he was gone, I'd be responsible for the well-being and safety of his cat.

Now here I was.

The shops were all dark. I looked up and down the street for any sign of movement, but I knew the best place to inspect first was the trash behind the butcher's. I slipped down a narrow passageway between two buildings and emerged into an alley behind the shops.

There were two giant blue Dumpsters parked side by side next to the back door of the butcher shop, with both their lids held slightly agape, one with bulging white garbage bags and the other with bundles of flattened cardboard boxes wrapped in twine. The sky was just beginning to lighten in the east, so it was still too dark to see clearly, but I'd already thought of that. I clicked on my penlight and peered over the edge of the Dumpster into the pile of white bags.

"Cosmo?"

I had to cover my nose. One of the bags had been clawed open, and some bloodied shreds of wax paper were pulled through the hole. There were bits of offal and cartilage strewn about, as well as a few other unidentifiable pieces of raw flesh. I found a stick on the ground and poked around the bags, watching carefully for even the slightest movement.

"Here, kitty . . ."

I crouched down on my hands and knees and directed the penlight under the Dumpsters, moving it slowly from one end to the other. All I could see was a couple of crushed plastic soda bottles and a half-decayed apple core lying under a glistening canopy of cobwebs clinging to the bottom of the Dumpster. I shut off the penlight and sat up on my haunches. If Cosmo had been here, he at least had supped on some tasty butcher's leavings, but I knew he'd be on the lookout for fresh water, too.

I looked up and down the alley. There were potholes here and there, still filled with rainwater from the day before, and I figured I might be able to see some paw prints around one of them, and perhaps even compare them to my memory of what the bloody prints across the counter had looked like. It was a long shot, but it couldn't hurt to try.

Just then there was a quiet click somewhere behind me. I jerked my head toward the sound and saw something move in the small window in the back door of the butcher shop. Then the door swung open and filled the alley with light, and framed in the doorway was the silhouette of a man, tall and bulky, wearing an apron and boots with a bulging bag slung over his shoulder. The tip of his cigarette glowed red as he took a drag, and then he flicked it into the alley, where it landed in a shallow puddle and fizzled out with a hiss just a few feet away from me.

I don't know why, but my first instinct was to scream. Luckily I gulped it back down my throat and slinked around to the dark side of the Dumpsters as the man lumbered down the steps off the back door. He raised the lid of the one I'd just been poking through. Then there was silence.

My heart bumped around in my chest like a raccoon trying to get out of a pillowcase. It felt like an eternity, but it couldn't have been more than a few seconds. I considered revealing myself and tried to come up with a reasonable explanation as to why I was out here rifling through his garbage in the dark. It's not like I was doing anything illegal, at least I didn't think I was, but I'd already hidden and now it was too late. I couldn't very well just poke my head over the back of the Dumpster and chirp, "Top of the mornin' to ya!"

Luckily I didn't need to. He mumbled something under his breath and then heaved the trash bag onto the pile and let the lid fall back. Then his footsteps went back up the stairs to the door. There was another clicking sound, and then the door closed and the alley went dark again.

I took a deep breath and let out a long, quivering sigh that ended with a quiet "Oh my God." Sometimes I open my eyes and look around and think to myself, *How in the hell did I end up here?* This was one of those moments, but I didn't care. I was determined to find that cat.

I checked up and down the alley to see if the coast was clear and then clicked my penlight back on and stepped around the Dumpsters toward one of the water-filled potholes.

"What the f—"

This time I did scream. Well, not really a scream. It was more like a high-pitched *whaaack!* — a cross between a newborn's first cry and the mating call of a pterodactyl. It surprised me even as it came out of my own throat. The man was standing on the landing outside the door, with a freshly lit cigarette in one hand, his feet shoulder width apart, like a man about to start a bar fight.

"Jesus Christ, lady, you nearly gave me a heart attack!"

I backed away from him with both hands over my chest. "I am so sorry, I didn't see you."

"You didn't see me? What the hell are you doing back here?"

I pointed up and down the alley. "I'm looking for a lost cat. I thought he might be rummaging around back here."

He glanced at the Dumpsters and then came down the steps toward me.

The sky was getting a little lighter, and now I could see the man more clearly. He was at least six feet tall, with unruly ringlets of black hair on his head that made him seem even taller. He was wearing jeans tucked into black rubber boots, with a tank top stretched over his rounded shoulders, and a white apron smeared with grease and bloodstains. He had puffy cheeks and a mustache, which I figured he grew to help hide his baby face.

"Hey, ain't you the lady that helped that guy in the car crash the other day?"

I nodded.

"Yeah, I seen you gettin' in your car with all that blood on your clothes. I told those cops you probably murdered that old guy from the bookstore. I guess I owe you an apology or something."

I managed a smile and stuck my hand out. "I'm Dixie."

He just waved at me. "Yeah, you don't wanna shake my hand. I'm Butch. This is my shop. Well, my old man's shop, but now it's mine."

I said, "So . . . you're Butch the Butcher?"

He grinned. "In the flesh. Nice to meet you." He made little quotation marks with his fingers. "*Meat* you. Get it?"

"Yeah. I'm sorry I scared you."

"Hey, we scared each other. No problemo!"

I cringed. In my experience, whenever people say "no problemo" and they're not speaking Spanish, it usually means they're speaking another language: Blowhard. He folded his arms over his chest, which by the way looked like two big slabs of meat.

"Hey, I seen a cat a little while ago."

"You did? What kind of cat?"

"Too dark to tell, but big. Light color. He went running off that way." He tipped his chin toward the bookstore.

I said, "It's actually Mr. Hoskins's cat I'm looking for."

He looked me up and down. "Oh yeah? Hey, you wanna give me your number or something? I mean, you know, just in case I see your cat?"

I probably should have, but something told me it wasn't a good idea. Maybe it was the blood on his apron, or the way he was leering at me as if I were a cow that needed processing.

I stammered, "Well, I'm in the neighborhood a lot, so . . ."

"Oh, you live around here?"

"Yeah, I mean, I work around here, so I'll just check in with you again. I'm sure he's around here somewhere."

He shrugged. "Yeah, sure. I'll ask around. What's he look like?"

I said, "I'm sure you've seen him. He likes to sleep in the window of the bookstore."

"Yeah, you probably can't tell from lookin' at me, but I don't spend a lot of time hangin' around bookstores."

"Oh. Well, he's orange and fluffy, with a patch of white at the tip of his tail, and he's kind of big."

"Well, he was definitely a big fella. I'll keep my eyes open."

He gave a little wave with one of his meaty hands and said, "Good luck," and then lumbered back toward the shop. When he got to the top of the stairs he lit another cigarette and then disappeared inside.

I made my way down the rest of the alley, inspecting each rain puddle as I went, but there were no cat prints, at least none that I could make out. There were a couple of barrel-sized trash cans behind the bookstore, but I didn't even look inside them. They both had metal lids, and I knew even a cat as big as Cosmo couldn't lift them up. I doubted he'd have been able to find anything worth eating in them anyway.

It was getting late, so I figured I'd better get on with my day, but at least now there was hope. As I made my way back to the car I had a pretty good feeling about my chances. If the cat that Butch the Butcher had seen actually was Cosmo, then that meant he was hanging around the bookstore — hoping like everybody else that Mr. Hoskins would come home soon. I hoped he didn't have too long a wait.

Morning was in full force now, and there was a little more activity on the street as I put the Bronco in gear and rolled out onto

Ocean. The sparrows and snowy egrets were out again, pecking around in the gutters and under the tables at Amber Jack's, and a couple of young, skinny girls in tank tops and short shorts were jogging up the sidewalk. It wasn't until they went by that I realized they weren't young, skinny girls at all. They were old, skinny girls with kick-ass bodies.

It made me smile. Just like there was hope for Cosmo, there was hope for me. I figured if I stopped lying around in a hammock eating frozen pizza, maybe one day I could be an old, skinny girl with a kick-ass body, too.

14

One of the perks of getting out early every morning is that I get to see the sun come up. A gob-smackingly glorious sunrise at the start of the day is practically a daily event around here, and every one of them is absolutely free of charge. Some of the full-timers, folks who don't retreat to the North in the dead of summer, barely even notice them anymore, but I always stop whatever I'm doing and take them in. I'd hate to think I'd gotten so jaded that I didn't recognize a gift from heaven when it was staring me right in the face.

As I turned off Ocean Boulevard and made my way toward the east side of the Key, the sun had finally come over the horizon, and the sky was ablaze with undulating streaks of deep rose and amber. It was the kind of sunrise that needs to be photographed, the kind that practically begs you to pull out your cell phone and capture its magnificent beauty for the benefit of generations to come — but it didn't fool me. I've learned the hard way that it's only when you take a picture and look at it later that you realize it's all an elaborate trick. The true glory of a sunrise is that it's fleeting. Try to freeze it in time, and the very core of its beauty is lost.

I wondered if Butch the Butcher was still standing at the back door of his shop and admiring the same sunrise. I doubted it. He didn't seem the type to goonily wonder at the morning sky and wax poetic about beauty. The image of his bloodstained apron sprang into view, and a cold shudder went down my spine. The thought of having to wake up at the crack of dawn and hack away at slabs of raw meat all day long . . . *Ick,* I thought to myself. No thanks. I'll take dirty litter boxes and fur balls over that bloody job any day of the week.

My last stop of the morning was Betty and Grace Piker, two retired sisters who live alone on Treasure Boat Way in a neatly appointed, low-slung bungalow with stucco walls painted the palest shade of turquoise and a sloping roof covered in terra-cotta barrel tiles, laid out in neat rows and painted pure white to reflect the sun's heat back up into the sky. There's not a single blade of grass in sight. Instead, the yard is a sea of tiny white pebbles, with little islands of arcing palms and broad-leaf philodendrons poking up here and there. Making my way up the driveway, the combined glare off the roof and the white-pebbled lawn was so bright I had to put on my sunglasses just to see where I was going.

As I slid my key into the lock I smiled quietly to myself, imagining what was waiting for me on the other side of the door. The Piker sisters have a long-standing agreement with each other. If one finds a stray cat and wants to bring it home, the other must stop her — using whatever means necessary, including physical force. They have eight cats, all rescues.

The latest addition was a petite tuxedo cat that Betty had found shivering in the toolshed just behind their house. She was all black except for a white splash on her chest and four white mittens on her paws. They'd named her Stevie, after Betty's favorite poet, Stevie Smith, and it wasn't long before they felt like she'd been a central part of their lives for years.

When I opened the door there was a soft-pawed stampede that came from somewhere in the back of the house and straight down the front hall, and then I was so busy giving out kisses and scratching ears that at first I didn't even notice there were only seven cats vying for my attention instead of eight. I looked up to find Stevie waiting patiently just beyond the fray, with a look on her face that said, "I'll say hello when you're done with all the riffraff."

I've heard people say that black-and-white cats are smarter than other cats. I'm not so sure. Every cat I know is smart in its own particular way, but one thing is certain: Betty and Grace were instantly impressed with Stevie's talents. For one, if you toss a crumpled-up piece of paper across the room, she'll come trotting back with it in her mouth, dutifully drop it at your feet, and then stand there with her tail twitching, waiting for you to throw it again. Even more impressive, she responds to all kinds of commands: sit, stay, lie down, roll over. Dogs are big show-offs at heart, but most cats wouldn't be caught dead participating in such vulgar displays of subservience to humans. For a while Betty and Grace even thought she might be a runaway circus cat, but no one at Ringling reported anyone missing, so Stevie had been welcomed into the family with open paws.

Now, having eight cats is mostly eight times the wonderful of having one cat, but there are a few disadvantages. For one, I can't even imagine what Betty and Grace must spend on cat food — not to mention kitty litter — and then there's the boundless supply of cat hair. They go through a package of vacuum cleaner bags at least once a week. Of course, none of that outweighs the one big advantage: There's a lot of joy in the Piker house, and the cats couldn't be happier. There's never a lack of playmates, so they never get bored, and the backyard is completely screened in, so they have free run of the garden. There's even a small pond in the back, so sometimes I'll find all eight cats lined up at the pond's edge, watching in utter rapture as the goldfish and koi swim around in slow, wary circles.

I served breakfast in eight identical bowls, conducted eight beauty makeovers with a fine-bristled cat brush, and then did a quick walk-through of the house for any kitty damage. Surprisingly, everything was in order. I wondered if perhaps Stevie wasn't patrolling the house when Betty and Grace were away, making sure everyone behaved in a respectable manner. When I left, they were all in a pile on the sofa in the screened-in front porch and sound asleep, all except Stevie, who winked slowly at me as if to say, "Thanks, I'll take it from here."

I'm always in a good mood when I leave the Piker house, but as I opened the door to the Bronco I made the mistake of glancing at my watch. It was 11:45 A.M.

I slumped into the driver's seat and put my forehead down on top of the steering wheel. McKenzie was expecting me at the sheriff's station at noon. I'd almost forgotten, and now I really didn't want to go. The thought of being back in that station made my stomach ball up in a knot. Why in the world had I agreed to meet her there? What could she possibly have to tell me that required a face-to-face meeting?

I put the car in gear and rolled out of the driveway and down the street, remembering the very first time I'd met Detective McKenzie. It was at a crime scene, another one of those times when I managed to situate myself in the wrong place at the wrong time, right after she'd taken over as lead homicide detective. She'd been hammering me with questions about what had happened and what I'd seen, and then out of the blue she looked me squarely in the eye and said, "I was with the FBI for twenty-five years. My husband was murdered nine years ago. I have a sixteen-year-old daughter. Her name is Eva."

Just like that.

Of course, I knew right away that somebody must have told her my whole story, probably somebody at the station, about how I'd lost my family and my badge and my career. She was trying to say that she understood me, that she knew where I was coming from, that she *felt my pain.* At that point, if people even hinted at the idea that they felt my pain, I had two responses: one, I curled up into a ball, or two, I started throwing punches. Still, something in the way she'd said it so matter-of-factly, as if it were just the most normal thing in the world, had kind of broken my heart a little bit.

In the years since Todd and Christy died, one thing I've learned is that losing a loved one makes you an instant member of this strange, underground club, a club that only people who've lost someone they truly, deeply love can join. Once you're a member, all you have to do is let your guard down a little bit to see that there are fellow members everywhere you go. At the gym, at the grocery store, in the line for the dressing room at Marshalls, and like it or not, you can never unjoin.

In that moment, when McKenzie had laid her pain out for me so plainly, a bond had been established between us, an unspoken bond, but a true bond nonetheless.

By the time I rolled to a stop at the end of Treasure Boat Way, I half wondered if McKenzie wasn't trying to ease me back into the station. Maybe she thought it would help me move on, or help me get over the painful memories of the last time I'd been there. If that was her plan, I wanted nothing to do with it.

Suddenly I had a flash of brilliance. I remembered my mystery caller from the night before. I was supposed to be at 9500 Blind Pass Road at two o'clock, but I figured a little white lie wouldn't hurt anybody.

McKenzie answered the phone with a short "Ready when you are."

"Yeah, about that, is there another place we can meet? Maybe somewhere closer to me? I have to meet a new client down at the end of the Key, and I'm worried I'll be late."

There was a pause. I could tell she was thinking it over.

"Dixie, the problem is I've got too much going on here. I want you to see something, but I can't leave the station for long. I suppose we could meet at Payne Park, but that's not exactly in your neighborhood."

"No, that's perfect," I lied. "I'm near there

now. I'm just finishing up with a client that lives right behind the high school. I can be there in no time at all."

"Okay, then. I'll meet you at the park in ten minutes."

"Great," I blurted out. "No problemo!"

As I flipped the phone closed, I caught a glimpse of myself in the rearview mirror, with a smile as fake as a three-dollar bill still pasted on my face.

"Really?" I said out loud. *"No problemo?"*

I decided right then and there that if I ever said "no problemo" again I'd go directly to the nearest Treatment Center for Blowhards and check myself in.

It wasn't until I pulled back out on the road that I realized — Payne Park is basically a two-minute walk from the sheriff's building. Why it was better to meet there instead of McKenzie's office made absolutely no sense at all.

She was onto me.

15

As I headed out for Payne Park, I had to force myself to drive north instead of down to the beach pavilion, mainly due to the fact that I was starving. Normally I can't go anywhere near Siesta Key Beach without grabbing at least one hot dog at the food stand, and by "at least one" I mean *two,* but there wasn't enough time, never mind the fact that technically it was still morning and it just seems wrong to eat a hot dog before noon.

So I took Higel at a respectable speed all the way up to the top of the Key, and then once I was on Siesta I stepped on the gas and sped across the north bridge onto the mainland. Normally I drive as slowly as possible so I can gawk at all the waterfront mansions on San Remo Terrace as I come off the bridge, but this time I cruised on by and turned right on Tamiami Trail.

On our little island there's not a single

fast-food joint, but Sarasota is a whole different story. First I drove by Crusty's Pizza and the Chicken Shack. Then I drove by them again, except this time in reverse order because I'd gone the wrong way and had to make a U-turn. Then I passed Beethoven's Steakhouse, Big Top Burgers, Aztec Grill, Vito's Subs, China Palace, and Taco Depot. After sitting through a green light next to the Waffle House I decided I'd better keep my eyes on the road, but my stomach was whining like a hungry dog.

When I pulled into the lot at Payne Park, McKenzie was already there, sitting at one of the wooden benches that overlook the tennis courts. She wore a plain beige blouse tucked into a faded blue-jean skirt with big round sunglasses and an oversized straw hat to keep the sun off her pale skin. When she saw me, she wrapped something up in a piece of shiny foil and put it down in her briefcase. I wondered if it would be rude to ask what she'd just been eating.

"Thanks for coming, Dixie."

I sat down while she pulled out a laptop computer and opened it on the bench between us. She wasted no time in clicking a couple of keys, and then a video popped up and started playing.

"I want you to watch this and tell me what

you think."

In the video, there was a group of people eating in an outdoor café, with other people walking by on the street behind them. It was a little blurry and the colors were washed out, so at first I had no idea what I was looking at, but then I saw something familiar in the background. It was a dusty, maroon van with a logo on its side. It read, BEEZY'S BOOKSTORE.

I realized that what we were watching was the webcam feed at Amber Jack's, with a view of Beezy's Bookstore across the street. I said, "Oh, wow, is this live?"

She shook her head. "No, it's a recording from the night Mr. Hoskins disappeared, and as you can see, we've got a clear shot of the bar with a north-facing view of the street beyond, and just to the right of that van is a perfect view of the doorway to Beezy's Bookstore."

She was right. Occasionally a truck would go by or a waiter would linger in front of the camera, but for the most part, the front door and the display window of the bookstore were in plain view. Just then a truck pulled into the frame, and McKenzie clicked the pause button.

"Recognize it?"

I looked closely. It was a big dump truck

with forest green doors. I shook my head, but then, in the very upper-right corner at the back of the truck, were three identical cocoa brown columns rising up out of the frame. They were palm trees.

I pointed and said, "That's —"

McKenzie nodded. "That's the truck that was involved in the head-on collision, correct?"

"Yes. That's it."

She sped forward a little bit, and I watched it without blinking. I didn't want to miss a single frame. Next an ambulance rolled by with its lights flashing, and I knew right away it was the ambulance that had come to take Baldy to the hospital.

"No one comes in or out of the bookstore until . . ."

She paused the video again, and there, just entering the left-hand side of the screen, was a white blur.

McKenzie said, "Tell me if you've seen this person before."

A gray-haired woman wearing a white dress made her way along the sidewalk outside the bookstore. Her gait was slow and labored. She paused at the window. I could see she was carrying something, like a small cardboard box, about the size of a toaster. She stood there for a few moments, her head down as if she were catching her breath or maybe reading something printed on top of the box, and then the front door opened and Mr. Hoskins appeared.

I knew it was him right away. The big wraparound sunglasses were a dead giveaway, and even though the picture was blurry and the colors washed out, I recognized the red button-down shirt and the bright red beret. I felt a lump form in my throat, thinking how much he had reminded me of a cute little bridge troll or an elf, and how I thought I'd made a new friend.

They exchanged a couple of words, and then Mr. Hoskins stepped back, holding the door open, and the woman disappeared inside. Mr. Hoskins looked briefly up and down the street and then closed the door behind him.

McKenzie stopped the video and turned to me.

"It's a bit blurry, but no, she doesn't look familiar at all."

She frowned. "Are you sure?"

"No idea who she is."

She clicked again and the video played on. "I want you to be absolutely certain. The main reason is that, with the exception of here . . ."

She stopped the video. All I could see was

a black-and-white checkerboard filling half the frame.

"What is that?"

"It's the uniform shirt the waiters wear at Amber Jack's. Except for here where the view is blocked by the waiter for approximately seven seconds, no one comes in or out of the bookstore until . . ."

She forwarded the video a good bit now. All the cars whizzed by and the people in the bar raced around in superfast motion, completely unaware that this mundane moment in their lives would soon be evidence in a potential homicide investigation, every second of it intensely scrutinized. Just as another person appeared on the left-hand side of the screen, she clicked the pause button.

This time I knew exactly who it was.

A slim woman in her early thirties with straight blond hair. She was standing in front of the bookstore, looking at the display in the big picture window. I recognized her immediately because everyone else on the street was wearing flip-flops, shorts, and tank tops, but this woman was wearing a black zip-up hoodie that was easily ten times too big for her.

It was me.

We watched as I approached the front of

the display window, and I remembered thinking how artfully all the books had been arranged, how I'd smiled at the stack of dictionaries in the corner with its fluffy top of orange fur. I lingered in front of the display for a few moments and then pushed open the door to the shop. Seeing myself in the video, the first thought I had was *I am not broad in the beam.*

Luckily I kept that to myself.

McKenzie then sped forward again, this time to the point where I came out of the shop, and I watched myself leave the frame of the video and head back north toward my car, holding my new book under my arm.

McKenzie said, "That's it."

I turned to her. "What do you mean that's it?"

She sighed. "Just watch."

The video sped forward as she folded her hands in her lap. Soon it got dark and the crowd at Amber Jack's thinned out. Then all the waiters raced around clearing away glasses, flipping the chairs over on the tabletops, and mopping the floors. Finally there was only one person left, probably the owner, sitting on one of the tables and drinking a beer as the occasional car passed by in the street. Then he set his empty bottle down and moved out of view, and a few moments later all the lights in the bar went out.

Now, everything was completely dark — everything, that is, except Beezy's Bookstore. The big window and the front door glowed yellow. The lights inside had been left on, and they stayed on, all night long.

As the video sped forward, the sky eventually started to brighten again, and a few early-morning commuters appeared in the street. Then, sure enough, pulling in to the spot next to Mr. Hoskins's van was a white truck with a short flatbed full of bundled newspapers. A man hopped out and carried one of the bundles over to the sidewalk in front of the bookstore.

McKenzie stopped the video. "Dixie, with the lights on inside, the front door of the bookshop is clearly visible. After you left, no one went in or out that front door until the next morning when the paper man arrived."

I nodded. "So the woman in the white dress, she must have left when the view was blocked by the waiter, right?"

"Yes. That's a possibility."

"And whoever it was that took Mr. Hoskins, they came in the back door after I left."

She nodded, but she didn't look convinced. I couldn't think of any other explanation. "Maybe someone saw something in the alley?"

She pulled the screen of her laptop down, and it made a little click as it closed. "Well, as a matter of fact, Dixie, someone did."

"Who?"

She slid her computer back down into her briefcase. "The butcher."

I was beginning to think ol' Butch the Butcher was as good as Amber Jack's webcam when it came to recording what happened in the street around his shop. I started to say as much, but the look on McKenzie's face stopped me. She was staring off in the distance.

"He told me that after he locked up the butcher shop, when he saw you getting in your car, he immediately went out back to the alley —"

I said, "Yeah, he smokes back there. He probably went out to light up."

She paused and blinked a couple of times, either because I'd just interrupted her or because she was wondering how I knew so much about what went on in that back alley. Either way I figured I'd better keep quiet and let her talk.

"He saw a car, an old station wagon. It was pulling away from the back of Beezy's

Bookstore. He said a couple of times he'd caught kids parked back there, making out in their cars, and he'd chased them off. But he said this car sped away before he even had a chance. He said he immediately got the feeling that something was wrong."

I sat up, "So, whoever took Mr. Hoskins, they probably watched the front and waited until they knew the shop was empty. Then they came around the back and broke the door in, grabbed Mr. Hoskins and shoved him in their car. Then when the butcher came out, they sped away so he wouldn't be able to identify them."

Of course, that didn't quite explain the blood on the counter, but I turned to see her reaction to my brilliant analysis anyway.

She just nodded. "When you left the bookstore, how long do you think it took you to get to your car?"

I wasn't sure what that had to do with anything, especially since I'd just solved a pretty big part of her case, but I figured I'd humor her. "Well, it's probably less than a minute's walk, except I probably did it in about twenty seconds or so."

Now she took off her big sunglasses. "Oh? Why is that?"

"Well . . . I was skipping."

She raised one eyebrow. "You were skipping?"

I nodded. "Or running. Sort of half skipping, half running. I was kind of excited about the book and Mr. Hoskins, and I was in a hurry to get home and take a shower."

She looked away. "After the butcher locked his front door, how long do you think it would have taken him to get to the alley?"

"His shop's not that big. I'd say ten to fifteen seconds tops."

Without pausing she said, "So from the moment you left the store to the moment the butcher saw a station wagon speed away in the alley, a period of roughly thirty-five seconds elapsed?"

I said, "Um . . ."

"So your theory is that someone watched the front of the store until they thought it was empty, and then they went around to the alley, broke in the back door, grabbed Mr. Hoskins, and then ferried him into a waiting car . . . in thirty-five seconds."

I should have known. McKenzie seemed to get some kind of perverse pleasure in letting me know what an utter moron I was whenever she got the chance.

Well, that was it. I decided I'd had just about all I could take of her games, and

214

besides I still had work to do. I threw my hands up and shrugged. "Well, the only other way it makes sense is if they did it while I was in the store, in which case I would have been in on the whole thing. Did you ever think of that?"

I turned to find her watching me. There was a look in her eye, a hard gleam, and I knew right away: That's exactly what she was thinking. Suddenly it felt like I was fixed in the sight of a shotgun, or more precisely a magnifying glass.

I gulped and said, "Oh."

We sat in silence for a while, both of us staring straight ahead, McKenzie with her hands folded neatly in her lap and me with my mouth hanging slightly open.

On the tennis court in front of us was a tall, gangly young man with copper red hair and long arms giving a tennis lesson to a group of children, seven- or eight-year-olds, all holding their pint-sized tennis rackets in front of them at ninety-degree angles to their little bodies.

They were all watching the young man intently and copying his every move. When he bent his knees slightly and swung his racket to the right, they all immediately did the same. When he swung his racket to the left, they quickly followed suit. Every once in a while he would pause a bit, flash the kids a mischievous grin, and then let his racket fall to the ground with a clatter. All the kids would look wide-eyed at each other for a couple of seconds and then let their rackets fall, too, bursting into fits of happy giggling.

I looked at McKenzie out of the corner of my eye. There was absolutely no way she could possibly think I had anything to do with Mr. Hoskins's disappearance or the blood on his front counter, or that I had seen something and was hiding it from her, but I knew she was considering the same thing I was — anybody else who saw that video would probably think otherwise.

The fact that I was the last person to be seen going in or out of the bookstore, coupled with the butcher seeing a suspicious car pull away from the back door immediately after seeing me basically run to my car . . . I'd suspect me, too, if I didn't know better.

McKenzie interrupted my train of thought. "Is it possible, Dixie, that the woman in white was in the back room when you arrived?"

"Huh," I said.

Suddenly an entirely different scenario opened up before my eyes. The woman in white wasn't a customer. She was a friend, perhaps even more than a friend, perhaps even . . . a lover? It was a little hard imagining befuddled old Mr. Hoskins involved in a little early evening hanky-panky in the back of the store during business hours, but I had to admit it was possible. I remembered his hastily buttoned shirt and untied shoes. Maybe he wasn't so befuddled after all. Maybe he was just rattled by my interruption.

"You said you heard a noise from the back room right before Mr. Hoskins appeared?"

I had completely forgotten. "Yeah. Like a thud."

"And what do you think that could have been?"

I shook my head. "I don't know. Maybe they were on that couch, the one with the gold tassels. Maybe when they heard me Mr. Hoskins jumped up and bumped into something?"

McKenzie frowned. "On the couch?"

I shrugged slightly. "Well, I mean, it seems like if they were doing anything, you know . . . the couch would be the most comfortable place for it."

The slightest hint of a smile played across her lips, and then I thought of the blood on the countertop next to the register. I was still casting about for a reasonable explanation for everything, like a fish who refuses to accept she's been hooked, but McKenzie didn't seem convinced. She was watching the kids on the tennis court with a distant look in her eyes. They had all lined up in a row along one of the lines on the court, and now the tall red-haired man was handing a single tennis ball to each one of them.

I sighed. "You think that woman hid in the back of the store until I left and then murdered Mr. Hoskins, don't you?"

I didn't like saying it out loud like that. It meant giving up hope that Mr. Hoskins was alive and well, drinking sangria on a cruise ship in the Caribbean.

Her expression didn't change. She leaned over and picked up her briefcase as she stood up. "Dixie, I think until we find a body, we can't begin to know what happened." She shook my hand with a wan smile. "Let me know if you remember anything else."

I nodded as she turned and headed back for the sheriff's building. When she got to the edge of the tennis court she turned and said, "Oh, and Dixie, if I were you I'd keep looking for that cat. I got the lab results back this morning. The blood on the countertop . . . it's human. *Which* human, however, is still up in the air."

On the way to my next appointment, I stopped at Vito's Subs and got an Italian with extra hot peppers, and as I crossed back over the bridge to the Key, it was still sitting on the seat next to me, untouched.

What Detective McKenzie was suggesting had made every neuron in my head go to mush, and all the way down Higel my feeble brain did its best to wrap itself around it. I tried to imagine everything that had happened as if it were a painting hanging on the wall, and the picture it made was pretty clear. There was blood on the countertop, *human* blood. There was a missing person. There was a suspicious-looking figure dumping what might have been a body off the Sunshine Skyway Bridge into the bay. Considering all that, it wasn't too far-fetched to come to the conclusion that something had happened in Beezy's Bookstore that night . . . something bad.

I guess I must have been distracted, because instead of taking the dogleg at Higel and shooting straight down to Midnight Pass, I took a left on Ocean Boulevard, which of course took me right by the bookstore. I'd like to think I didn't do that on purpose, that what I really meant to do was get on with my day and forget about the whole bloody mess and let Detective McKenzie take care of it on her own.

But I'm not sure.

As I approached the bookstore, I slowed down and studied the front entrance. The police tape was gone, which meant the bookstore was officially no longer an active crime scene. I could see the display of books through the front window, and the stack of dictionaries on the side where Cosmo liked to nap.

I pulled over to the side of the road and stopped. There was a CLOSED sign hanging in the window, and the lights were off. I wondered what the chances were that in the seven seconds the webcam's view had been blocked by the waiter at Amber Jack's, the woman in white had come out of the bookstore before I got there.

I looked at the door and tried to calculate how long it would take. I imagined someone pulling it open, exiting the store, and walking down the sidewalk. *One-one thousand, two-one thousand . . .* Then I stopped.

In the video, the woman had walked into the frame on the left-hand side just as I had, from the north. When she came out of the store, if she'd gone back in the same direction, it would have taken her much longer than seven seconds to leave the webcam's view, and we would have seen her in the video as soon as the waiter moved out of the way. The angle of the camera didn't provide as long a view going in the other direction. If the woman in white had turned south when she came out of the store, she would have disappeared out of frame in less than four seconds, giving her more than enough time to leave without being recorded.

That was one possibility. I pulled back out on the road and tried to imagine the other option, that she'd gone out the back door instead. Maybe she'd parked back there, or maybe she just felt like taking a tour of the alley . . . No. I'd been in that alley. There was no place to walk and no designated parking spots, and anyway it was filthy. No woman in her right mind would go walking around back there willingly.

The reason it mattered how the woman in white left the store, and the reason I was so distracted now, was that Detective McKenzie was suggesting something that sent a chill down my spine. Yes, the blood on the countertop was human, that was certain, but McKenzie had said "*which* human." All this time I'd been asking myself, who could have murdered Mr. Hoskins? I'd missed another possibility altogether.

McKenzie was suggesting that if the woman in white had left the shop by the back door, it might very well mean that she was the murderer. On the other hand, it could just as easily mean she was the victim.

If that was true, sweet old Mr. Hoskins had a very good reason to disappear.

16

As I made my way south toward the end of the Key, the sun was dead center in the sky and there were wavy lines of heat radiating off the asphalt up ahead. My mind was swimming. Could there have been something about Mr. Hoskins that I had overlooked? Something he was hiding? He had seemed so harmless and sweet, even grandfatherly.

Of course, the fact that I liked Mr. Hoskins should probably have been a little red flag. I don't know why, but I seem to be drawn to people who give off a certain kind of energy, people who are just a little bit unhinged. I'm not sure if they're the flame and I'm the moth or vice versa, but I do know one thing: People that are a little bonkers can be a lot of things, but they're rarely boring. Unfortunately for me, there's a very fine line between crazily interesting and interestingly crazy, and it occasionally gets me in trouble.

The point is, I had liked Mr. Hoskins right away. He just seemed to have a good soul. The idea that he might have been busily hiding a dead body in the back of the store while I browsed around the aisles made the hair on the back of my neck stand up. It just wasn't possible. It's true that Mr. Hoskins had seemed a little eccentric and odd, but he certainly didn't seem capable of that kind of evil, not to mention hoisting a deadweight over the railing of the Sunshine Skyway Bridge.

Then again, I know from firsthand experience that with a strong enough dose of adrenaline pumping through its veins, the human body is capable of almost anything.

I decided to make a quick stop at the drugstore across the street from the diner. Murderer or not, Mr. Hoskins had an agreement with me, and I felt like I'd let him down. The fact that he was wholly unaware of our agreement didn't deter me in the least, and I had a plan to fix it. All I needed was some supplies: a pack of bright construction paper, some big markers, and a staple gun.

My plan was to put signs up all along Ocean Boulevard, and maybe all over the Key. I didn't have a picture of Cosmo, but I felt as if I'd gotten a pretty good look at him, or at least good enough to come up with a fairly accurate description of his two main traits: big and orange. I didn't much like the idea of putting up signs with my phone number for every loony-tune on the street to see, but I didn't think I had much of a choice — I had to do everything in my power to find that cat.

I even considered calling Detective McKenzie and asking if she might consider getting me back in the bookstore to look for a picture of Cosmo I could use for the signs. Perhaps Mr. Hoskins had a photo in that desk in the back room, or failing that there might even be a pen-and-ink drawing of him hanging somewhere in the store.

Either way, I thought, how many big fluffy orange cats with white-tipped tails could there be running around Siesta Key? It's a small island, and if it was possible that Butch the Butcher had seen him, the chances that someone else could have seen him too were pretty strong.

I decided once I found Cosmo, if Mr. Hoskins hadn't turned up by then, I'd take him to the Kitty Haven, a cat kennel and rescue center run by my friend Marge. I knew without a shadow of a doubt that under these circumstances, Marge would take Cosmo in free of charge.

When I came out of the drugstore with all my goodies, I thought of one more thing I might try.

Gia was sitting behind her little window in the vet's office. She had just hung up the phone and was writing something down in a notepad on her desk. There was only one person in the waiting room, except he was so big he took up at least three seats. A young man with muttonchops and a crew cut, he looked like he weighed at least three hundred pounds. I figured he was probably a linebacker for the Sarasota Thunder, our local football team, but lots of professional sports teams come to Sarasota for summer training, so he could have been from anywhere. His arms were as big around as my waist, and it took a couple of looks for me to realize that there was a tiny white Shih Tzu sitting primly on one of his gigantic knees.

Gia has dark cropped hair framing a cute gamine face with deep green eyes like a woodland nymph's. When she looked up to find me standing in front of her window she said, "Oh my gosh, Dixie, what's wrong?"

I said, "Shut the front door. Do I look that bad?"

She laughed. "Sorry. You just look pretty

worried is all."

"I guess I'm a little preoccupied. I have a friend who lost his cat a couple of nights ago. I was hoping if somebody saw him they might have called you."

She shook her head. "Nobody's called saying they *found* a cat, but tell me what he looks like and I'll keep my ears open."

"He's big, long-haired, orange, with a white-tipped tail. His name is Cosmo."

I tried to remember if he'd been wearing a collar in the store, but Gia frowned and pulled her notepad toward her.

"Hold on. I think somebody just called about the same cat."

My face lit up. "Did they see him?"

"No, but they said they were looking for him, too."

I felt my heart start beating a little faster. Was it possible it was Mr. Hoskins?

I said, "Was it an older man?"

She shook her head and leaned forward, as if she had some juicy gossip to share and didn't want anyone to hear. "No. It was Mrs. Silverthorn."

I said, "Huh?"

"The cat lady. She's that old woman that everybody says is crazy and lives in that haunted mansion down at the end of the Key. She said she was looking for a large tabby with a white-tipped tail, and that it answered to the name Moses Cosmo Thornwall."

I said, "You're kidding me."

"Nope. It has to be the same cat, don't you think? I mean, what are the odds? And to be honest, she didn't sound all that crazy. She said whoever found him would be handsomely paid. Those were her exact words, 'handsomely paid.' Weird, right?"

I nodded. "Yeah, weird."

Handsomely paid. Where had I heard those words before? I remembered Ethan saying that Mrs. Silverthorn owned some of the buildings along Ocean Boulevard, including the bookstore. Detective McKenzie had probably gotten in touch with her to find out if she knew anything about Mr. Hoskins, and being a certified "cat lady" she must have decided that until her missing tenant was found, Cosmo was her responsibility. Any cat lover would do the same.

Gia crinkled her nose. "Dixie. You sure you're okay?"

I realized I'd been standing there staring off into the distance, completely lost in thought. "Yeah, I'm fine. I just remembered I have an appointment with a new client. Will you say hi to Dr. Layton for me?"

"She'll be out any minute. Do you want

228

to wait?"

I headed for the door. "No, I've gotta run. But if anybody else calls about that cat, can you let me know?"

I didn't hear her answer. I was already out the door and headed for the car.

I always like to meet with new clients in their homes before their humans go away. It helps the animals know I'm welcome, and I get to see how they interact with their owners and what their routines are. Plus, I just like to know who I'm working for. In this case, I was pretty sure I'd already figured out that part.

I had written the address down in the notebook I keep in my backpack, and I was watching the street numbers as I headed south on Midnight Pass. The numbers get bigger the farther south you go, so I knew it had to be well past my house, near the very end of the Key. Down here, the island gets more and more narrow and finally divides into two parallel spits of sand like the sharp tines of an olive fork. Midnight Pass forms one of the tines. It comes to a dead stop at the very tip, and just before that, Blind Pass Road branches off and forms the other tine.

It's mostly small vacation bungalows and little hotels scrunched up next to each other, but I had a feeling where I was headed was a bit different. I was keeping an eye on the numbers on the mailboxes when, sure enough, I came to an ancient stand of pines in a lush bed of saw palmetto on the right side of the road, with two stone pillars and a narrow, weedy lane that disappeared into the woods.

There was a rusty iron gate swung partially open off the left pillar, but the other half of the gate had been taken down and was leaning against the pillar on the right. I had a feeling it had been standing there for quite some time — it was choked with invasive cat's-claw and rosary pea vines.

I slowed down to check the address. The tangle of vines near the base of the pillar on the right had been cut away to reveal a weather-stained marble placard embedded in stone. Carved deeply into its surface was the number 9500.

I looked over at my notebook lying open on the passenger seat. It said 9500 Blind Pass Road. Even though I'd pretty much figured it out already, my jaw dropped open and I let the Bronco crawl to a stop.

I was at the gates of the Silverthorn Mansion.

17

Low-hanging branches caressed the hood of the Bronco as I inched down the winding driveway. It was paved in an intricate pattern of diamond-shaped red-clay bricks and covered in weeds. There were stucco walls that undulated along the sides of the lane like lizard tails, but as the road curved gently to the right, they crumbled into defeated heaps of pink-and-white rubble, and the view opened up to the ocean.

Standing before me like a queen at her coronation was a towering mansion of white limestone, at least four stories high and nearly encased in a woody green tangle of the same vines that were overtaking the front gate. They snaked around an army of massive columns that formed an elegant portico along the entire width of the front entrance and then weaved their way through the stone parapets on each of the floors above, finally twining all the way up a cluster of towering openwork spires and reaching up gracefully to the sky. Where the roof wasn't concealed under a blanket of decaying leaves, I could see a patchwork of crumbling slate tiles the color of faded dollar bills.

Spread out in front of the house was a sweeping circular courtyard around a massive marble urn in the center that looked like a giant's chili bowl, and off to one side was an open rectangle, formed by a low, vine-covered colonnade that I took to be the parking area. I pulled in and cut the engine.

I felt like I'd wandered into a fairy tale, where a castle had been picked up in a faraway land and plopped down on the beach, which of course is exactly what it was. I tried to imagine what it must have cost for the Silverthorns to dismantle a house like this, bring it all the way from the English countryside to a remote corner of a tiny Florida key, and then rebuild it piece by piece. It was probably more money than I'd ever see in my entire life. For the Silverthorns, it was probably just a drop in the bucket.

I grabbed my backpack and slipped my notebook down in the side pocket. As I headed across the courtyard, weeds brushing against my ankles, I had the distinct feeling that someone was watching me. All the windows looked like panels from a cathedral, with intricately shaped pieces of colored glass glittering in the sun, but I couldn't see any light or movement inside. The giant's chili bowl in the center of the courtyard was filled with fetid, brackish water. It looked as if it had once been a magnificent fountain, but now it was just a playground for a bazillion mosquito larvae.

Just then someone appeared from around the portico, an older man, with gray hair and a pale complexion. When he saw me he paused and straightened his jacket, which was black and slightly worn but formal looking, almost like a tuxedo jacket, over a crisp white dress shirt. I saw the gleam of a silver cuff link at his wrist as he walked over and extended his hand.

"Oliver Silverthorn. How very kind of you to come."

I said, "Oh, thanks. Except I don't really know why I'm here."

"Ah yes, the eternal question. My wife will fill you in on the details. I'm just off to repair a broken screen, but Janet will see you in."

He motioned to a long expanse of marble steps leading up to the front entrance and was about to turn away when he paused, leveling me with his deep gray eyes. His tone was suddenly serious.

"Miss Hemingway, I know we've only just met, but I wonder if I might ask you a favor. My wife is a rather secretive woman, always has been. She's going to ask that you keep the nature of your employment here a secret from me. I'd be most grateful if you'd play along."

I thought, *My employment here?* That sounded like I was the new full-time cat nanny — and then I remembered Ethan saying he'd heard the mansion was filled with hundreds of cats. Of course, my first instinct was to ask him why in the world she'd want to keep it a secret from her own husband, but I figured for now I'd just shut up and nod politely.

He smiled. "I know, it's unusual. My wife tends to worry too much, especially when it comes to cats. She feels a certain kinship to them and always has. I'm afraid I don't quite share her love for our feline friends, but I understand that her heart is in the right place. I've always been more inclined to the canine species myself."

I nodded. "I think it says a lot about a person what kind of pets they're drawn to."

"Really? Do tell."

"Well, I can only speak for myself, but I'm drawn to dogs because they make you feel loved no matter what. They're always there; they love you unconditionally. But then at the same time, I'm drawn to cats precisely because they do have conditions, so if a cat loves you, you know you're something special."

He folded his hands together and chuckled. "Well, then, I suppose the best of all worlds would be to have the love of both, wouldn't it? In my younger days, I was very active with our local dramatic society. We destroyed a nineteenth-century classic, *Charley's Aunt,* myself in the title role, and to get ourselves back in the good graces of the community, the entire cast volunteered at the local animal shelter. I've still got more than a few cat scars on my arms to prove it. So I do admire their beauty, but I prefer to admire it from a good, safe distance."

I nodded. "Well, I admire any man who volunteers at an animal shelter whether he likes cats or not."

He stood a little taller now, and I could tell in his younger days he'd probably been quite handsome. His hair was long and silvery, combed straight back over his head, and his gray eyes were speckled with ocean blue so it seemed like they were constantly glittering. There was a genteel, almost royal air about him. In my cat-hair-covered shorts and T-shirt, I felt a little bit like a country bumpkin in the presence of the king.

"Well, don't let me keep you, Miss Hemingway. I believe you and Mrs. Silverthorn are going to get along splendidly. She loves cats, and she also has a weakness for chocolate. It's served daily with tea."

He winked and bowed slightly and then headed across the courtyard toward the far corner of the house. I took a deep breath and sighed. He seemed like a very nice gentleman, but so far the Silverthorn Mansion was turning out to be just as strange and mysterious as I had always imagined it would be.

"Well," I muttered to myself, "at least there'll be chocolate."

Avoiding the cracked sections, I went up the sweeping marble steps to the front entrance, where I was greeted with a pair of brass elephant's heads, oxidized in the moist, salty air with a pearlescent coating of emerald green and verdigris. They were hung one each on a pair of arched wooden doors painted a mossy black, flanked by fluted marble urns spilling over with dead weeds and twigs. I was looking for the doorbell when I realized the elephants' heads were actually giant door-knockers.

I wasn't sure which door I should use, so I just guessed. I took a deep breath and raised the trunk of the elephant on the right and let it fall back to the door with a solid thud. Little green flecks of oxidized metal chipped off on my fingers. I would have expected the trunk to be polished to a golden shine from years of use, but it was just as green and mottled as the rest of the elephant's head.

I was about to raise the trunk again when the round handle on the opposite door made a click and then turned slowly. The door swung open to reveal a woman in her mid-twenties, with long dark hair tied in pigtails hanging limply down her back, wearing a simple black skirt and a pearl gray blouse under a white apron. She was alarmingly thin, with broad, bony shoulders and lips stretched into a taut line, as if they were holding something in.

I said, "Hi, I'm Dixie Hemingway. I have an appointment with Mrs. Silverthorn?"

The woman's eyebrows rose slightly, but she didn't say a word as she stepped back and opened the door a little wider. Her face was hardened beyond its years and pale — I don't think she'd seen the light of day in months — and her eyes looked red and swollen. It occurred to me that she'd been crying when I knocked on the door.

We stepped into a large cathedral-like foyer, with vaulted ceilings, parquet floors of faded black and white, and a sweeping staircase big enough for a herd of buffalo to go up and down comfortably. All around the perimeter of the foyer were royal blue velvet drapes, easily twenty feet long, their dusty bottoms ballooned on the parquet floors like a southern belle's party dress. Every ten feet or so they were bunched open with gold ropes and tassels, revealing tall panels of silvered mirrors, framed in gilded wood. More than a few of the mirrors were cracked, and some were missing altogether, revealing a crumbling layer of horsehair plaster and lathing underneath.

The girl nodded silently, which I took to mean that I should wait here, and then she turned to one of the mirrored panels, which slid open to a long hallway lined with stained-glass windows on one side, but I didn't see much more than that because she quickly slid the door closed behind her.

I looked around. Ethan had been right. It was obvious the Silverthorns were struggling to keep the whole place from falling in around them — from all appearances, they were holding on to it like a dog to a chew-toy. The floor was filthy, covered in a thin layer of dust and grime, and there were clouds of cobwebs arching across the ceiling, dotted with the desiccated bodies of insects trapped in suspended animation.

I heard three short chirps, like a telephone bell, come from somewhere upstairs, and then I noticed a pathway in the grime on the floor that led from the sliding door the girl had disappeared through across the foyer and up the right side of the staircase. I don't think the floors had been mopped in years. It made me thankful for my teeny little apartment. I can basically mop the whole place with a couple of wet paper towels.

I thought, *If only Michael could see me now.* We'd spent practically our entire childhoods fantasizing about what this house looked like on the inside, making up stories about ghosts and missing children locked inside its numerous underground torture chambers, and now here I was, smack-dab in the middle of it, about to meet with the infamous Mrs. Silverthorn, live and in person.

So far, though, I hadn't seen a single cat.

As if on cue, a woman appeared at the top of the steps. She was long limbed and tan, with a scarlet wrap tied around her head, sky blue capri pants over a flesh-colored leotard, and a long flowery scarf tied around her tiny waist. She practically floated down the stairs and extended her hand to mine in one single fluid motion. She was barefoot.

"Oh, Dixie Hemingway, how kind of you to come. I'm Alice Ann Silverthorn."

She was in her mid-seventies at least, but her skin was taut and shiny, and her hair was shimmering silver and beautifully coifed in sculpted waves. For a moment I wondered if all her money didn't go to hairdressers and plastic surgeons, but then I noticed a thin wisp of straight, mousy gray hair peeking out the back.

She was wearing a wig, and her hair underneath must have been pulled back so tightly it was pulling the skin of her face taut. I had to admit, she looked pretty damn good for a woman her age. I decided right then and there that the very moment my hair started thinning, I'd go out and get myself a couple of wigs. Her cheeks were lightly dusted with fine powder, and she'd freshly applied to her lips a thin layer of burgundy lip gloss.

With a firm handshake, she said, "It's a pleasure to meet you. Won't you come in?"

I wasn't quite sure how to respond since I was already in, so I just smiled and said, "Oh, thank you."

She turned toward the mirrored sliding door and caught her own image. "Janet, we'll take tea in the reading room." She smoothed the scarf around her waist down with the tips of her fingers and then turned back to me. "I feel a day isn't worth living without a cup of tea."

Before I could respond she turned and headed up the stairs. I didn't know if Janet had heard her or not, nor was I sure it mattered, so I followed mutely, taking care not to step on the scarf trailing behind her. Parts of the stairs were crumbling and separated at the joints, and at one point she said softly, "Keep to the right, my dear."

The "reading room" turned out to be a massive ballroom, with fully stocked bookshelves lining every wall from the floor all the way up to the arched ceiling, which must have been at least twenty-five feet high at its peak. The perimeter of the room was fitted with an iron track and rolling ladders to reach the books on top, and hugging one wall was what looked like a gigantic Egyptian rug, rolled up and covered with layers of yellowing newspaper and thin plastic dry-cleaner bags.

Mrs. Silverthorn pointed to the far corner of the room where there was a low coffee table and said, "We'll sit by the window.

The light is brilliant this time of day."

The entire room was crowded with chairs of all sizes, shapes and colors. Dining chairs, club chairs, hassocks, rocking chairs, even an old wheelchair with a woven cane back. There were so many chairs, in fact, that I wasn't exactly sure how we'd navigate through them to the table in the corner. I thought perhaps they'd been stored here temporarily, maybe from other parts of the house that were being painted, but Mrs. Silverthorn acted as if they were a permanent fixture. I followed as she expertly weaved in and out of them in a predetermined path, like a ballerina in an obstacle course.

Tucked in among the chairs here and there were old buckets and copper pans, each partly filled with dingy gray water. I looked up to find long strips of crumbling paper and green plaster hanging from the ceiling, like dripping stalactites in a cave. I wondered if perhaps all those woody vines on the outside weren't actually holding everything up and keeping the whole house from collapsing in on itself.

We finally reached the coffee table and sat down opposite each other in a pair of button-tufted armchairs covered in pale lemon silk and a fine layer of dust. I considered discreetly brushing some of it away, but I didn't want to embarrass anybody, so I ignored it.

Mrs. Silverthorn arranged her long trailing scarf into a little bouquet in her lap and then sighed with a charming smile. "Now. Dixie Hemingway, I do hope you won't mind my little trick, but I worry that tongues will wag whenever the Silverthorn name is bandied about, so I'm afraid I wasn't entirely honest when I spoke to you on the telephone."

I said, "I completely understand. It's not a problem at all."

She smiled. "Good, and please pardon the mess. As you can see, the roof is on the fritz. My footman is in charge of repairs, but I'm afraid he's gone missing."

I had never once heard anyone say the word "footman" in real life, but I just smiled nonchalantly as if it were the most normal thing in the world and said, "Oh no, not at all. It's a very beautiful house. I've always wondered what it looked like, I mean, on the inside. I grew up here on the Key, so as kids we used to make up all kinds of stories about it."

She threw her head back and laughed. "Oh, how delightful. What kind of stories?"

Luckily for me Janet came in carrying a tray. I didn't think Mrs. Silverthorn would be too happy to hear how the whole town thought she was crazy and that her house was filled with hundreds of cats and ghosts and secret torture chambers. She stood up and waved her scarf in Janet's direction. "We're over here, darling."

Janet was wending her way slowly through the chairs, keeping her eyes on the tray so as not to spill anything, and I thought to myself that her name didn't fit her at all. She didn't look like a Janet one bit. I would have guessed something darker, like Gerta or Morticia. Without looking up she said glumly, "I see you."

Mrs. Silverthorn cleared a dirty ashtray and a stack of faded gossip magazines from the coffee table to the floor next to her chair. The cover of the top magazine had a blurry snapshot of a shirtless man on a yacht, with a caption that read, "Burton Finds Liz with Another Girl's Hubby!!??"

Janet set the tray down on the table. It held a small silver teakettle sitting next to a matching sugar bowl, with a couple of lace napkins, two mismatched porcelain cups filled to the brim with steaming tea, and a tiny plate with two chocolate wafers.

Mrs. Silverthorn handed me one of the cups and said, "Dixie Hemingway, I do hope you won't take cream in your tea, because I'm afraid we're all out."

She had a funny way of saying my name, as though it were all one word — *Dixahemingway.* I wondered if I shouldn't correct her, but at that point I was still trying to adjust to my new surroundings and I didn't quite trust my own judgment. I finally understood what Alice must have felt like in Wonderland. I'd smoked pot a few times in my rebellious teenage years, but I avoided the harder drugs like the plague, so I don't have firsthand experience of what a bona fide drug trip feels like, but this had to be pretty damn close.

As I took a sip of my tea, I prayed that Janet hadn't slipped some kind of potion in it, or at the very least had rinsed the cup out first. It was mint, with just a touch of lemon, and actually quite tasty.

Mrs. Silverthorn settled back into her chair and nodded at the back of Janet's head. She was already halfway across the room. "That will be all for now, Janet darling, thank you."

I heard Janet say, "I know."

Mrs. Silverthorn said, "And now, we can finally talk."

I had set my backpack down on the floor next to my chair, and I was pulling my notebook and pen out of the side pocket. I said, "Mrs. Silverthorn, I think I may already know why you called. And you're right about those wagging tongues. I stopped in at the vet's office right before I drove here. They mentioned you were looking for a missing cat."

She shook her head. "Mr. Peters?"

"What?"

Her eyes widened with alarm. "Janet, where is Mr. Peters?"

Of course, Janet had already gone. Mrs. Silverthorn then raised one hand and solemnly held it in the air, like a student raising her hand to get the teacher's attention.

She said, "Never mind. Whenever I think a troubling thought, I am to raise my hand in the air and name it. We'll call that one 'Oh, bother.' "

I nodded, relieved.

"You see, Mr. Peters is my only cat with outdoor privileges, and I'm afraid I worry about him too much. Hadley tells me I'm going to put myself in an early grave. I'm sure wherever Mr. Peters is, he's perfectly safe. He's probably out hunting crickets in the garden."

I half expected her to tell me that Mr. Peters was a Cheshire cat. I said, "Oh, is Hadley your footman?"

She waved her finger in the air as if to say

"no no no" but instead said something completely different. "Dixie Hemingway, you may or may not know there's been a terrible incident in town. It would appear that one of my tenants has gone missing, and the authorities suspect foul play."

"You mean Mr. Hoskins?"

She arched one eyebrow and nodded slowly. "So you do know. I want you to help me find him."

As much as I would have liked to find Mr. Hoskins, I shook my head immediately. I'd promised myself I wouldn't get more involved in the case than I already was, and anyway it would have been completely irresponsible for me to snoop around behind Detective McKenzie's back when she was already conducting an official investigation of her own.

I said, "Mrs. Silverthorn, I'm sorry, but I'm a cat sitter, not a missing persons detective. You'll have to call someone else. I can't help you."

She pursed her lips and swiveled her head toward me like a hoot owl. "Young lady! Mr. Hoskins's cat is missing. Are you aware of that in your impertinent head?"

I gulped. "Oh. I'm sorry, I . . . I didn't mean to be rude. Yes, I do know his cat is missing. In fact —"

"Good. Then it's settled. You'll help me find him."

"Huh?"

"Moses Cosmo Thornwall — he's a marvelous animal. The police tell me he's lost, but I believe he can't have gone far. In fact, I believe he might still be inside that bookstore. I want you to find him."

Sometimes I think we're all just bags of molecules, randomly bouncing and bumping around the universe, and then other times I think somewhere, something or someone is in charge, pulling all the strings and making sense of all the chaos. Here I'd been sneaking around in the alley, looking for Cosmo and wondering how I could get inside that store, and now the universe was literally handing me the keys. Mrs. Silverthorn was pulling them out of a small blue velvet pouch.

"I spent practically the entire night looking for these keys only to find them in the exact spot they were supposed to be. Of course I could have sworn I'd already looked there, but such is the burden of an aging mind. Now, this long one with the round head opens the front door. The smaller one opens the back. There are all kinds of nooks and crannies in that store, and cats are very quick and crafty, so he could be hiding anywhere."

I started to remind her that I did actually know a thing or two about cats, being a professional cat sitter and all, but she held one hand up to stop me. "Now, let's not talk about money. It's so vulgar. There is, however, one delicate matter that I feel I must ask of you." She glanced toward the door and then lowered her voice.

"I've explained to Mr. Silverthorn that you're here to care for Mr. Peters. I'm afraid my reputation as a cat-obsessed recluse is not entirely unearned, and I'd prefer my husband think I'm not so far gone as to employ a professional to help track down a tenant's cat. Anyway, it's only a half-lie. Mr. Peters is a rascally tom and constantly gets into trouble, and without my footman I'm at a total loss. I can't be out traipsing about the property at my age, and Mr. Silverthorn is no spring chicken himself. So I'll spare no expense to keep my peace of mind about Mr. Peters. He's my favorite, you know."

I tried not to sound too nosy. "So . . . you have other cats?"

She made a gesture with her arm that seemed to encompass the entire mansion. "Oh, of course, dear, but not on this floor."

She dropped the keys back down in the pouch and held it out to me, but I still wasn't convinced. If Cosmo was still inside the store, I didn't think he'd be hiding. By now he'd be as hungry as a tiger, pacing in the window and trying to get out — someone would have seen him. Plus, I didn't know the first thing about finding missing animals other than tacking up signs on telephone poles, and it seemed wrong to take money from a woman who was clearly a little off her rocker and broke to boot.

She said, "I know what you're thinking — the ravishing yet crazy cat lady has no money."

"No, I'm not thinking that at all. It's just that if Cosmo was still inside the store —"

She interrupted me. "No, dear. He won't answer to just Cosmo any sooner than I'll answer to just Alice. It's Moses Cosmo Thornwall."

"Okay," I said, "if he was still inside the store, I think I would have seen him. I've already looked in the window a couple of times, and there's no sign of him. I think he might have gotten out of the store. In fact, I think he may be hiding in the street somewhere."

She tipped her chin and studied me. "And why were you looking in the window of the bookstore?"

I said, "Mrs. Silverthorn, I was in the store

the night Mr. Hoskins disappeared. It's possible I was his last customer. The police are looking for him, but no one's looking for his cat. He seemed like a very sweet man, and I felt it was the least I could do — and I know animals."

Her eyes narrowed. "Then you know exactly how I feel, and you're clearly the right woman for the job."

She held the velvet pouch out again, and this time I took it.

18

I was standing in front of the big display
window at Beezy's, trying to look incon-
spicuous. The sun was low in the sky,
threatening to plunge into the ocean, and
the shops were all still open, so the street
was busy. A couple of college kids, a boy
and a girl, came meandering up the sidewalk
holding hands. The girl was tall and slightly
plump, with short frizzy hair and a flowing
hippie skirt, and the boy was a good deal
shorter, with black-framed glasses and a
seventies-style goatee.

They slowed, and the boy said, "Ma'am,
are they still closed?"

I nodded. "Yeah."

The girl said, "Bummer," and then they
made sad, grumpy faces at each other.

I mad a sad, grumpy face at myself in the
reflection of the window as they walked on.
Since when did kids get so goddamned
polite? I decided if one more person called

me "ma'am" I would sock him in the mouth.

I was a little worried about being seen going into the bookstore. I didn't want to have to answer any questions about what I was doing there, or what had happened to Mr. Hoskins. Since Mrs. Silverthorn had asked that I not tell her husband about our arrangement or what I was doing, I was pretty sure she didn't want me telling anybody else either.

Also, I was a little scared.

Even though I knew Detective McKenzie would have ordered a cleanup crew to get rid of the blood on the counter, just the fact that something terrible could have happened inside the store made me a little wary of going in alone. I took a walk down to the end of the block just to calm my nerves, but I didn't want to linger on the sidewalk too long. The more I hung around the more likely it was that I'd run into somebody I knew.

As I passed the butcher shop I saw Butch in the back, wearing a bloody apron and a white chef's hat. I wondered if it was possible he'd seen that cat again. If he'd gotten a good look at it and could confirm it was Cosmo, maybe I wouldn't need to go in the bookstore at all. I half hoped he'd tell me that he'd caught the cat he'd seen and taken it to the Kitty Haven, but that was probably asking for too much.

I pushed the door open, and a blanket of cool air wafted over me, mixed with the pungent smell of raw meat and bleach. The whole place was probably about the same size as the bookstore, but the front area, the part for customers, wasn't much bigger than my kitchen. It had a white tile floor, with chalkboards on the walls listing prices and the day's specials, and a long refrigerated display case separating it from the back, where all the meat was prepared for sale.

The display case was filled with row upon row of fresh, glistening meat, lined up with artistic precision in neat, parallel rows. There were turkey breasts, ground beef, sirloin, pork chops, sausage, thick-cut bacon, Cornish hens, sliced ham, roasting chickens, and a whole slew of other cuts of meat I didn't even recognize. I don't much like going in butcher shops — all that raw flesh just reminds me that my hamburger patty used to be a living, breathing thing walking around in a field and munching on grass and dandelions. I like it much better when it's laid out in front of me on a plate already cooked, and preferably by somebody else.

Butch was behind the case, standing over

a worktable and expertly sharpening a butcher's knife that looked at least fifteen inches long. He was holding it out in front of him and slicing its edge along a honing steel, his hands flying with such speed and precision that he looked like a mad conductor leading an orchestra in the final frenzied moments of a symphony. The shimmering ring it made was so loud I didn't think he heard me come in, and it turned out I was right, because when he finally saw me standing there he looked momentarily shocked.

I said, "I was just in the neighborhood. I thought I'd stop in and see if maybe you'd seen that cat again?"

He put the knife down and came over to the counter, wiping his hands on his apron. "Yeah, yeah, they found him already."

I said, "What? They did?"

"Yeah. A lady came in here this afternoon asking if I'd lost a cat. She said they found him hiding in the alley out back. Big orange fella, right?"

"Yes, that's him! Did she say where she was taking him?"

He shrugged and cocked his head to the side. "Nope. I told her about you, but since you didn't give me your number . . ."

I was relieved that someone had found Cosmo, but I could have kicked myself. If

I'd given Butch my number when he asked for it I could have been halfway back down the Key by then, with Cosmo in a cat carrier in the seat next to me. I could just see the delight on Mrs. Silverthorn's face when I delivered him into her arms not more than an hour after she asked me to find him.

Butch was unrolling his sleeves. "Well, I guess you don't gotta worry about finding him now."

I pulled one of my business cards out of my backpack and handed it to him. "I guess not. But could you do me a favor? If you happen to see that woman again, would you mind giving her this and asking her to give me a call?"

He grinned. "Sure thing."

I winced as he pushed my card down in the front pocket of his apron, imagining it getting stained and soggy. I guess when you work with dead meat for a living, you get used to things being bloody, just like I get used to being covered with fur all day long — it just comes with the job.

Outside, I made my way slowly back toward the car, dodging passersby on the sidewalk and muttering under my breath. Even though I didn't think I had a choice, I wasn't happy about giving Butch my card. I'd been thinking about getting a post office box for a while, but I just couldn't justify the expense. I don't get a lot of business-related mail, and usually people just pay me in person, but every once in a while clients want to send me something, like a check or their travel itinerary, so I'd included all my contact information on my business cards. I barely knew this man, and here I was giving him my name, my private cell phone number, and my home address. I might as well have handed him the key to my front door, too.

Then I thought of Mrs. Silverthorn and raised my hand up in the air. I said out loud to myself, "Oh, bother," hoping no one was watching. Butch may have been a little rough around the edges, but he certainly wasn't a criminal, and most important of all, Cosmo was safe and sound. He wasn't lurking around in a filthy alleyway, scavenging for food in a garbage Dumpster or hiding behind a box of dusty old books, scared and alone.

That, as far as I was concerned, satisfied my contract with Mr. Hoskins.

As for Mrs. Silverthorn, all I needed to do now was give her a call and let her know that Cosmo had been found and that she didn't need to worry any longer. Although, when I tried to imagine that conversation, I knew it might not go so easily. Mrs. Silverthorn didn't seem the kind of woman to just leave it at that. She'd want to know who had found Cosmo. Where was he now? Was the woman planning on keeping him? Or had she put him in the pound with the hundreds of other abandoned pets, hopelessly waiting for a home . . .

I paused in front of the bookstore. I could see the big claw-foot table in the middle of the store, and all the boxes and stacks of books along the aisles. I smiled, remembering how Cosmo had whipped past my feet and disappeared under the counter in a flash. He certainly was fast, and he certainly knew how to hide. I should have been happy somebody had been able to catch him, but when I saw the little stack of dictionaries with its head of orange fur, I burst into tears.

Well, that's it, I thought. I'd finally gone off the deep end. I was becoming one of those crazy people who walk around talking to themselves and swinging from one extreme emotion to the other, laughing hysterically one minute and sobbing uncontrollably the next. I figured the next logical step would be to collect all my belongings in shopping bags and move to a cardboard box in the park.

Maybe Deputy Morgan had been right;

maybe I did need to lighten up, take a vacation or something. I shook my head and dabbed at my eyes with the hem of my T-shirt, and that's when I saw something move inside the store.

It was white, like the tip of a pointed shoe or a crumpled piece of paper or, perhaps, the very end of a fluffy cat tail. It was at the end of one of the aisles midway toward the back of the store, just around the corner of one of the bookshelves, and then it was gone.

I stepped up to the door and peered in. Everything looked completely still. I couldn't quite see all of the countertop from the outside, but I could see the big antique cash register and all of Mr. Hoskins's drawings arranged on the walls.

I glanced across the street at Amber Jack's. It was strange to think there was a live camera pointed at me for anyone with a connection to the Internet to see, and I wondered who might be watching me this very instant.

You'd think I'd have known better. In the past I've gotten myself mixed up in all kinds of stupid and dangerous situations without the vaguest idea how I ended up there, but now . . . I was beginning to recognize those moments when things took a turn.

Maybe it was the way my breath quickened slightly, or the vague tingling that started at the base of my spine and inched its way up to the back of my neck. Right then, standing on the sidewalk outside Beezy's Bookstore, I realized I had a choice. I could just walk away. I could go home and have a perfectly normal, uneventful evening. I could make some popcorn or a frozen pizza. I could fall asleep in the hammock with my new gardening book draped over my face.

I took a step back from the door and sighed.

Then, with a quick glance up and down the street, I reached into my pocket and pulled out the blue velvet pouch that Mrs. Silverthorn had given me.

19

It was completely quiet inside the bookstore except for the fading ring of the bell over my head and the steady, pounding beat of blood in my ear. There was an added note of disinfectant mixed in with the dusty smell of all the books, and the bloody paw prints that had been on the counter by the register were now completely gone.

I put my backpack down by the counter and flicked on the lights, then moved through the store slowly, aisle by aisle, carefully studying every shelf up and down. At the aisle where I thought I'd seen something move, I paused for a good long while and waited, but there was nothing.

I was about to move on when I heard a tiny rustling sound. It was coming from the end of the aisle, where there was an air-conditioning vent, with half its grille missing, cut into the baseboard at the bottom of the wall. A tiny brown mouse poked its head out and sniffed the air tentatively. When it saw me it froze, and we locked eyes for a moment; then in a blink it hopped out of the vent and disappeared through a crack between the bookshelf and the wall.

For an instant my mind flashed to my mother. I was about five years old, and we were just getting home from church. As we walked into the kitchen, she let out an earsplitting scream. There was a mouse running along the toe-kick of the kitchen sink, and at the sound of my mom's screeching it hopped a good foot in the air and then slipped under the stove. I turned around to find a pair of white high-heel shoes, sitting perfectly still on the floor where she'd just been standing.

"Dixie, honey."

I looked up. My mother was perched on top of the kitchen table, holding her skirt up around her knees and shaking like a leaf. She had literally jumped right out of her shoes.

"Go get your father."

My dad was certain that poor mouse had been just as terrified of my mother as she was of it, and we laughed so hard that my sides ached for hours. There are a lot of things I inherited from my mother. Unfortunately, fear of mice isn't the worst of them.

I waited a little while longer to see if anything else poked its head out of the vent, but nothing happened. I glanced at the AC unit built into the wall over the front door and then back at the open vent. It must have been a remnant of an old air-conditioning system, probably broken down at some point and never repaired. I moved on.

At the back of the store, I went through the low swinging door and searched every inch of the office, under the green velvet sofa with tassels, behind the big mahogany desk, even in a little broom closet, though it was closed and latched. Inside there was nothing but a tiny sink and faucet with some old mops and a stepladder. On the floor under the desk were a couple of bowls, one empty and the other with a tiny bit of water left at the bottom.

I'd expected there to be a litter box somewhere in the back of the store, but there wasn't. I figured Cosmo must have been in the habit of being let out in the alley to do his business, but if he was locked in the store now without a litter box, he'd have found an alternative.

I brought the ladder out and used it to look on the tops of all the shelves in the store, which took a while. There was a gap of about a foot below the ceiling, but just like the rest of the store it was crammed with more books and boxes, so I had to move the ladder at least three or four times per aisle and slide things around to get a good view of everything. By the time I made it to the first aisle at the front of the store, I had lost all hope.

More than likely, the orange cat that someone had found in the alley was indeed Cosmo, and whatever I'd seen moving inside the store was either a reflection in the window or a mouse or my own imagination. The mind sees what it wants to see, and I knew I'd be much happier if I found Cosmo now as opposed to worrying about whether he'd been taken to the pound, but it didn't look like that was going to happen. I decided I'd finish searching this last aisle and then go home and start calling shelters.

I was balanced on the very top rung of the ladder, steadying myself with one hand on the top of the bookcase. When I slid a box over to one side and peered over the top, I saw a man framed in the doorway.

He was outside. At first I didn't recognize him, but when he pressed his forehead against the glass I realized it was Butch the Butcher. He had changed out of his white butcher's apron and black boots and was wearing faded jeans and a black T-shirt. He cupped his hands around the glass and squinted, sweeping his eyes all around the inside of the store.

I froze. It would have been difficult to explain what I was doing in the store without betraying Mrs. Silverthorn's confidence, especially since Butch had just told me Cosmo had been found, but it had also been Butch who told the deputies he'd seen me leaving the scene of the crime covered in blood. There's no telling what he'd think if he caught me snooping around inside the store now.

But what was he doing here? Unless he'd been lying about someone finding Cosmo, why on earth was he looking in the bookstore? I kept myself as still as possible, hoping if I didn't move he wouldn't see me. Eventually he stepped back and folded his meaty arms over his chest. He looked up the street a couple of times and then walked back down the sidewalk toward his shop.

By the time I got the ladder folded up and back into its broom closet in the office, I knew what he was up to. More than likely I wasn't the only one around here with an ego the size of a Texas bull. He probably thought his chances of figuring out what had happened to Mr. Hoskins were just as good as anybody else's. Maybe he thought he'd notice that one detail in the shop that no one else had seen — that one tiny clue that explained everything. Either that, or I wasn't the only person Mrs. Silverthorn had hired to find Cosmo.

As I latched the door of the broom closet, my cell phone rang. I think I was probably still a little nervous to be alone inside the store, because I yelped like a baby seal. Probably if I'd been wearing high heels, I would have jumped right out of them. I pulled my phone out of my pocket and looked at the screen.

It was Ethan.

I shook my fist and whispered, "Oh *shhhoot!*"

We hadn't talked all day, which wasn't completely unheard of, but getting rarer and rarer. I had a feeling it was probably due to "the letter" — the one from Guidry, the one still sitting in a basket on my kitchen counter, the one I still hadn't opened. The fact that I'd let it sit there this long gave me a sick feeling in the pit of my stomach. I'm an old pro when it comes to hiding things from myself, but it wasn't fair to Ethan. He was probably just as worried about the can of worms that letter might open up as I was.

I sat down on the green velvet sofa, took a deep breath, and flipped the phone open.

Cheerfully as possible, I said, "Hey, what's up?"

He said, "I was just about to ask you the same thing. What are you doing?"

I wondered what he might say if I told him I'd been hired by Mrs. Silverthorn and that I was sneaking around in Beezy's Bookstore looking for a missing cat. Then I thought, *Well, there's only one way to find out.*

"Umm, you might want to sit down for this."

He sighed. "Uh-oh. Now I'm sorry I asked."

I laughed. "No, really, it's fine. Ask me where I am right now."

"Do I have to?"

"I promise it's not that big a deal."

"Okay, where are you right now?"

"I'm in Beezy's Bookstore."

"What the hell? Really? Did Mr. Hoskins turn up?"

"Unfortunately no. The owner of the building hired me to find his missing cat."

There was a pause. "The owner of the building . . ."

"Yup."

"No way."

"Yes way."

"You mean Mrs. Silverthorn?"

I nodded, "Yep. I'm pretty sure somebody already found the cat, but I was walking by and I thought I saw something move inside, so I came in to check it out just to be on the safe side. I think I must have been seeing things."

"How did you get in?"

"Mrs. Silverthorn gave me the keys herself."

"Wait a minute, are you telling me you actually met her?"

"Impertinent man!" I said, doing my best impersonation of her. "We didn't just meet. We had tea in the library at the Silverthorn Mansion!"

There was silence.

I said, "Hello?"

"Uh, yeah. I was just picking my jaw up off the floor. I've been working with the Silverthorn family for years and I can barely get that woman to talk to me on the phone."

I shrugged, "Well, we're old pals. Maybe I'll introduce you sometime."

"I'm not so sure I like the idea of you being in that store alone."

"Oh poppycock!" I said, doing my Mrs. Silverthorn again. "Don't be ridiculous."

"I guess I'll just have to trust you on this one," he said, but then the tone of his voice changed. "Listen . . ."

I winced. When Ethan starts a sentence with the word "listen," it usually means something very important is on his mind, but I already knew what it was.

I said, "Wait, I know what you're going to say, and I'm sorry."

"What are you now, a mind reader?"

I said, "Sort of. It's about that letter, right?"

He sighed. "Yeah. Listen, I don't want to pressure —"

"Ethan, I promise I'll open it tonight. I don't know why I've been putting it off."

"Listen, it's none of my business if —"

"No, *you* listen. It's completely your business. I'm just not in the habit of thinking about anybody but myself, and it's been so crazy the last couple of days, and I know you think things were left up in the air with Guidry and me, and I know you know I wouldn't want to do a thing to make you —"

He interrupted. "Hey."

"What?"

"First, stop talking. Second, would you like to have dinner tomorrow night?"

I took a deep breath and smiled. "Yes. I'd like that very much."

"Sweet. I'll pick you up at eight, but promise me one thing."

"What?"

"If you see anything weird in that store, call me right away."

I said, "I promise."

Suddenly it felt as if a huge weight had been lifted off my shoulders, a weight I'd been carrying around ever since that letter had arrived. For a long time, everything that had happened to me, big or small, happened to me and me alone. I was beginning to realize that no matter what Guidry had to say in that letter, I wouldn't have to deal with it by myself now.

That was a feeling I hadn't had in a very long time.

After I hung up, I pulled a Baggie of kibble out of my pocket and filled the empty bowl under the desk, and then I topped off the water bowl, too, just in case.

As I headed up toward the front of the store, I'd already planned my course of action. First of all, I'd phone Mrs. Silverthorn and tell her Cosmo had probably been found, and if she wanted me to confirm it I'd be happy to check with the local shelters. If he did turn up, I'd take him to the Kitty Haven, where I knew he'd be safe until we figured out what happened to Mr. Hoskins.

Second of all, I'd go home and open that letter. If Guidry was writing to say he'd changed his mind, that he missed me, or that he was unhappy with his new job and leaving New Orleans to come back to me, I'd just have to tell him it was too late, that I was with Ethan now and nothing could change that.

I was just about to get to "third of all" when something stopped me dead in my tracks. I was standing at the front door, my backpack slung over my shoulder, with the cash register and counter just to my right.

My fingers started to tingle.

I took a step back and looked down.

There on the floor, just a few inches from the edge of the counter, was a single, glistening red paw print.

My mind went numb. I gently pulled my backpack around and pulled out my penlight. Then, as quietly as possible, I put the backpack down on the floor and slowly lowered to my hands and knees. I clicked the light on with my thumb and directed its beam into the gap under the counter.

There were a few pennies lodged in a bed of dust and cobwebs next to a yellowed pencil, its edges pocked with teethmarks. To the left, tucked into the corner, was another air-conditioning vent, its metal grille covered in dust and lying on the floor in front of it. The vent opened up into the crawl-space beneath the big picture window, and as the light moved across the opening, I saw from deep within the reflection of two gleaming points of yellow, floating in the dark and staring back at me.

"Cosmo?"

I lay down flat on my stomach and pulled myself even closer under the counter. If I turned my head just so, I could wedge myself close enough to the vent opening to see all the way inside the space under the window. I squeezed my arm through and maneuvered the point of the penlight into the vent.

It illuminated an unfinished crawl space, directly beneath the big display window. It was less than two feet high, about four feet wide, and only about three feet deep. It was the perfect size for a nice kitty hideout, but as I swept the light from one corner of the space to the next, I felt a tremor start to well up from somewhere deep inside my body. The two yellow points of light weren't cat's eyes.

They were the shiny brass buttons on Mr. Hoskins's shirt.

His lifeless body was folded into a crumpled pile in the corner, lying in a pool of half-dried blood, his red beret laid across his face like a death mask.

20

It's hard to say exactly how long I sat there on the floor, my legs folded under me, leaning back against the front of the counter. A kind of calm took over my entire body, as if I were sleepwalking and everything I'd just seen was a dream.

After a while, I pulled myself up off the floor and went out on the sidewalk. My legs were rubber, and I had to lean against the side of the building to steady myself as I pulled my phone out of my pocket. I was covered in dust and cobwebs, but at that point I didn't really care. There was pulsing reggae music playing across the street at Amber Jack's, and the crowd of revelers there was so loud and boisterous I wondered if Detective McKenzie would think I was at a party when she answered the phone.

As usual, she picked up on the first ring. "McKenzie here."

I took a deep breath before I realized I

hadn't figured out how to tell her what had happened. I had just dialed her number automatically without even thinking.

I said, "Detective, it's Dixie Hemingway. I'm not sure what to say, but . . . I'm standing outside Beezy's Bookstore. I just found Mr. Hoskins."

Without skipping a beat she said, "Is he alive?"

I tried to answer as calmly as possible. All I had to do was say one word, but when I tried it choked in my throat. After a couple more tries, McKenzie said, "Oh, Dixie . . . I'm so sorry."

I blinked. I hadn't expected that. Why she was apologizing to me, I had no idea.

"Where is he?"

I swallowed hard. "He's hidden in the crawl space beneath the display window."

There was a long pause. Then she said, "Dixie, I don't know how you got in that bookstore, and for the love of God I'm not sure I want to, but don't go back in until I get there."

She rang off, and I almost laughed out loud. The first thing that popped into my head was *No problemo* — from that moment on I had absolutely no intention of ever setting foot in Beezy's Bookstore again.

■ ■ ■ ■

It felt like an eternity, but within a few minutes one of the sheriff's patrol cars arrived with its lights flashing red and blue, and then a deputy in full uniform stepped out and looked up and down the street. It was Morgan. He reached into the car through the open window and pulled out his deputy hat, which might have seemed strange on such a hot day, but I knew why. Except for at funerals and official events, deputies aren't required to wear their department-issued hats, but it's a symbol of reverence and respect. He also took his mirrored sunglasses off and slipped them down in his breast pocket.

I held my breath and kept completely still as he walked up to the front of the bookstore and looked through the window. Then he scanned the street again.

I'll admit it wasn't the most mature thing in the world, but I just couldn't talk to anybody yet. I needed more time. I needed a little breathing room. At first I had considered sneaking over to Amber Jack's and downing a shot of whiskey and a beer or two. Or three. Instead I just climbed into the backseat of the Bronco and slumped down with my legs stretched out over the center console.

Basically, I was hiding — and that's where I stayed until McKenzie's unmarked sedan pulled up a couple of minutes later, followed by another patrol car and an ominously silent ambulance.

The whole time, I couldn't stop thinking about what McKenzie had said on the phone. *Oh, Dixie, I'm so sorry . . .* as if Mr. Hoskins had been my father or my dearest friend. As if finding his body would be a devastating blow to my delicate sensibilities. It was only later, when the street was cordoned off with police tape once again, and forensic workers, crime technicians, and Sarasota cops were swarming around the bookstore, that I realized: McKenzie must have thought seeing a dead body would bring up long-lost memories of Christy and Todd.

I couldn't blame her, but it didn't. I don't have memories of Todd and Christy, at least none like that, and anyway, if those memories do exist they're locked away so deep in the caverns of my mind that nothing could ever dislodge them.

I stayed in the Bronco until I didn't think I could hide any longer without coming off looking like a complete imbecile. One of the cops saw me approaching and said, "Sorry, ma'am, this is a crime scene, you'll have to go around."

I just nodded. "Yeah. Detective McKenzie is probably looking for me."

I can barely remember what happened next, but I know I must have told McKenzie everything, how Mrs. Silverthorn had hired me to find Cosmo, and how I'd seen something move in the bookstore window as I walked by. When I told her about the bloody paw print below the counter, she just nodded quietly, watching me with a pained expression on her face, and she only asked a few short questions, which was not like her at all. I wondered if she wasn't a little embarrassed that I'd been able to find what she and her deputies hadn't, but I couldn't exactly take credit.

It was just dumb luck.

After I talked to McKenzie, I stood just outside the police tape and watched the proceedings. I overheard one of the deputies saying that the panel under the display window had been attached with just a few screws, which meant that someone had opened up the crawl space, hidden the body inside, and then simply screwed the panel back in place.

Then shortly after that, one of the deputies noticed an open vent in the alley. There were cat prints inside it and in the dirt right below, which confirmed that Cosmo — at least I hoped it was Cosmo — was probably traveling around in the abandoned duct-work. I imagined he'd been going in and out of the store on his own for years, using the vent as his own private entrance. That explained why there was no litter box in the store, but it also gave me hope. It meant he might come back.

Right about then one of the deputies pulled the police tape aside, and an ambulance backed up to within a couple of feet of the front door, which meant they were about to bring the body out.

I retreated to a bench down the street, the same bench, in fact, where the burly doctor had helped me carry Baldy after the accident. A crowd had formed across the street, most of them from the bar, and I'm sure the sight of Beezy's Bookstore surrounded with emergency vehicles — twice in a matter of days — had people coming up with all kinds of theories about what was going on. I didn't want to hear it.

Eventually a news van from the local TV station pulled up, and a smartly dressed woman with slicked-back hair popped out with her camera-carrying minion close behind. Anybody who knows me knows I don't have the best track record when it comes to dealing with the press, so all the better that I stayed at a safe distance from the center of things.

My mind was wandering around like a bumper car without a driver. Why? Why would anyone want to kill Mr. Hoskins? He had seemed like such a kind, gentle person. I couldn't figure out why anyone would want to hurt him . . . except for the money. McKenzie had mentioned the cash register had been emptied out. Immediately my mind flashed to the woman in white.

I pictured her hiding somewhere in the store, crouching behind a box of books at the end of one of the aisles, waiting until she was certain there was no one else in the store but Mr. Hoskins. Then she surprised him just after I left, aimed a gun at his head, and told him to put all the money in a bag. Maybe he had resisted; maybe he had tried to run and she'd shot him before he could get away. Even then, she had seemed so small and frail in that video. How was it possible she could have opened up that crawl space and dragged his lifeless body . . .

I closed my eyes. I just couldn't think about it anymore.

I decided it was high time I sat myself

down for a little reality check. I told myself that Mr. Hoskins's death and how it happened had nothing to do with me. For the millionth time I told myself that McKenzie was a perfectly capable detective and if anyone could figure out what had happened it was her. For the bajillionth time I told myself that I was no longer an officer of the law; I was a pet sitter, dammit, and pet sitters in their right minds don't go around trying to solve murder cases.

I stared up at the stars and nodded. *Good, then,* I thought to myself. *It's settled.*

I closed my eyes, took a deep breath, and imagined myself on the gentle bank of a beautiful babbling stream, bathed in dappled sunlight with flowers and birds and butterflies flitting about all around me. I imagined there was a path of ten smooth stepping-stones leading down to the water, and with every step I imagined myself getting calmer and calmer. One, two, three . . . *swoosh!* an orange tabby shot past me and leaped over the imaginary brook, disappearing into the make-believe brush on the other side.

So much for mind control. I couldn't stop myself. I clambered down the imaginary steps and chased after him.

Could it have been a different orange

tabby that someone had found in the alley? Maybe Butch had figured that out, which would explain why he was snooping around the bookstore. Then again, if that was the case, why hadn't he called me right away to let me know I should pick up my search for Cosmo again?

Right then, instead of entertaining every random thought and theory that rattled around in my head, I should have been calling Mrs. Silverthorn. I knew she was probably anxious to hear from me, especially since I'd told her I planned on heading straight to the bookstore to look for Cosmo after we met, but I'm a terrible liar, and I knew I wouldn't be able to tell her I hadn't found Cosmo without telling her what I *had* found, and I wasn't sure Detective McKenzie would want that information public yet. Plus, there was another problem: how Mrs. Silverthorn would take the news that Mr. Hoskins had been murdered.

I decided I'd spare her the anxiety for just a little while. I told myself it was too late to call her, even though it wasn't much past eight o'clock, but I ignored that part. I'd call her in the morning.

Just then I heard voices. A couple of frat-boy types had wandered out of the bar and were walking by on the sidewalk, their arms around each other's shoulders. I heard one of them say, "Dude, let it go. She's not worth it," and the other one said, "Dude, she totally is."

I had to smile in spite of myself. It felt like the universe was giving me yet another gift on a silver platter — a lesson on how everything in this world is random and temporary. Here were two half-drunk college boys trying to fathom the mysteries of life, and less than a hundred feet away, a sweet old man was lying in a pool of his own blood and no one knew why . . .

I shook my head and tried to give it one more try. I pictured that babbling brook again, but this time without the birds and the butterflies, which might attract curious cats. I took a deep breath, imagining all of the crap from the last couple of days dissolving away like grease in soapy water. I sat down at the edge of the stream and dipped my toes in. It was freezing cold, so instead I sat Indian-style and said "Ommmmmm" in a low droning voice, trying to tune out the music from Amber Jack's wafting over me.

Wastin' away again in Margaritaville
Ommmmmmm . . .
Searchin' for my lost shaker of salt
Ommmmmmmmmm . . .

Thankfully after a little while McKenzie walked over. She probably figured I'd fallen asleep, but I opened my eyes as she was approaching the bench.

She shook her head. "There's no sign of Cosmo."

"I know. I didn't think he'd show himself with all the people around."

"He must have gone out to the alley. We'll leave that vent open in the back just in case. I've given everyone specific instructions to call me right away if they see him. I imagine he'll come back sooner or later . . . How are you?"

I pretended I didn't hear. "I put food and water in his bowls. They're under the desk in the back office."

She nodded. "I saw. I'll make sure nobody moves them. I've asked one of the deputies to follow you home."

I shook my head. "No. That's stupid. I'll be fine."

Just then a patrol car pulled up in the street behind her. She cocked an eyebrow. "I've asked one of the deputies to follow you home."

I drove down Midnight Pass with the squad car following at a discreet distance, and when we got to my driveway, I slowed a bit and honked a short thank-you. It flashed its headlights and waited until I was well down the driveway, then pulled back out on the road and made a quick U-turn toward town. I wondered which deputy had been given the exciting task of following the poor shell-shocked ex-deputy home. I sort of hoped it was Morgan.

The carport was empty. I was so dazed I didn't even bother to get my backpack. I just left it on the passenger seat. Walking across the driveway, my legs were so heavy that the crushed shell felt like quicksand, and the only thing that got me up the stairs was the sight of Ella Fitzgerald in my window, her tail twitching in anticipation. When I opened the door she hopped down and did figure eights around my ankles and chirped, *"Mek mek mek!"*

I swooped her right up and made a beeline for bed.

I could barely sleep. Every time I started to doze off I'd hear a noise, like a branch blowing in the breeze or a ship's horn in the distance, and then I'd jerk awake and remember the sight of Mr. Hoskins, crumpled up like a bag of garbage and stuffed under that display window. I couldn't get the image out of my head.

Sometimes being alone with your thoughts is the best cure for loneliness, but lying there in the dark and staring at the ceiling, I felt more alone than I'd felt in years. I figured if I knew what was good for me I'd drag my butt out of bed and go make myself a cup of tea.

Then I remembered Ethan telling me to call him if I saw anything weird in the store. Well, I had definitely seen something weird, but I didn't think I had the energy to explain the whole story of what had happened, at least not tonight, and I didn't want him to worry about me, and I knew he'd just want to come over.

So instead I just lay there in bed and didn't move a muscle — as still as a turtle. One thing I'm really good at is pulling all my protruding parts deep inside my shell.

I've had a lot of practice.

21

The next morning I woke to the sound of monk parakeets chattering excitedly in the treetops, which could only mean one thing. I had overslept. I jumped up and scrambled for my watch, staring with bleary eyes as I tried to focus on its face, but it was only a little past six o'clock. Sometimes the parakeets conspire to wake me up early, especially if the morning is warmer than normal or there's an early crowd of lovebugs and dragonfly nymphs to hunt, but a bank of fog was rolling in off the gulf, and the air had enough of a chill to it that I figured something must have startled them.

I stumbled into the bathroom and splashed cold water on my face, taking care not to look at myself in the mirror. I knew I looked like crap, and I didn't want to see it, so I just stared at the sink while I ran a brush through my hair. Then I got dressed in a clean pair of shorts and T-shirt and slipped a light sweater on just in case the fog lingered around for a while. Then on my way out, I slipped Guidry's letter into my back pocket.

I felt like I was in a daze all morning, as if the air were thick and syrupy and I had to push my way through it just to get around. I thought about Tanisha and how she always has a smile on her face, but no matter how hard I tried I couldn't really do it. Plus, I could barely concentrate. I drove all the way over to Tom Hale's condo and even had my key in the door before I remembered he'd taken Billy Elliot to Lake Okeechobee to visit his brother and wouldn't be back for a week. Then, driving down to check on a couple of blue Abyssinians whose owners were away on a river cruise, I ran right through a four-way stop sign. Luckily it was early enough that the roads were still deserted, but I eased over to the side of the road to pull myself together.

Detective McKenzie was right. Seeing Mr. Hoskins's body had apparently thrown me for a loop, and all I wanted to do was go home and crawl back in bed. I knew lack of sleep wasn't the problem, though. What I needed was a good dose of old-fashioned TLC, and I knew exactly where to find it.

■ ■ ■ ■

Judy put a hot cup of coffee in front of me as I slid into the back booth of the diner, and Tanisha threw me her customary wave and smile from the kitchen. Just seeing her face made me feel a little better. Judy plopped down into the booth opposite me and gave me her signature "WTF?" look. I knew right away the word was out.

"Dixie, was it you?"

I tried to look as innocent as possible and took a sip of my coffee.

"Was it me what?"

"Was it you that found him?"

I sighed and nodded. "Yes. The building's owner hired me to find his cat. I was snooping around in there, and one thing led to another . . ."

"Oh, Dixie, I'm so sorry."

I felt a jab in my side and sat up straight. "Why does everybody keep saying that to me?"

"Saying what?"

"That they're sorry, like they need to treat me like I'm some sort of fragile flower. I didn't know Hoskins from a hole in the ground! And I've seen a dead body before, by the way. If you'll recall, I used to be a sheriff's deputy. I've seen much worse than that."

I knew I must have sounded like a mewling baby, but I couldn't stop myself. The words rushed out of my throat as if they were fleeing a burning building. I could feel people turning toward me and staring.

Judy looked me straight in the eye. "Honey, nobody's saying you're a fragile flower. You found a dead guy. Believe it or not, that doesn't happen every day around here, even to you. And it's definitely not easy and it's not good, no matter what you've seen or done. In my world, when something bad happens to somebody, like finding a dead body, for instance, we say 'I'm sorry.' "

I sighed. She was right. I put my coffee down and cradled my head in my hands. "I know. I just don't like people tiptoeing around me, thinking they have to treat me with kid gloves just because of whatever crap has gone down in the past, acting like I'm some kind of . . ." I trailed off. I couldn't think of the right word.

Judy said, "Human being?"

I laughed. "Yeah, that's it."

She stood up and headed for the kitchen. "I'm gonna bring you some bacon."

I brought my fist down on the table triumphantly. "That's why I'm here!"

Just then, the door of the diner swung open and in walked Ethan, carrying a briefcase and dressed in a tailored suit the color of lightly creamed coffee with a pearlescent teal tie that was almost the exact same color as the booths in the diner.

As he made his way down the aisle, practically every female, not to mention a few non-females, stopped midsentence to watch him pass and then struggled to remember what they were just talking about. As he stopped at my table, a woman across the aisle looked him up and down, mentally trying him on for size as she sprinkled a packet of sugar on her scrambled eggs.

Judy slid my breakfast down on the table, along with a platter of extra-crispy bacon, just as Ethan slid into the booth opposite me. For a second I couldn't decide which made me feel better, Ethan or the bacon.

Judy winked. "What can I get you, handsome?"

"Nothing for me. I just stopped by to say howdy."

She fanned herself with her notepad. "Well, thanks, Ethan, that's so very sweet of you."

As she sauntered off, Ethan's smile fell away and he lowered his voice. "What did I tell you on the phone last night?"

I flashed him a face that was half grimace, half disarming cuteness, but he just sat there, waiting for an answer.

"Umm, you said if I found anything weird in the bookstore to call you right away."

"Yes, that's exactly what I said. And did you find anything weird?"

"So . . . you heard."

He was trying to keep his voice low, but I could tell he was upset. "Dixie, why didn't you call me?"

"I know. I'm sorry. I should have called you right away. I just didn't want you to worry about me, and it was late . . . and I don't know, I just wanted to go home and go to bed. I should have called you, though. I barely slept all night."

He put his hands on top of mine. "Dude, I am really sorry that happened to you."

I looked into his eyes and decided I'd thank Judy later. "Thanks. And don't call me dude."

We sat like that for a bit, his hands resting on top of mine. I eyed the plate of steaming bacon not five inches from my fingers, but I didn't want to ruin the moment.

I sighed. "I just can't believe it. And I'm so sad for his daughter, too. I can't even imagine what she must be going through right now."

He slid my coffee over and took a sip. "Who in the world do you think could have done something like that?"

My mind flashed again to the image of the woman in white disappearing inside the bookstore, but I just shook my head. "No idea. That's for the detectives to figure out, I guess."

He turned his head to the window but watched me out of the corner of his eye. "Right."

I took a deep breath. "Anyway, let's change the subject. Are we still on for tonight?"

"I'm on if you're on, but you've had a rough couple of days. Maybe it would be better if we stayed home tonight?"

It actually seemed like a good idea, but I didn't want to be a party pooper.

I shook my head. "No, no, I'll be fine. But Ethan, listen . . ."

He raised an eyebrow.

I said, "I have an admission to make. I didn't open that letter yet. I know I said I would, but I was so beat when I got in last night. I didn't even brush my teeth. I just went straight to bed."

I started to pull it out of my back pocket, but he shook his head. "No, it's not my place to say whether you should open that letter or not. That's between you and Guidry. Believe me, I totally get it. All I want to do tonight is have dinner and hang out and stuff."

"Stuff?"

He grinned. "Yeah, you know . . . fun stuff."

As I looked into his dreamy brown eyes, I took a bite of Tanisha's bacon. It really was a toss-up. The bacon was mighty tasty, but . . .

He looked around and then leaned closer to me. "Hey, I shouldn't tell you this, but I was talking to a guy I know in the DA's office. The cops ID'd your friend."

"What friend?"

"That guy in the car accident."

"Mr. Vladim?"

He shushed me. "Yeah. They took fingerprints and ran them through the national database. He's a bank robber."

I gasped. "A what!"

"Yep. A Russian bank robber. He and his wife have been on the run for more than a year. They came here a couple of years ago and then found out their kid had cancer. Apparently they didn't have money or health insurance, so they went on a tear from one end of Florida to the other, holding up small-town banks to pay for the treatments."

I shook my head. "That is truly, truly terrible."

"I know. Can you imagine? Sick kid, no insurance, no money, no friends . . ."

"That poor man. So where's his wife?"

"Nobody knows. And he's not talking."

I shook my head. "Who knew people still robbed banks? I thought that just happened in the movies."

He reached for a piece of bacon, but I swatted his hand away. "It happens more than you'd think. Banks get robbed all the time. I think it's mostly small stuff, but your friend and his wife racked up a ton of cash, which I guess they just handed right over to the doctors — they're like the Russian Bonnie and Clyde. But look, don't tell anybody. They're keeping it under wraps until they find his wife. They figure she has to be somewhere nearby."

I shook my head. "Ugh. I hope they never find her."

"Yeah. You and me both. But hey, look on the bright side. You saved the guy's life. And maybe you'll get a big reward for catching him." He picked up his briefcase and winked at me. "You're . . . I mean, we're rich."

I rolled my eyes. "Is that supposed to

make me feel better?"

He bent down and kissed my forehead. "I'll work on it."

As he strolled out, all the other women in the diner, Judy included, craned their necks and practically sighed out loud as he walked by. I probably would have done the same thing except that with what he'd just told me about Baldy, I felt like I'd been hit over the head with a rolling pin.

I looked down and thought, *Really? A Russian bank robber?*

There was a tiny crumb of bacon left on my plate, sitting all by itself. I picked it up between my thumb and forefinger, and right before I popped it in my mouth, I said, "Huh."

When I was done with my afternoon rounds, I pulled into the parking lot at Siesta Key Beach. I figured I had avoided calling Mrs. Silverthorn long enough and it was time to bite the bullet. I sat there with the engine idling quietly and watched the gulls play in the waves while I tried to figure out what to say to her.

I had decided that it wasn't my responsibility to tell her about Mr. Hoskins. If she didn't already know about it, I would keep that part to myself. Anyway, I knew Detective McKenzie was probably planning on talking to her. She was Mr. Hoskins's landlord. It was entirely possible that she might know things about Mr. Hoskins that no one else did.

As for Cosmo, I decided I'd just tell her exactly what Butch the Butcher had told me, that someone had found an orange cat in the alley, and that I couldn't be sure it was him yet. I'd promise her I'd keep asking around and let her know if I learned more.

I was half hoping she wouldn't pick up and I could just leave a message, but by the tenth ring I realized she probably didn't even have an answering machine. For a split second it put a tiny smile on my face. I've spent most of my adult life avoiding electronic gadgets like the plague, but Mrs. Silverthorn was clearly way more old-school than I.

I was just about to hang up when a woman answered with a breathless "Good afternoon. The Silverthorn residence."

I said, "Oh . . . Mrs. Silverthorn?"

"No, this is Janet. Who may I say is calling?"

I knew it wasn't Janet. I recognized Mrs. Silverthorn's voice immediately, even though she seemed completely out of breath. I pictured her running from one end of the mansion to the other to get to the phone in time. Why she was pretending to be Janet I had no idea, but I figured I'd just play along.

I said, "Oh, hi, Janet, this is Dixie Hemingway."

She said curtly, "Please hold," and then there was a short pause and a shuffling sound, followed by a whispered "Dixie, I can't talk to you right now."

I said, "Oh, I was just calling about Cosmo."

She said, "My —" and then stopped herself. It suddenly occurred to me that she wasn't out of breath at all. She was crying.

I said, "Mrs. Silverthorn, are you okay?"

She said, "I've just been speaking with an unfortunately bland woman from the sheriff's department."

I said, "You mean Detective McKenzie?"

"Yes. Wretched woman. Horribly dull. And oh, my dear, how horrible for you. I just can't imagine . . ." Her voice trailed away, and then there was a muffled sob.

"Mrs. Silverthorn, I'm so sorry. Were you close to Mr. Hoskins?"

She took a deep breath. "Oh, darling, it's too late now. No use crying over spilt milk, as they say, but I'm afraid there's still the matter of Moses Cosmo Thornwall and your payment. Come to the house this afternoon for tea — four o'clock. I'll be better by then. And I'll let Mr. Silverthorn know you're coming so he can write a check for your efforts so far."

"Mrs. Silverthorn, I —"

But she'd already hung up.

I sat staring out at the beach. There was a group of girls hitting a volleyball back and forth on one of the courts set up in the sand and a gaggle of boys in board shorts cheering them on. Just beyond the court was an elderly couple in big straw sunhats, pulling an ice chest behind them and making their way down to the water's edge. I closed my eyes and shook my head.

Poor Mrs. Silverthorn. I hated hearing her cry. She seemed like such a strong woman, but I knew what she was thinking. The thought of Cosmo, scared and alone, guarding the body of his dead owner . . . it was enough to make me cry, too.

I tried not to think about it. If anything, it made me want to work harder to find Cosmo. I decided I wouldn't give up no matter what. I'd keep searching the neighborhood and asking questions and putting up signs until I could either deliver him directly into Mrs. Silverthorn's arms or assure her without a doubt that he had found a good home and was being taken care of.

For the rest of the afternoon, I did my best to stay positive. I thought about Tanisha again and forced myself to smile as I finished up my rounds for the day. It actually worked, at least until I opened the front door at Meg Kerry's house on Oxford Drive. Sammy, her bluepoint Siamese, was waiting in the hall, paws spread and tail twitching. He took one look at me and hissed.

He wasn't buying my fake smile for a second.

I didn't take it personally, though. In fact, that's one of the best things about cats. They don't walk around pretending to be something they're not — they just tell it like it is. A cat will never betray you. It might scratch you, it might bite you, it might pee in your suitcase, but it will never look you straight in the eye and lie to you.

That's more than I can say for most humans — in fact, if you've got a friend as faithful as a cat, you should thank your lucky stars.

22

When I stepped out of the elevator on the sixth floor, Cora was waiting for me down at the end of the hall in front of her apartment door. She held one freckled arm high over her head and waved excitedly. She's not much taller than five feet, with a little wisp of cottony silver hair that floats on top of her head like an afterthought, and glittery blue eyes that never fail to put me in a good mood. She was wearing a pale pink housedress with a scooping neckline, and white fluffy house shoes with puffballs on the toes.

The way we came to be friends is a long story — her granddaughter was a client — but except for the very negligible genetic factor, she feels more like a sister to me than anything else, and I like to think she feels the same about me. I always stop by Cora's whenever I feel my batteries need a little recharging, which these days is at least once a week, sometimes more. Plus there was the little matter of Guidry's letter, and Cora was the best person on earth to give me advice in that department. She may look like a sweet little old lady, but she's sharp as a tack and doesn't pussyfoot around.

As I came down the hallway, she was teetering on her toes and grinning from ear to ear, which she always does, but this time I was particularly happy to see it. Just a few weeks before, I'd gotten a call from Vickie, the concierge in the lobby at Cora's building. She had called to let me know that they'd taken Cora to the hospital for heart palpitations. I was already racing down the stairs when she said Cora was back home and doing fine. At first I considered driving over to Cora's building and wringing Vickie's neck for not having called me sooner, but of course it wasn't her fault. If anyone needed a good neck-wringing it was Cora. If I get so much as a mosquito bite everybody hears about it, but Cora is a card-holding member of the stoic, suffer-in-silence generation.

She told me later she hadn't called me because she didn't want anyone to make a fuss or worry about her, which I couldn't very well argue with since it sounded exactly like something I'd do myself. Even so, I made her promise that in the future, if she didn't want my wrath raining down on her like a plague of sand fleas, she'd call me right away if anything like that ever happened again.

Most people would think that given the fifty-year difference in our ages we wouldn't have much in common, but they'd be wrong. I wouldn't be the relatively sane person standing before you now if it weren't for her.

She was practically beaming at me. "Oh my goodness, dear, you look pretty as a picture."

I said, "Ha. You're just saying that because you know I have goodies for you."

She held the apartment door open with one skinny arm. "Well, you're right about that. I've got you nicely trained, don't I? All I have to do is tell you how pretty you are, and you show up with all kinds of treats."

On the way over I had stopped by the market and grabbed some of Cora's favorites — chicken noodle soup, a big fat slice of cornbread, and a fruit salad with fresh sliced kiwi, strawberries, and mango, plus other sundry supplies for the week. While Cora shuffled in behind me, I unpacked everything on the kitchen counter and put the soup in the refrigerator.

Cora's apartment is bright and cheery, with pale pink tile floors and walls a slightly deeper shade of coral. To the left is a small galley kitchen behind a bar with folding louvered doors to close it off, and to the right through an arched doorway is a modest bedroom. The living room has a marble-topped coffee table, with a sofa covered in fern green linen and two pink chintz armchairs that nobody ever sits in. Instead, there's a little ice cream table with two chairs in front of the sliding glass doors, which open up to a narrow sun porch overlooking the bay and spilling over with potted plants and cooking herbs.

Cora said, "I'm so glad you're here. There's hot tea, and I made a little surprise for you."

The "surprise" was Cora's world-famous chocolate bread, which I know for a fact she makes every single day whether I show up or not. When I first met her, she only made it about once a week, but demand was so high now with all her friends in the building that she'd been forced to step up production.

The recipe is top secret. All I know is that she makes it in the bread machine her daughter gave her for Christmas one year, and she could probably make it in her sleep.

At some point in the middle of the baking process, she opens up the top of the bread machine and pours in a cup of semisweet chocolate chips. The result is a deliciously crusty bread, with chewy rivers of rich, creamy chocolate running through every slice. It's scrumptious fresh and it's scrumptious a week later cold from the refrigerator, but Cora serves it the best way possible: Fresh out of the oven, torn off in steaming chunks and slathered with melting butter.

As she laid the tea tray down on the ice cream table, I took one bite and closed my eyes, drifting off into a state of heavenly bliss. I saw a vision of frolicking kittens flying across a star-filled sky, leaving behind a trail of rainbows and unicorns. It was that good.

Cora sat down across from me and said, "Sometimes I wonder if I stopped making that chocolate bread if I'd ever see you again."

I nodded, my mouth full of buttery chocolate goodness. "You probably wouldn't. I'd head right over to the Lido Key Bridge and jump right off. I don't think I could bear a world without your chocolate bread."

"So, tell me all about that beau of yours."

"Cora, don't say 'beau.' It makes you sound like an old lady."

"Well, I am an old lady. What do you want me to say? How is that *dude* of yours?"

I pulled Guidry's letter out and plopped it down on the table between us.

"What's that?"

"It came in the mail earlier this week."

"Who's it from?"

"J. P. Guidry."

She frowned. "Oh, dear. I thought you were looking a little peaked. What's it say?"

"You said I looked pretty as a picture!"

She flicked her fingers in the air as if she were drying her nails. "Never mind. What's it say?"

I sighed. "I have no idea. I'm afraid to open it."

She nodded solemnly and took a sip of tea. Cora knows everything there is to know about Guidry. When I had first met him, I was like a hermit crab that never came out of her shell. I'd spent so many years mourning the loss of Todd and Christy that I didn't know how to feel anything even remotely close to love. Cora had helped me see that it didn't have to be one or the other. I could hold Todd and Christy in my heart and still let somebody else in at the same time; all I had to do was make a little more room. Cora taught me that the heart is expandable.

She said, "Well? What are you waiting for?"

I said, "What if he's changed his mind? What if he still wants me to come to New Orleans? What if he's coming back here?"

She rolled her eyes. "Oh my goodness! All these what-ifs! What if he's made of cheese?"

"I know it sounds stupid, but . . ."

"Sweetheart, what are you so afraid of?"

I thought for a moment. "What if Ethan's not *the one*?"

"The one? Oh, Dixie, we've already been down this road."

I groaned. "I know, I know, I know."

"You actually think God hides our 'One True Love' somewhere, and then he plops down on earth and says 'ready, set, go!' and then we're supposed to go running willy-nilly all over the planet trying to find him before we die, like a game show?"

"I don't know."

"Oh, phooey. Love isn't a game of chance. It's a feat of strength." She balled her fist up and tapped it on the table for emphasis. "A tour de force! You find a man that you love, and you *make* him the one."

I grinned. "Maybe you should get a computer and set up one of those matchmaking sites. You'd probably make a fortune."

She wrinkled her nose. "Oh, I don't care

for computers."

"I'm right with ya, sister. As far as I'm concerned they're totally unnecessary."

"Oh, no, dear, they're absolutely necessary. One day they'll be all that's left of us."

I said, "Huh?"

She smiled. "When I was a little girl, in the field behind our house my daddy had an old apple orchard — well, that's what he called it — it was really only about ten trees or so, but he was extremely proud of it, and we always had a nice crop of fresh apples. Every spring, just when the ground was starting to warm up, he'd take his old Louisville Slugger out there and bang away at all those tree trunks. He'd give each one of 'em at least ten good whacks. I remember asking my mother what in tarnation he was doing out there hitting those trees with a baseball bat, and she said, 'He's telling those trees their time is up!' "

She poured us both another cup of tea. "Well, I know what you're thinking, but my daddy wasn't crazy. He was just giving those apple trees a good scare. If you bonk the base of an apple tree with a baseball bat, its little apple tree brain thinks the end is nigh, so it puts all its energy into making as many apples as possible — every last one of them chock-full of seeds, filled with every blessed

307

piece of information that old tree can think of. And when it's dead and gone, somebody can plant one of those seeds and make a whole brand-new tree just exactly like the original. Believe me, there's nothing a living thing wants more than to keep on living."

"Cora, what the heck does that have to do with computers?"

"Well a computer is nothing but an apple seed."

"Huh?"

"It's the seed of Planet Earth, which is just a big living, breathing organism, if you ask me, and Mother Nature is busy loading it up with all the information in the world, all our books and languages and genetic codes and songs and religions, putting it all on a computer chip that keeps getting smaller and smaller and smaller. And then one day, when the earth is all used up and gone, some alien from outer space will be flying along and find that chip and take it home. All they'll have to do is figure out the right soil to grow it in, and then there you go — they'll re-create our whole world."

She took a sip of her tea and winked at me over the rim of her cup.

I said, "Cora, that is hands down the looniest idea you've ever had. You better not go around saying that to too many people or they'll lock you up in a funny farm."

Her eyes sparkled. "That's what they said to Galileo."

I had to admit, what with global warming and oil drilling and ocean pollution, if the earth is a living thing, I wouldn't be a bit surprised if it felt like somebody was beating it to death with a baseball bat, but Cora had already moved on to another subject.

"Sweetheart, there's something else we need to talk about."

I got a little nervous. There was a look in her eye that I'd never seen before.

She propped her elbows up on the table and folded her hands together. "Now, I told Kate Spencer that when I'm gone she can have my bread machine."

I sighed. "Oh, come on. I do not want to talk about this."

"Well, you're gonna have to, Dixie. Now, Kate Spencer is a perfectly nice woman, but she can barely boil an egg, and she's dumb as a box of flip-flops. And the woman's ten years older than me anyway, so I don't know where she got it in her fool head that she'll still be here after I'm gone. So if something should happen, I want you to come straight here first thing. I want you to pack up that bread machine and take it home with you."

"Cora —"

She held up one hand to stop me. "Now, I don't want to hear it. You can give it to your brother if you want, but somebody has to make that bread when I'm gone or you'll go jump off that bridge, and I don't want that hanging over my head for all eternity. And another thing — I'm gonna hide my bread recipe in a shoebox under the bed. I want you to take that, too, and guard it with your life."

"Alright already," I said. "Let's change the subject." I slid Guidry's letter closer to her. "What about this?"

"What about it?"

"Tell me what I should do."

She looked out at the bay, and her eyes softened. There was a congregation of yachts and sailboats anchored in the middle of the marina, and the water was glittering and gleaming in the sun like a big bowl of emeralds. As she took another sip of tea, a mischievous smile spread across her face, and her cheeks fractured into a million tiny, fine lines.

She said, "You should damn well grow up is what you should do."

23

There had been another quick afternoon thunderstorm, which seemed to have cheered up the Caesar weed and spike sedge growing through the cracks in the redbrick drive at the Silverthorn Mansion. They looked a good foot taller than they'd been on my first visit, and the big marble fountain in the center of the courtyard was filled to the brim with fresh rainwater. As I walked by, a bright green frog pulled itself up onto the fountain's rim and eyed me with unveiled contempt.

I looked at my watch. Perfect timing. Mrs. Silverthorn had asked, well, more *demanded,* that I arrive at four o'clock. I made my way up the cracked steps of the front entrance and was steeling myself for Janet's down-in-the-dumps greeting when she opened the door and stepped out. She seemed genuinely startled to find me there, but before I could say anything, Mr. Silverthorn stepped out behind her.

I could swear they were both wearing the exact same clothes they'd worn on my first visit to the mansion. Standing there together, they looked like the couple in that *American Gothic* oil painting, except instead of a pitchfork, Mr. Silverthorn was holding an old, rusty flashlight with a handle almost as long as a French baguette. Unlike Janet, he seemed genuinely pleased to see me. "Ah! Miss Hemingway, fancy meeting you here."

I shook his hand and glanced at Janet. There was something markedly different about her — dark circles under bloodshot eyes with lines of worry across her forehead. She was listing slightly to one side, as if it took every ounce of strength she had just to stay on her feet.

Mr. Silverthorn cleared his throat and said, "Janet, won't you please let Mrs. Silverthorn know that her guest is waiting downstairs."

Janet nodded sullenly and disappeared inside, leaving the door open behind her.

He leaned in and whispered, "I gather you're here to file a report on Cosmo."

I gulped. This whole time I'd been operating under the assumption that my search for Cosmo was strictly undercover. "Umm, I . . ."

He winked. "Not to worry. Mrs. Silverthorn can't keep a secret to save her life. She spilled the beans after the detective was here yesterday afternoon. I understand you've had a very productive week."

"Well, I think I may have some good news."

His face brightened. "Oh? Did you find our fugitive feline?"

"No, unfortunately, but it's possible someone else did. You know the butcher shop two doors down?"

"Yes, of course, that's one of our buildings."

"Oh, right. Well, the butcher told me someone found an orange cat in the alley a couple of days ago."

"Oh, good news, indeed."

"Yeah, except the problem is it might not have been Cosmo. The main reason I went in the bookstore yesterday was I thought I saw something move inside, and then I noticed a cat print . . ."

His face fell. "Yes, the detective told us all about it. How ghastly for you. Luckily I managed to persuade the detective to omit the more unsettling details when she spoke to my wife, and I'd prefer you do the same.

It would only worry her more."

I knew it wasn't my place to ask, but I couldn't stop myself. I said, "Mr. Silverthorn, when I talked to your wife on the phone earlier, she seemed really upset. Was she close to Mr. Hoskins?"

He nodded sadly. "I know. And yes, I'm afraid she was. My wife's fondness for cats is equaled only by her love of books, as I'm sure you have already gathered by her rather monstrous collection in the ballroom, so she knew Mr. Hoskins quite well. She's probably the best customer he ever had."

I shook my head. "That's terrible. He seemed like such a nice man — of course she's upset."

"Unfortunately they seemed to have had some sort of falling-out recently. She had been favoring a bookshop in Bradenton, and I think that may be weighing quite heavily on her. Probably something silly, the price of a book, or whatnot. You may be aware, Miss Hemingway, that my wife can be rather . . . *impetuous.*"

I tried to hide a smile, but he could tell I understood completely.

"Well, don't let me keep you." He held the rusty flashlight up. "If you're wondering what this old thing is for, I'm afraid you're not the only private investigator my wife has enlisted in this matter. My orders are to search every nook and cranny in the alley behind that bookstore."

I said, "Oh, that's good. The more people looking for him the better."

"Yes. I'm afraid my indifference to cats is quite outweighed by my undying loyalty to my wife. I don't like to see her worry, but also I can assure you that one doesn't lightly cross paths with Mrs. Silverthorn. I've learned over the years that when she makes a request, if it has anything to do with cats, it's always best to simply nod and obey."

"Well, I admire a man who obeys."

He smiled. "Yes, most women do."

"I can tell you one thing, though. The detectives will still be there now that it's a crime scene again, so I doubt they'll let you inside the shop."

"Yes, I thought as much."

"But there's an old air-conditioning system that's not used anymore, and the detectives saw paw prints just outside one of the vents in the alley, so I think there's a good chance he's going in and out that vent."

He nodded thoughtfully. "What a clever cat."

"I left a bowl of kibble and some water for him in the back office, so he won't have to worry about food, and there was a bowl of chocolates by the register, which is poisonous to cats, so I asked the detective in charge to remove it just in case."

He nodded. "A wise decision. I'd hate to think what would have happened if he shared your weakness for chocolate."

I nodded. "Well, I can tell you from personal experience, Mr. Silverthorn, it's torture. I wouldn't wish that on my worst enemy."

He chuckled, but then his eyes softened and a blush spread across his face, "Miss Hemingway, I'm sorry to change the subject so abruptly, but . . . you know . . . there's no money."

I looked down and nodded. The cuffs of his pants were slightly worn, but he had polished his shoes to a glossy sheen. "Mr. Silverthorn, I was looking for Cosmo long before your wife called me. I couldn't bear the thought that Mr. Hoskins's cat might be roaming the streets alone and hungry, so there's nothing to worry about. I'm more than happy to help."

He smiled wistfully. "Thank you, Miss Hemingway. It's a difficult subject. I appreciate your kindness. I'm afraid this whole mess may serve as more fodder for gossip and rumor — if nothing else we still have our good name to uphold, and it weighs heavily on my wife. If Mr. Hoskins's cat can be found it will be one less thing for her to worry about."

He reached down in his pocket and pulled out a set of car keys, and I noticed there was a silver medallion with a colorful coat of arms and a crown on top. "Ah, and here's Janet."

I turned to see Janet through the open doorway, standing motionless at the bottom of the stairs and waiting.

I said, "Mr. Silverthorn, please call me if you see anything back there. I'm pretty good at coaxing cats out of their hiding places."

He bowed slightly and then headed down the portico toward the side of the house, where I assumed there was probably a beautiful old stone garage, covered in vines and falling in on itself, probably housing a collection of vintage Rolls Royces and Cadillacs in various states of disrepair.

As I watched him go, I suddenly felt a wave of . . . I wasn't sure. Anxiety or confusion, or maybe sadness. I could tell it had taken every ounce of strength in his body to swallow his pride long enough to discuss the matter of money with me, and the sight of his polished dress shoes broke my heart. He was doing everything he could to keep up appearances. Of course, it was a little hard to feel sorry for a man who'd lived his entire life in the lap of luxury, but I wondered if losing it all might be harder than never having had it.

Janet led me up the stairs to the library, where Mrs. Silverthorn was waiting in the same spot we'd had tea before, the little table at the far side of the chair-filled ballroom. The floral scarf that was tied around her waist when we first met was now fitted around her head like an Indian turban, and instead of a flesh-colored leotard she wore a bright red one-piece bathing suit with a white caftan hanging off her shoulders. Her long, beautiful tresses of shiny gray hair would have been impressive except I knew right away it was another one of her wigs.

As I made my way through the mélange of chairs, she talked a blue streak.

"Dixie Hemingway, I am so relieved to see you! You can't imagine what I've been through in the past twenty-four hours. The most dreadful woman from the sheriff's department was here yesterday with a demeanor so wretched that I felt sad for the entire world. She told me everything that happened and insisted on asking the most unsettling questions — how long have I owned the building, how long did I know

Mr. Hoskins, where was I on the night he disappeared. I told her I've much better things to do with my brain than use it as a virtual appointment calendar."

As I sat down in the chair opposite her, she pulled a tissue from the sleeve of her caftan and dabbed it at her eyes. "I cannot tell you how terrible I feel to have pulled you into such a mess. And when I think of that poor cat, waiting . . . all alone and helpless . . ."

She lowered her head and mumbled, "Oh, bother," and raised one trembling hand in the air.

Now I finally understood how fragile her nerves could be. I wondered if she hadn't slept at all since Detective McKenzie had been here.

I said, "Mrs. Silverthorn, cats are very strong, resilient creatures, and they're experts at surviving difficult conditions — and one thing you should know, we think he's going in and out of the store through the old air-conditioning system, and I left food for him in the back office, so I think it's only a matter of time before we find him. I'm sure there's absolutely nothing to worry about."

She raised her head, her eyes filled with tears. "Thank you, Dixie Hemingway. You've done a great deal to ease my mind. I don't know what I would have done without you. I've asked Mr. Silverthorn to write you a generous check."

I looked down at the floor and nodded. "Yes, I ran into him on my way in. That's all taken care of now."

Just then, the phone rang. It was an old beige princess phone, sitting on the floor next to the stack of magazines by her chair, except it wasn't a normal ring. It was three bright chirps.

Mrs. Silverthorn raised one thin finger in the air and said, "One moment, dear. That will be Janet." She leaned over and picked up the phone.

"Yes, darling?"

There was a pause, and then her eyes rolled upward and she put the one finger she'd been holding in the air to her right temple and massaged it in a slow circle as she spoke. "How high . . . oh, damn it all . . . Yes, I understand. Alright, stay where you are and I'll send the girl down."

I wondered who else was in the house that she planned on sending down — perhaps there was a cleaning woman hiding with the cats somewhere — and then I wondered how it was that the Silverthorns managed to keep so many domestic servants and yet still couldn't quite muster up the cash to pay for my services.

She laid the phone back down in its cradle and turned to me with imploring eyes. "Dixie . . . may I call you Dixie?"

I nodded mutely. I think I'd just figured out which "girl" she was sending down.

"Dixie, darling, that was Janet. I'm afraid Mr. Peters has climbed up a tree again and won't budge. Silly Janet has a ridiculous fear of heights, or so she says — I'm not sure I believe a word that comes out of that woman's mouth, but no matter. The point is, I was wondering . . . do you think you might . . . ?"

I'm not a big fan of heights myself, but it didn't seem right to just flat-out refuse. Hesitantly, I said, "Of course, but . . . how high is he?"

She smiled. "Not to worry. Mr. Peters is a very good climber, and he has quite an adventurous streak — I can vouch for that — but Janet tells me he's well within reach. He's in the old magnolia tree in the West Garden."

I sighed. "Yes, of course."

"Oh, thank heavens, you're a dear. He's never climbed that particular tree before — what an adventurous fellow he is. Normally, of course, I'd never ask you to do such a thing, but with the footman having run off God knows where, there's no one else to ask. Janet's waiting for you downstairs. She'll direct you to the ladder."

"Ladder?"

She nodded. "It should be in the garden shed. That is, if the footman didn't steal that as well. Janet will show you."

She sat and watched as I made my way through the chairs, and when I got to the door I looked back. She was still sitting there, her back ramrod straight. She unwrapped the flowered scarf from her head and waved it at me.

I couldn't tell if she was waving good-bye or telling me to get a move on, but I waved back and smiled. Now, I thought, in addition to "Missing Pets Detective," I could add "Girl" to my job description.

I wondered if that meant I'd get a raise.

24

Janet was waiting for me by the front door, staring at her shoes. We walked out to the porch, and I followed her down the portico and around to the right side of the house. The gardening shed turned out to be an ancient dry-stone building with a peaked slate roof, topped with a weather vane in the shape of a chicken, its wings spread wide to catch the wind. It was set in the middle of an undulating sea of weeds and rosary pea vine, covering a series of raised beds and low walls made with the same red brick as the driveway. There was a maze of overgrown shrubs surrounding the entire yard, with vine-covered statues here and there, and I could tell in its heyday it had probably been a very impressive display garden.

Janet led me down a beaten path through the weeds to a narrow gate set in stone, and as we made our way along it I tried to strike up a conversation.

"I take it Mr. Peters likes to climb trees a lot?"

She opened the gate and pointed at an extension ladder inside the shed. "Yes."

I nodded and thought to myself, *Alright, then, good talk!* Janet was about as personable as a soggy bar coaster.

She pulled on a chain just inside the door, and an old hanging lamp illuminated the interior. The floor was covered in dried leaves and hay, and along one wall was a stack of clay pottery and broken pieces of an old trellis. Next to the ladder were shelves with dusty mason jars filled with various seeds and fertilizers and covered in cobwebs, and in the corner of the top shelf was a huge squirrel's nest made of twigs, woven through with scraps of paper and shredded bits of lavender-colored fabric.

Janet helped me carry the ladder out, which wasn't completely necessary since it was aluminum and actually quite light, but it was a little awkward getting it through the shed's small doorway, so I was thankful for the help. She led me across the yard to an ancient magnolia tree as big as a mountain, which stood at the far end of the garden like an emperor surveying his vast holding of lands. It was in full bloom, and the heady scent of the flowers filled the air.

Looking a bit like the Ghost of Christmas to Come, Janet raised one thin arm and pointed up into the tree, where, perched on a branch at least twenty feet off the ground, was a snow white cat with piercing blue eyes. He was gazing down on us with an expression that was part curiosity, part utter disdain.

I said, "Oh, wow, he's really up there isn't he?"

Janet curled her lip briefly and then made her way back toward the house without saying a word. I leaned the ladder up against the massive trunk of the tree and muttered at the back of her head, "Oh, Janet, you jokester you!"

She didn't answer. She was probably headed back to her servant's lair somewhere deep in the bowels of the mansion, where she sat staring in the mirror and practicing her stink-eye. Of course, if the Silverthorns were paying her anywhere near what they were paying me, I'd be in a foul mood, too.

The ladder was actually two ladders joined together on a sliding track, with a yellow rope attached on one side to a pulley that could be used to extend the length as needed. I pulled on the rope and hoisted the extension ladder up until it reached as far as it could go, which was about twenty-five feet.

The trunk of the tree was easily ten feet around, with braided ropes of bark winding their way up into the canopy. The north-facing side of the trunk, where it received the least amount of sunlight, was covered in a fine carpet of green moss, and there was a column of tiny black ants traveling up and down a two-lane highway.

On my way up the ladder I had a few more choice words for Janet, and by the fifth rung or so, only five or six feet off the ground, my heart started skipping and I made a point of grasping the rails a little tighter. I couldn't imagine Janet's fear of heights being any worse than mine, but since it was in the service of rescuing a cat, I forged ahead.

Moving slowly, I climbed all the way up to the top of the ladder, where the glossy magnolia leaves formed a darkened cavern. I immediately knew why Mr. Peters might want to hang out here. He could lie about in the cool comfort of the shade while spying on all the birds flitting from branch to branch. I hoped for the birds' sake that he was only enjoying the view and not hunting for a late-afternoon snack.

Mr. Peters watched me with a bemused twinkle in his eye, as though he'd done this a million times before and knew the drill.

When I got to his branch, he twitched his whiskers and tipped his chin as if to say, "Evenin'."

I said, "You know, Mr. Peters, this would be a lot easier if you'd just come down to me."

He didn't say a word. Cats are perfectly engineered for climbing up anything they can sink their claws into, but coming down is a whole different story. I reached down into the pocket of my cargo shorts and pulled out the little plastic bag I'd grabbed from my backpack on the way out. I figured a few irresistible kitty treats might give him the extra bit of encouragement he needed, and it turned out I was right.

I held a cube of cheddar cheese between my thumb and forefinger and held it out so Mr. Peters could see it. He sniffed the air and then tentatively put one paw forward.

I said, "That's a good kitty. Come and get it."

He stood up now on all fours and crept down the branch about a foot, and just when I thought I'd have him in my arms in no time, a gray squirrel, its mouth full of strips of paper, popped out of a hole in the trunk not half a foot from my head. It scared me so bad I nearly fell right off the ladder.

For a brief moment, the squirrel and I just looked each other in the face, each of us equally flabbergasted. I giggled silently when I realized the strips of paper in his mouth had an archaic-looking print on them.

I said, "Well, it looks like Mrs. Silverthorn isn't the only one around here with their own private library." Mr. Peters ignored me and took a few more steps forward. He was just as interested in the squirrel as he was in the cheese, if not more so.

Suddenly the squirrel hopped out of the hole and scampered down the tree, and Mr. Peters and I watched as he ran across the tangled lawn of vines and slipped into a hole near the foundation of the gardening shed. I turned to Mr. Peters. Now I knew what he'd been up to.

I said, "You know, it's not very nice to go around hunting poor defenseless squirrels, especially when you have a devoted owner who I'm sure keeps you very well fed with the finest cat food available."

He gazed at me, unblinking, and I wondered if that was even true. If the Silverthorns' financial situation was as dire as it appeared, it was possible Mr. Peters was wholly responsible for rustling up his own dinners.

I held the cube of cheese up again, cooing softly at him, and even though he eyed me suspiciously the entire length of the branch, it only took a little more encouragement to get him to come all the way down and gingerly take it from my fingers. As he gobbled it down and licked his chops, I could see his eyes were even more beautiful up close. They were an impossibly clear baby blue, like something an artist could only come up with in a dream.

He flashed me an expectant look, so I took that opportunity to make my final move — one more tiny offering of cheese, which worked like a charm. He fluttered his tail in the air and rubbed his cheek up against the back of my hand, purring like a tiny salad spinner. Now I knew I'd won him over completely, so I gently scooped him up in my arms and handed him another morsel. He barely argued, which was a good thing since I had no idea how I would have managed to climb down that ladder and hold on to a flailing cat at the same time.

Just then, I noticed one of the strips of paper hanging halfway out of the squirrel's hole. It had perfectly aligned bite marks all the way down one end, but that's not what caught my attention. It was the color of the paper — a pale, creamy yellow.

I have no idea what possessed me to do what I did next, because in my mind, every nook and cranny in the entire state of Florida is teeming with venomous snakes just waiting for an opportunity to strike, but sometimes my curiosity gets the best of me. Cringing, I reached my arm down into the hole and my hand fell on something at the base of it, something fluffy, like a cheerleader's pom-pom, but solid underneath. I closed my hand around it and slowly drew it out.

My jaw fell open and my eyes must have grown ten times bigger.

Now I knew exactly where I'd seen that paper before, plus the old-fashioned print. I was certain. The bottom half was nibbled and shredded, and the whole thing was wrapped in a water-stained lavender scarf, which was also pulled and chewed through, but I knew without a doubt that it was the missing chapter from *The Furry Godmother's Guide to Pet-Friendly Gardening,* by V. Tisson-Waugh.

I said, "Huh," and pursed my lips together, making a little sucking sound of air through my teeth.

Mr. Peters cocked his head to one side and stared up at me quizzically.

"Mr. Peters," I said. "I have no frickin' idea."

Part of me knew it was wrong. Part of me knew I should have dropped the stupid thing right back in its squirrel hole and never thought of it again, but I didn't care. In a way, it was mine. I folded the whole fluffy mess up as neatly as possible and was tucking the wispy ends of the scarf between the pages when something slipped halfway out the bottom.

It was a drawing — a pen-and-ink drawing, to be exact — of an attractive woman with long dark hair cascading off her shoulders. She was sitting on a couch, her knees drawn up beneath her, with one arm draped casually over the side cushion, and looking straight at me with a slyly seductive look in her eyes. I recognized her immediately.

It was the same woman in the drawings hanging behind the register at Beezy's Bookstore, the same woman with the diamond ring and the tiny kitten in her lap. This drawing, however, was a little different from the rest — the woman was completely naked.

When I got to the bottom of the ladder and was back on solid ground, I turned to find Janet standing behind me, her arms folded over her chest.

I gasped. "Good Lord, you scared me to death! I thought you went back inside."

She narrowed her gaze. "I came back."

Something in the way she was staring me down made my palms break out in a sweat. I could probably have freed Mr. Peters right then and there and said my good-byes before she started asking questions, but I just couldn't be sure he wouldn't run right back up the tree, and I definitely didn't feel like climbing that ladder again. Janet stepped forward and held out her hand with an expectant, almost accusing look in her eye. I took a deep breath.

She said, "I take cat."

I handed Mr. Peters to her. He tried to squirm out of her arms, but she held on to him with a firm grip and then glanced in my general direction.

"Thank you," she said and then turned back toward the house.

I'm not sure what came over me then — maybe the adrenaline from having stuck my hand down in a potential snake's lair — but there was something about her voice, her accent, that made something click in my brain.

I said, "You're welcome . . . Mrs. Vladim."

She stopped and turned to me. In that instant I knew. I could see it in her eyes.

She was Baldy's wife, the Bonnie to his Clyde, the woman the police were looking for — and Mrs. Silverthorn's missing "footman" was none other than Baldy himself.

Her eyes widened, and she smiled politely. "I'm sorry? My name is Henson. Janet Henson."

Then she turned and continued toward the house, her pace slightly quicker now. Not knowing what else to do, I followed her through the garden and around the corner through the portico, and when we reached the front entrance Janet opened the door and bowed her head. "I will tell Mrs. Silverthorn that you are gone." Then she closed the door behind her.

I stood there dumbfounded, staring blankly into the eyes of the weathered green elephant door-knocker, my mouth hanging open like a boxer who's just received a good left hook, followed directly with a heavy jab from the right. My hand fell down to the side pocket of my cargo shorts and closed around the tattered edge of the missing section of my book.

There appeared to be a whole host of things hiding at the Silverthorn Mansion.

25

It felt like I was waking from a dream as I made my way through the labyrinthian maze of hallways and stairwells at Sarasota Memorial. I hadn't exactly planned on going there, but speeding up Midnight Pass from the Silverthorn Mansion, I found myself turning right onto Stickney Point and crossing over the bridge to Tamiami Trail. Then the next thing I knew I was circling around inside the multilevel garage next to the medical building looking for a parking place, and then suddenly I was headed straight for Baldy's room.

I told myself I wouldn't stay long. I was already in deep enough and I had my own life to think about — specifically, my date with Ethan that night. I wanted to keep it short and sweet so I could go home, take a shower, and get ready for a nice evening out with my man. Of course, even as I made my way through the lobby, I had no idea why I was there or what I was planning on being so short and sweet about.

When the elevator doors slid open at Baldy's floor, it dawned on me that in some strange way I felt responsible for him. Sure, he'd put himself in the hospital with his crazy driving — that was nobody's fault but his own — but I was the one who had pulled him out of his car, just the way you might free a chick that's too weak to break out of its own shell. And just as a baby chick forms a never-ending bond with the first thing it lays eyes on, Baldy had taken one look at me and decided I was his dear, loving wife.

As far as I was concerned, it was my duty to see that he at least made it out of the hospital okay. Plus, I had a feeling that where he was headed next, kindness would not be in full supply.

When I rounded the corner to his room, I was surprised to find an armed guard sitting in a chair just outside the door. I should probably have expected that. Baldy was a criminal with probably a very high flight risk. My shoes squeaked on the shiny linoleum floor as I came to a stop. I considered turning right around and heading back for the elevator.

The guard stood up out of his chair and

eyed me down the bridge of his nose. He wore black pants with white stripes down the outside seam, with a cop-blue, short-sleeved shirt with pockets on the chest. There was a black leather holster strapped to his waist, with the shiny black handle of a pistol poking out the top. He was big and muscular, the type of man you might find escorting a busty movie star through a crowd of frenzied paparazzi or standing next to a presidential candidate on the campaign trail.

His voice as deep as a bullfrog's, he said, "Sorry, miss. No visitors."

I said, "Oh, I'm Dixie Hemingway. Baldy . . . I mean, Mr. Vladim knows me."

He held his hand up like a guard directing children at a school crossing. "I'm under strict orders. No one is allowed in this room unless authorized by hospital staff."

I said, "No, you have to let me in. It's important. Tell him Dixie Hemingway is here. I'm the one that —"

He interrupted. "I don't have to do anything. If you want access to this room you'll have to talk to the doctors."

Just then I heard a voice over my shoulder. "What's the problem?"

I turned to see a burly man with short-cropped black hair coming down the hall toward us. He was wearing green surgeon's scrubs under a white lab coat, and when he saw my face his dour expression brightened.

He stopped in his tracks and held his arms open. "Hey, look! It's Super Woman."

I would never have recognized him in his surgeon's clothes. It was the man from the head-on collision, the doctor who had helped me get Baldy out of his car.

The guard said, "This woman wants to visit Mr. Vladim, but I explained to her there's no one allowed in this room but medical personnel. She's leaving now."

He nodded and then turned to me. From the pained expression on my face, he must have known right away that I wasn't just there to shoot the breeze, because without missing a beat he thrust his open hand toward mine and said, "Dr. Hemingway, I'm Dr. Dunlop. I believe we've met before?"

As we shook hands he gestured toward Mr. Vladim's door and said, "Shall we?"

The guard stepped back a little as Dr. Dunlop reached past him and opened the door to Baldy's room. I met the bewildered guard's suspicious frown with a solemn, doctorly nod. It took every ounce of self-control in my body to keep from sticking my tongue out at him, but I figured I would never have made it through medical school and become an important, world-renowned physician at the Sarasota Memorial Hospital by acting like a spoiled, immature brat, so instead I closed the door behind me with a polite smile and kept my tongue, quite literally, to myself.

Mr. Vladim was asleep on the hospital bed. His breathing was a little raspy, but slow and steady, and his complexion had improved since I'd first visited — it was rosier, and the bruises around his neck and face were almost gone. I was relieved to see that all the wires and IV lines had been taken away. Just a single tube remained, strapped to his left arm and leading to a clear bag of liquid on a hook behind his bed. I assumed it was probably a morphine drip.

I turned to Dr. Dunlop and whispered, "Thank you so much for that. I just wanted to see how he's doing."

He smiled and whispered back, "My pleasure. The guard is just a precaution. This guy's not gonna hurt anybody. He might steal your wallet, but he's on enough drugs to put an elephant to sleep. Anyway, he probably wouldn't even be alive if it weren't for you."

"Well, thanks. I can't believe you recognized me."

He folded his arms over his chest. "How could I forget the woman that made me feel like a complete horse's ass?"

As innocently as possible, I whispered, "Who, me?"

"Yeah, you. I'm a doctor. After that car accident, I was more worried about my BMW and my next appointment than this poor guy, especially the way he was weaving in and out of traffic. I don't know what you do for a living, supermodel or something . . . ?"

I smiled. "Ha. I'm a cat sitter."

"Right, you're a cat sitter. Of course. The cat sitter jumps out of her car and saves a man's life. The doctor sits on his ass and checks his voice mail."

I shook my head. "No, you showed up just at the right time. I don't think I could have gotten him out of that car if you hadn't helped me. You did the right thing."

He smiled. "Thank you for that. I'll go ahead and pretend I believe you."

He stepped over to the side of Baldy's bed. "Mr. Vladim, you have a visitor."

Baldy opened his eyes and looked around the room. When he saw Dr. Dunlop, he smiled slightly. "Hello, Doc."

"How's the pain, buddy? Okay?"

He thought for a moment. "Level three."

"Alright. I'll leave you alone, then. Miss Hemingway is here to see you."

Baldy's eyes flashed at me, and immediately a look of fear spread across his face. He turned back to the doctor and said firmly, "I talk to her now."

"Okay, then, I can take a hint. I was just leaving. I'll be back to check on you later." Before he closed the door he gave me a look and winked. "Let me know if he gives you any more trouble."

I wasn't sure if he meant Baldy or the guard or both. I pulled a chair up next to the bed, and Baldy rolled his head to the side and looked me up and down.

"I know you are not wife."

I nodded. "No, I'm not. I tried to tell you."

"Yes. But drugs, they make me dream bad things."

"That's okay. You got banged up pretty good, so they have you on a lot of painkillers."

"You safe me from car, yes?"

"I did, and Dr. Dunlop was in one of the cars behind you. He helped me carry you out. Your car was crushed in on one side and there was a lot of smoke, so we lifted you out and I stayed with you until the ambulance came. You're in a lot of trouble apparently. If it weren't for Mr. Dunlop, they wouldn't have let me in this room."

He nodded. "Yes, I think so."

I leaned a little closer. "Mr. Vladim. I have something I need to talk to you about."

"Yes, I know."

"It's about your wife."

His eyes widened. I could tell he hadn't been expecting that. He looked around the room and then shook his head, nervously running his fingers over the edge of his blanket. "I don't know where she go. She leave me. We are not couple now."

"No . . . you see, I'm a professional cat sitter. I got a call from —"

He eyed me warily. "Cat sitter? I don't know this."

"I look after people's pets when they're away on business or vacation. I got a call earlier this week from a woman who wanted me to help her find a friend's missing cat."

His eyes narrowed to slits. "You look at cats, for money."

I nodded.

"Why you tell me this?"

"This woman, the one that called me, her name is Alice Ann Silverthorn."

His expression didn't change; he just turned and stared up at the ceiling. In a couple of moments his eyelids fluttered slightly and his eyes welled with tears.

"I don't know this name. I am tired now."

"Mr. Vladim, are you sure?"

He pushed himself up on the pillow and glared at me. "I will call nurse. You are not allowed here. I am criminal."

I said, "Listen, I haven't told anyone anything, but your wife is very, very upset. I think she has no idea where you are."

He had reached for the call button, but then he stopped and rested his head back down on the pillow. "No. I don't know this. My wife is gone from here. We are not couple."

I took a deep breath. "I think you should know that I lost my child when she was three years old. She was hit by a car and died instantly. There was nothing I could have done to save her, but believe me, Mr. Vladim, if there had been, I would have done it. Anything."

He didn't respond, just stared at the ceiling, and we sat there for a while like that, not talking. The IV drip's timer made quiet clicks and sucking sounds every once in a while, and at one point there was a burst of laughter from the nurses' station down the hall, but otherwise the room was completely silent except for Mr. Vladim's slow, steady breathing.

Finally, he said, "We take boy to miracle

doctor in Houston. They make promise he will find cure. But we must pay cash. Four thousand dollars every month."

He paused, and I could tell he was trying to keep his emotions under control.

"If we don't pay, he don't help. This doctor. He lied. He was devil." He turned to me. "Cat looker, you will deliver message?"

I nodded, fighting with all my might not to burst out in tears, because for the first time I realized that their child had not survived. "I'll do whatever you need."

"Tell her I am okay. They will take me to jail. I will tell police that I make her do everything."

"And Mr. and Mrs. Silverthorn . . . do they know who you are?"

He nodded slowly. "My wife. She is third cousin of Mrs. Silverthorn. They help us, and for this we work for them. At first it was good arrangement, but now we are slaves. But Dixie, you must not tell."

"I promise I won't. Your wife will be very relieved to know that you're okay."

"Please tell her I have no choice. If I call they trace phone and take her to jail."

"I'll tell her. And if there's anything else you need, let me know." I stood up and put my chair back in place. "I'll leave you alone now, Mr. Vladim, and I'm glad you're feeling better."

I turned and headed for the door, but he stopped me.

"Dixie. What you do with chocolate?"

I turned back to him. "Huh?"

"Chocolate. What you do with it?"

I said, "I'm confused. What chocolate do you mean?"

He raised one eyebrow, as if he thought I must be the dumbest person in the world. "The chocolate I put in your bag. What you do with it?"

I walked back to the side of his bed. "Mr. Vladim, I have no idea what you're talking about."

He shook his head as his face flushed red and his voice grew louder. "These women. They don't listen. I told you don't eat!"

"Mr. Vladim, I think perhaps you dreamed that. The drugs you're on are very strong, and they can cause all kinds of —"

Just then the door opened and a nurse poked her head in. I could see the guard standing behind her. It was a different nurse this time, a skinny, older woman with spiky black hair and drooping eyes. Mr. Vladim was visibly shaken. His eyes flashed at the nurse and then at me.

The nurse frowned. "Excuse me, who are you?"

I said, "Um, Dr. Hemingway?"

She shook her head. "No, I'm afraid you can't be here. There's no one allowed in this room but medical staff. The guard should have told you that."

I nodded, "He did, but Dr. Dunlop said it was okay."

"Ma'am, I don't know anything about that. All I know is you need to leave right now. If Dr. Dunlop wants you on the visitors list, he would need to talk to me. And the last time I looked, there were exactly zero approved visitors for this room."

I turned to Mr. Vladim and nodded. "Don't worry."

He looked away, as if he didn't want the nurse to know he had even talked to me at all.

The nurse tapped her foot and said, "Ma'am? Right now."

I touched Mr. Vladim's hand lightly and headed for the door while the nurse glared at me. I thought about how I'd made a promise to myself that the next time somebody called me ma'am, I'd sock them right in the mouth. I can't say it was my proudest moment, but sometimes action speaks louder than words. As I passed by her, I made a face and stuck out my tongue.

26

About ten feet outside Baldy's room I started having second thoughts. Then in the elevator down to the lobby, I was quietly mumbling to myself while my fellow passengers pretended not to notice. Then by the time I made it through the lobby and outside into the fresh air, I didn't care who saw me — I was straight-up talking out loud and giving myself a good, stern disquisition on the basic standards of reasonable behavior.

I'd gone too far. I should never have promised to deliver Baldy's message to his wife. He was a grown man. He could do it himself. Don't get me wrong — I knew without a doubt that what he and his wife had been through was unimaginably heartbreaking, but it just wasn't my responsibility, and it was crazy of me to even consider delivering messages back and forth between two wanted criminals. Except . . .

346

I thought of Janet, all alone in that sprawling mansion, crying herself to sleep every night, isolated from the outside world, and with no earthly idea where her husband was or why he had disappeared. For all she knew he was dead, and now I understood why she always looked so exhausted and tortured — her life was a living hell, and all because she had tried to save her child.

Except, I thought, lots of people deal with sick children, and they don't all go around robbing banks to pay their medical bills. Not to mention the fact that if I didn't report Janet's whereabouts to the authorities, I would essentially be committing a very serious crime.

As I unlocked the Bronco and jumped into the driver's seat I mumbled to myself, "It's called aiding and abetting, you dummy."

No. I just couldn't take that kind of risk, not even for Janet.

Except then I thought of the pain she must have been in — to lose her child like that, and now the only thing standing between her suffering and a little bit of relief was me. Except I knew without a doubt that if she turned herself in right away she'd have a much easier time in court . . . and it wasn't like she and Baldy were murdering

thieves. They were just small-time bank rob-
bers, right?

Except how exactly had they robbed all
those banks? Had Janet held a gun to the
teller's head while Baldy filled a bag with
cash? I mean, robbing a bank is one thing,
but robbing a bank with a deadly weapon
could mean life in prison for both of them.
Except they just didn't seem capable of that
kind of violent crime . . . except what did I
know? They could just as easily have been
cold-blooded killers, except . . .

Except, except, except!

In the car all the way home, I shook my
head and sighed so many times I must have
looked like a bobblehead doll. Yet again I'd
managed to get myself tangled up in a seriously complicated mess, but there was no
way out. I'd given my word to Baldy. I
couldn't very well change my mind now and
turn his wife in to the police. That would
have been wrong, no matter how hard I
tried to justify it.

I told myself that if Baldy and his wife
had fallen into a life of crime as a way of
paying for their child's medical bills, then
that meant they'd been abandoned from the
get-go, that society had turned its back on
them. No parent should ever be put in that
kind of situation, no matter who they are or

348

where they come from or how they got here, and I knew I'd never be able to look myself in the eye again if I betrayed my promise to Baldy. My only choice was to deliver his message to her.

I just hoped I wouldn't go to jail for it.

Meanwhile, the whole time I was engaged in that mental game of tug-of-war, there was a little voice in the back of my mind, repeating the same words over and over again: *What you do with chocolate? What you do with chocolate?* I shook my head like an Etch A Sketch that needs erasing. The man was on enough painkillers to down an elephant, that was all. Somehow he'd gotten chocolate on the brain, a condition I could completely understand, and with all those drugs, not to mention the head trauma, he had just hallucinated some crazy scene where he gave me chocolates . . . some chocolates that for some reason he didn't want me to eat.

As I pulled into the driveway, I had to laugh at the absurdity of it all. I'm not exactly the most religious person in the world, but I do believe that we each have some kind of higher power — some presence that watches over us all, pulling the strings and keeping everything spinning. Whatever it is, I was beginning to think that my higher power had a very mischievous sense of humor. On top of all the craziness that had unfolded in the last few days, the moment I had decided to go on a diet it seemed like there was something tempting me to break it every five minutes. I was beginning to feel like a character in a book, where everywhere I turned the author put some chocolate in my path just to torture me.

As I came around the curve and saw the carport under my apartment, I breathed a huge sigh of relief. Michael's car was in its regular spot, and so was Paco's. As an undercover agent, Paco rubs elbows with all kinds of shady characters — corporate embezzlers, drug dealers, gang members — and as for Michael, fighting fires isn't exactly the safest activity in the world, so a full carport always means one thing: I can rest a little bit easier. It's like a big ball of tension in the pit of my stomach just starts melting away.

Of course, a full carport usually means I'm probably getting a gourmet meal for dinner, so that feeling in my stomach could just be hunger.

Either way, as I crunched across the driveway to the steps, the sight of Michael and Paco busily moving around in their kitchen helped take my mind off everything. I decided that, at least for tonight, I'd just let it all go and try to have a nice, relaxed evening with Ethan.

He was taking me to Yolanda, the Spanish restaurant where we'd had our very first official date, so I definitely didn't want to spend the whole night thinking about Baldy and Janet and Mr. Hoskins and Cosmo. It helped that I didn't have Mr. Silverthorn's number; otherwise I would probably have been calling him every half hour to find out how his search was going. I didn't even know if he owned a cell phone at all, but I had already decided that it wouldn't hurt to sneak away at some point during our date and give Mrs. Silverthorn a quick call, just to see if there was any news.

Once inside, I dropped my backpack in the middle of the floor and sat down on the couch. There was just one more little thing I needed to take care of if I really wanted to have a nice night and focus all my attention on Ethan.

I reached down in the side pocket of my cargo shorts and pulled out my souvenir from the Silverthorn Mansion — the shredded remains of my book's missing chapter.

I laid it down on my lap and whispered,

"Okay. How in the world did you end up in that tree?"

Given the week I'd had, I half expected it to answer me, but of course it didn't. It just sat there all shredded and mute — clearly it wasn't giving up its secrets that easily — so I unfolded the loose covering of lavender fabric and drew out the pen-and-ink drawing.

"And who the hell are you?"

The woman peered back at me, tight-lipped and sly. I flipped it over. It wasn't signed anywhere, but I knew it had to have been one of Mr. Hoskins's drawings. The only difference was that it looked almost like a preliminary sketch. The style was the same, but it wasn't as detailed and intricate as the other drawings.

I studied the woman's face, hoping there might be something I recognized, some identifiable feature, like a mole or a tattoo, but there was nothing. She could have been any pretty young woman with long dark hair . . . but of course, I had my theories.

The top page was mostly intact. Even though the lower portion was nibbled a bit at the ends, and the paper was all buckled and water stained, I could still make out the chapter title. It was "Gardeners Beware."

I read the first paragraph.

Now let the reader turn to Figure 9, where such a beauty as *Abrus precatorius* is depicted. If the reader wishes to preserve his muscle for other household chores, he may allow such a vine to o'ertake his fields, which it will do in short order, smothering all other plants in its path and establishing a garden that is, if not attractive, forever free of fret and fidget. We hasten to add, however, that the fruit from which this industrious vine gets its common name, rosary pea, is quite deadly. It is in fact considered the most poisonous seed of them all, so unless the gardener has less charitable uses in mind, he would do well to avoid the cheerily colored berry altogether.

I hadn't even finished the last sentence when I grabbed my cell phone off the coffee table and punched in Detective McKenzie's number.

"McKenzie here."

I said, "Detective, this may sound crazy, but has the coroner determined Mr. Hoskins's cause of death?"

She said, "Dixie, the cause of death is gun wounds. That was obvious from the beginning."

I frowned. "I know he was shot, but did

you run blood tests? Was there anything odd in his blood?"

"Dixie, what's going on?"

"Remember when I told you about that book I bought in the bookstore that night? Remember I said it was missing a section? Well, get this — I was in the top of that big magnolia tree at the Silverthorn Mansion, and I found the missing section in a squirrel hole."

There was a pause. "A squirrel hole."

"Yes, a squirrel jumped out and it had a piece of paper in its mouth. They were using it as a nest."

"The squirrels were using the hole for a nest . . ."

"No, no. The book. They were using the book, chewing it up and building a nest with it in the garden shed. At first I couldn't figure out how it got there —"

"I'm trying to figure out how *you* got there, but go on."

"It's a long story. I didn't have a chance to look at it until now, but listen — it's all about poisons. The whole chapter is plants that gardeners should avoid if they have pets."

She sighed. "Dixie, it sounds interesting, but I don't see the connection."

I said, "The very first paragraph is about

rosary pea vine. It's like the most poisonous seed in the world, and it's growing all over the Silverthorn Mansion. It's basically covering everything that doesn't move."

"Yes?"

"So, I mean, don't you think that's kind of weird? There's a book in Mr. Hoskins's store that's missing the last chapter, and then the next thing you know Mr. Hoskins is dead and the missing section is all about poisons and it's hidden in a tree surrounded by poisonous vines? I know it seems crazy, but you're just going to have to trust me on this one. If you run those tests, you'll find poison in his blood."

"Dixie. We ran tests. His blood was clean. There were no foreign substances at all. No poisons. No drugs. Nothing. There was head trauma, so we think he was knocked unconscious first, and then he was dragged into the crawl space and shot once in the chest. We know how he died."

I winced. I wished I'd been spared that detail. "Are you sure?"

"Dixie, I wish you were right, I really do. I'd love to have a lead on this case, but I just don't see a connection. There was no poisoning."

I nodded. "Okay, but there's one more thing. Inside the book is one of Mr. Hoskins's drawings. It's a woman . . . and she's nude."

"Okay . . . go on."

"Well, doesn't that tell you something?"

"Dixie, what does it tell me?"

I sighed and shook my head, defeated. "I have no idea."

She thought for a moment. "You're sure it's one of Mr. Hoskins's drawings?"

"I'm not positive, but I think so. It's not signed or anything, but the woman looks a lot like the woman in a couple of other drawings in the store."

"Alright. Just to be on the safe side, I'll send an officer over first thing in the morning to pick it up. For now, keep it someplace safe. Though I must say, it's not exactly earth-shattering that you've got a book from Mr. Hoskins's bookstore with a drawing by Mr. Hoskins in it. Even given the strange circumstances of where you found it, there are a lot of reasons why someone might hide a nude drawing."

Half whispering, I said, "I know . . ."

I was thinking about Janet. If I was going to turn her in, now was the time. If I didn't tell McKenzie what I knew right away, it would be pretty hard explaining why later . . . but I just couldn't do it. I just couldn't shake the notion that, even though what Janet had done was completely wrong, I knew with all my heart that in her mind she felt there was no other choice.

"Was there something else you wanted to tell me?"

McKenzie's voice snapped me back to the present. I shook my head. "Um . . . no, that was it."

"You're sure?"

I could tell by the sound of her voice she knew there was something more, but I held firm. "Yep."

After we hung up, I laid the phone down on the coffee table and just stared at it. I was beginning to wonder if maybe Detective McKenzie didn't have a few psychically gifted ancestors of her own.

For the next half hour or so I managed to keep my mind off everything by straightening up the apartment. I got out some glass cleaner and my trusty bottle of bleach-and-water mix and cleaned the heck out of anything that was glass, porcelain, or chrome until all the accumulated grime was a distant memory. Then I took a long hot shower until all the accumulated grime in my head was a distant memory, too. Feeling completely renewed, I toweled myself off and padded naked into my closet to see if I could drum up a date-worthy outfit to wear.

I am not, by any stretch of the imagination, a fashionista. It's not that I don't like nice clothes, I do, but unlike most women I just don't like shopping for them. In fact, I'd be tickled pink if I never had to see another mall for as long as I live, even if it meant wearing the same clothes every day until they fell off in tatters and I had to go around stark-raving mad and naked to boot — which may very well happen one day. Standing in the middle of my closet and surveying my measly collection of outfits, though, I wished I had a slightly better attitude.

There were only a few viable options, one of which was a beautiful plum-colored evening dress, but I'd worn that the first time we'd gone to Yolanda and it didn't seem right to wear it twice in the same place, so instead I decided on something a little less fancy. I laid out a white silk blouse with mother-of-pearl buttons, a low-cut yellow cotton camisole, and a pair of cream-colored linen capris.

Looking in the mirror over the desk, I applied a little makeup, with just enough blush and eyeliner to make it look like I hadn't given it a moment's thought. That took me a good ten minutes. Then I pulled the hair dryer out from under the sink, blew off the dust, and coaxed my hair into a state of natural, windswept fluffiness — as if I'd just come in from a fun, carefree day at the beach. That took another ten minutes at least. Then I got dressed, which took another half hour because I changed my mind about what to wear ten times, and just when I'd given up and settled on my first choice — with a resolution to go to the mall as soon as possible — I heard Ethan's car rolling up the driveway. I knew I had just enough time to slip my bare feet into a pair of nice low-heeled sandals before he could climb the steps and knock on the door.

As I checked myself one last time in the mirror, I had a momentary lapse. I think it was the mother-of-pearl buttons on my blouse — for a second I saw the shiny brass buttons of Mr. Hoskins's shirt staring back at me in the darkness, but I closed my eyes and chased the image away before it had a chance to take over my whole brain. Then I just stood there and waited.

There was no knock. I went into the living room and looked through the window, thinking Ethan was waiting for me in the hammock, but he wasn't there. I grabbed my pocketbook and opened the French doors. Nothing. I looked over the balcony, and sure enough there was his car, parked just behind mine, but he was nowhere in sight. I went down the steps into the court-yard.

The tiki torches were all lit, except they'd been rearranged. Instead of surrounding the deck like they usually did, they were in a line leading all the way down to the beach. I looked in the kitchen window. It was empty. Drying on a rack next to the sink was a pile of copper pots and pans, but Michael and Paco were nowhere to be seen.

I went over to the edge of the deck and followed the line of torches down to the beach, where my eyes finally landed on Ethan, illuminated by the golden glow of the last torch. He was at the water's edge, standing next to a small table and two dining chairs. There was a white cloth spread across the table with a glass hurricane lamp in the middle, sending a flickering light over a sparkling arrangement of silverware, wineglasses, and gleaming white china.

He called out, "Hemingway, party of two?"

27

Every life has its milestones, those perfect moments that feel entirely right and familiar, as if you've been dreaming about them your whole life. Ethan was standing in the sand with the waves gently lapping over his bare feet, wearing a fitted black dress shirt and tan chinos rolled up to his calves. I immediately felt like I'd wandered into some kind of photo shoot for *Foxy Man Magazine* — and the theme was "World's Most Eligible Bachelor."

Most women presented with such a stunning tableau would have felt like a queen at her coronation, or at least Snow White waking up to her handsome prince, but not me. Both of my hands started to tingle, as if they'd fallen asleep, and my vision went a little blurry. I've only fainted once in my whole life, but I was a little worried it was about to happen again. It took all the strength I could muster just to make the rest of the trip down to the water — I distinctly remember making a conscious effort to put one foot in front of the other. As I came up to Ethan, my legs quivering and my head on spin cycle, he silently took me in his arms and kissed me.

I said, "What in the world is happening?"

He was beaming. "I decided we'd do something a little more special, and the food's much better here at Chez Ethan."

"Are you kidding me? Whose idea was this?"

"Well, yet again I'd like to take full credit, but it was a group effort. It's a good thing Michael and Paco are around or I'd be the lousiest boyfriend ever. We figured you could probably use a nice dinner at home after, you know, after everything that's happened this week."

There was only one word I could think of that was appropriate for this particular moment: *Whew!*

I'd just been on the verge of a full-blown panic attack. Tiki torches leading down to a beach, a beautifully appointed table, candlelight, romantic dinner for two, waves gently lapping at our feet . . . the only thing missing was Ethan getting down on one knee and then maybe some fireworks over the ocean and a harp player. Once I realized there was no ring involved, I felt like a fool, a very lucky fool, but a fool nonetheless.

I squeezed him tighter. "You have no idea — this is the perfect ending to an otherwise crazy day."

He kissed me again. "It's okay, then?"

I nodded. "Oh yeah, it is definitely okay. This is exactly what I needed."

"You looked a little pale there for a minute."

"I'm just surprised, that's all."

He pulled a chair out for me and we sat down, and then as if on cue Paco appeared out of the shadows, carrying two plates of food with a white napkin draped over his arm. I nearly fell out of my chair laughing.

He was wearing a tight black Speedo and black leather sandals, with a black tuxedo jacket over his bare chest and a red sequined bow tie around his neck. He looked like a Chippendale dancer delivering a strip-o-gram.

His cheeks were flushed red. "Don't laugh. The chef made me wear it."

I said, "You look fantastic. I think you should be required to wear that for every dinner."

Ethan patted his pockets. "Man, I'm all out of dollar bills or I'd throw you a couple."

Paco set the plates down on the table and

said, "Very funny."

Michael was right behind him with a bottle of white wine, wearing his regular khaki shorts and white tank top.

I said, "Wait a minute, where's *your* waiter uniform?"

He said with a grin, "Oh, I'm not a waiter. I'm the chef," and Paco rolled his eyes.

I said, "You guys aren't eating with us?"

"Nope. We don't want to crash your date, plus we have our own plans."

As he filled the wineglasses he described the menu — vegetable lasagna, with cremini and portobello mushrooms and a creamy bechamel sauce, served with a salad of baby greens and slices of fresh blood orange and ripe avocado. Later there'd be homemade key lime pie.

I started to get that feeling again — that everybody felt like I needed to be taken care of, that they had to pamper me and protect me and keep me happy as a baby so I'd forget about Mr. Hoskins and the accident and everything else that had happened. Sooner or later I was going to have to let everybody know that I didn't need to be coddled and spoiled, that I wasn't here to make them all feel like big, strong he-men taking care of a defenseless little girl.

I opted for later.

Dinner was absolutely delicious. Our grandmother always said you can improve just about any recipe by adding a pound of bacon to it, and I wondered if Michael and Paco didn't have some similar trick up their sleeve. Everything just seemed to taste better when it came out of their kitchen. They both reappeared every once in a while to refill our wineglasses or take plates away, and when we were done they headed back up to the house, their arms around each other's shoulders. As they disappeared into the shadows I heard Paco say, "Next time, you're the waiter and I'm the chef."

I turned to Ethan. "This has been about the nicest thing anybody has ever done for me."

He smiled. "I was hoping you'd say that."

He held up his wineglass and said, "To now," and then we clinked our glasses and each took a sip. Then he held up his glass again and said, "And to me being an awesome boyfriend."

I grinned and said, "I'll drink to that," and then we clinked our glasses once more and took another sip.

Then we just sat there for a while, not talking, just enjoying the wine and the company and the moon hanging over the ocean. I thought about my plan to sneak away and call Mrs. Silverthorn, but now, sitting here with Ethan, it didn't seem so urgent. I figured if Mr. Silverthorn had found Cosmo he would probably have called, and if he hadn't found him there wasn't anything I could do about it now anyway. Tomorrow I'd come up with an excuse to pay the Silverthorns a visit, which would give me an excuse to pull Janet aside and talk to her. Except . . .

Ethan interrupted the silence. "So, I wanted to tell you, about that letter from Guidry."

I took a deep breath, but he stopped me.

"No, just listen. I know what was going on when you met him. That was a rough time for you, and I know he made you feel happy for the first time in a very long time. So, I mean, it's pretty stupid of me to sit here and be all jealous just because he wrote you a letter. It's probably because of him that you're even here with me in the first place. So I figured I'd just go the mature route. No sweat. I don't need to be part of it. You can open it or not open it. Either way I'm good."

He sat back and folded his arms over his chest, then added, "Thus concludes my speech."

I smiled. "Thanks for that."

He winked. "Sure, babe."

Then I slid Guidry's letter onto the table between us. "Because I thought we should open it together."

His jaw dropped open and he pushed his chair back, holding his hands up in the air. "Whoa, whoa, whoa. I'm totally not ready to be that mature!"

I laughed. "Oh, come on! You have to help me."

"Why do I have to help you? That letter's for you, not me!"

I said, "Because we're a couple and that's what couples do. Now grow up and open it with me."

He shook his head. "No way."

"What about that speech you just gave me about not being jealous and taking the mature route?"

"That was all bullshit."

I cocked one eyebrow and stared at him.

He grinned uncomfortably. "Really?"

I said, "Ethan, I don't want to read it alone. I want to read it with you."

He sighed. "Ugh. What if he wants you back?"

"We'll say no."

"What if he wants you to come visit him?"

"We'll say no."

He picked up the wine bottle and split the

367

last remaining drops equally between our glasses. "Okay, let's open the damn thing already."

I picked up the letter, hoping Ethan wouldn't notice the slight tremble in my hands, and slid a fingernail along the edge of the envelope. I lifted the flap and looked inside. There was a single piece of paper, handwritten and folded into thirds.

I spread it open on the table, took a deep breath, and read it out loud:

Dixie,

I've been thinking about you a lot lately. I know you might find that surprising, but I do think about you a lot and hope you and Ethan are good (yes, the guys down at the station keep me up to date on all the gossip). I'm writing because I have something to tell you. I've picked up the phone a hundred times to call, but every time I do, I can't quite figure out how to say it. So I thought I'd just do the old-fashioned thing and write you a letter (or is it the cowardly thing?) Well, anyway . . .

I'm engaged.

I can tell you all about it later, if you want to hear it, but I didn't want to take the next step without letting you know first. Probably dumb, huh?

Guidry

I looked up to find Ethan staring at me, his eyes as big as an owl's. He said, "Whoa. Did *not* see that coming."

I had to admit, I hadn't seen it coming either, and to be honest I didn't know how I felt about it. Part of me was grateful Guidry had told me first — it would definitely have been strange to find out any other way — and part of me was just plain shocked. How was it possible he could so quickly have met someone, fallen in love, and decided to get married? It seemed like only yesterday that he'd left for New Orleans. Had I opened that letter alone, I would probably have sat down and cried for myself for a couple of hours, but with Ethan there with me, my ultimate reaction was entirely different, not to mention a little surprising.

Ethan downed the rest of his wine in one gulp and sighed. "So . . . what are you thinking?"

I picked up my glass, "I'm thinking . . . One, good for him. Two, I'm glad that's over with, and three, let's go inside, it's getting a little chilly out here."

He grinned. "That's it?"

I didn't think it would be quite so simple, but it was. I nodded. "Yep. That's it."

Looking a little relieved, Ethan stood up slowly and came around to my side of the table and pulled my chair out for me. Then we took our time and walked hand in hand back up to the house. When we got to the courtyard, Michael and Paco were in one of the chaise lounges my grandfather built, wrapped in each other's arms and sound asleep. We tiptoed up the stairs and closed the French doors behind us.

I wasn't sure what was coming next, but I didn't get a chance to find out. We hadn't been inside ten seconds when my cell phone rang.

I said, "You've got to be kidding me. Who in the world would be calling me at this hour?"

Ethan glanced at his watch. "Uh, it's nine o'clock, Gramma."

With the day I'd had, not to mention the miles of territory covered in Guidry's short letter — he was never a man of many words — I'd just assumed it was around three in the morning. My cell phone was on the coffee table in front of the couch, and when I read the caller ID, I turned to Ethan and frowned.

"It's Village Meats."

"Who?"

"The butcher up the street from the book-store."

As I flipped my phone open, Ethan whispered, "How the hell does he have your number?"

I held up one finger and said, "Hello?"

"Dixie, this is Butch from the butcher shop. I'm really sorry to call you, but this old guy just knocked on my window. He doesn't have a cell phone — that's how old we're talkin' about. He says he got that cat cornered out back in the alley. I said I'd give you a call."

I said, "Mr. Silverthorn?"

"Yeah, that's him. Old guy with gray hair. He said you're good at catching cats."

"Huh. Okay, thanks, Butch. Tell him I'll be right there."

Ethan's eyes widened. I flipped the phone closed and said, "This will take twenty minutes tops."

"Who is Butch? And where are you going?"

"He's the butcher. He said Mr. Silverthorn is there and he's got Cosmo cornered in the alley."

"He's Butch the Butcher?"

I picked up my backpack. "Would I make

371

that up?"

"So what does Mr. Silverthorn need you for?"

"Ethan, he's an old man and that cat is fast. There's no way he could catch him."

He sighed. "But what about dessert?"

I laughed as I kicked off my sandals and pushed my feet into a pair of Keds. "Oh, so *that's* what you're worried about!"

"Babe. It's Michael's key lime pie."

"I know, I know. We'll have it when I get back."

He followed me out to the balcony. Michael and Paco were still sound asleep on the deck. He said, "Well, I guess I better bring in that table anyway. If the tide comes in we'll never see it again."

"Okay. I'll be back before you know it. I promise."

He gave me a quick kiss at the top of the stairs and then watched me bound down the steps. As I hopped across the driveway I shouted, "If you eat all that pie I'll kill you!"

He grinned. "You better hurry, then."

28

I sped along Midnight Pass, thinking proudly that everything was falling perfectly into place. I had decided that once we had Cosmo safely ensconced in the cat carrier, I'd suggest we take him to the vet right away, and I'd call Dr. Layton to see if she could come in for an emergency checkup. Even though I'd left plenty of food for him, there was no telling what Cosmo had been eating these last few days, and I didn't want to take any chances.

Then I'd offer to pick Cosmo up in the morning and deliver him right to Mrs. Silverthorn's arms. I figured it wouldn't be hard to convince her to adopt him, and that way I'd have the perfect opportunity to visit the mansion one more time, and I could draw Janet aside and tell her where Baldy was. I'd do my best to persuade her to turn herself in, and I'd even drive her to the police station if she needed moral support.

My timing was excellent. I sailed right through all the lights, and in no time at all I was pulling into a parking place on the deserted street right in front of Beezy's Bookstore. There was a chill in the breeze off the water, so I grabbed Ethan's black hoodie from the backseat and then went around to the back of the car and took out one of my plastic cat carriers. I was just about to make my way to the alley when I remembered the cat treats.

I zipped my backpack open and pawed through it, feeling around for my little plastic bag of cubed cheese, but of course with all the junk I carry around in there it wasn't easy. I couldn't very well use my tried and true method of dumping everything out and combing through it — that would have taken too long, and Mr. Silverthorn was waiting for me. Plus, no animal likes to be cornered. I knew Cosmo would eventually make a run for it given half a chance, and I could just see Mr. Silverthorn's face when I explained why it took me so long to get to him.

I had worked my arm all the way down to the bottom of the backpack and was about to give up and dump the whole thing out in the street when finally my fingers slid across the crinkly plastic and my hand closed around the gumball-sized chunks of cheese inside. With a huge sigh of relief and a solemn promise to be less of a slob from now on, I wrestled the bag of treats out and stuffed it down in the pocket of my hoodie.

Even though the moon was casting a blue glow over the entire alley, it was dark. There was just one light on, midway down toward the north end, and I wondered why in the world Butch hadn't at least kept his back light on so we could see what the heck we were doing. I was thinking I'd have to go back again and fish around in my backpack for my penlight when I heard a crunching sound behind me.

"Dixie? Is that you?"

I turned to find Mr. Silverthorn, about twenty feet past the butcher shop, his face illuminated with the light from his rusty old flashlight. "We're over here."

I let out a sigh of relief as I made my way to him. "I'm glad you thought to bring that flashlight. I left mine in the car."

"Well, we may still need yours yet. The light on this one is getting dimmer and dimmer. I believe the batteries may be older than I am."

I smiled. "Sorry it took me so long, I had a little trouble finding my cat treats."

He directed the beam of the flashlight

down a narrow loading area cut into one of the buildings, at the end of which was a metal Dumpster with what looked like a small tool shed to the left of it. "I think you'll need them. He's taken up a rather strong position there in the corner behind that shed. Nothing I say or do seems to have even the slightest effect on him, and I'm afraid I'm too old to crawl under there and grab him."

I set the cat carrier down and patted the bag of treats in my pocket. "Hopefully we won't need to crawl under there at all. Even the most stubborn cat can barely resist a piece of cheese."

"Thank goodness you're here, Miss Hemingway. And what a turn of luck that the butcher had your number."

I nodded as I knelt down in front of the cat carrier. "I gave him my card and asked him to call me if he saw anything."

"That was smart. He was surprisingly interested in the news that I'd found Cosmo, although he seems to have disappeared now."

I opened up the front door of the carrier. "So if you can just stay close by with this, I'll try to coax him out with the cheese, and if that doesn't work and I can't convince him to come out on his own, I'll have to try to grab him. He won't be one bit pleased with me if it comes to that, so the sooner I can get him in the carrier the better."

He nodded firmly and handed me the flashlight as he picked up the carrier with both hands and readied himself. I had to smile. He seemed more than happy to follow orders, which shouldn't have surprised me. If I lived with Mrs. Silverthorn I'd probably get used to following orders, too.

The flashlight was pretty dim, but I knew it was strong enough to do the trick, so I crouched down and directed its beam of light along the ground toward the back of the passageway and under the Dumpster. There, in the very back corner at the end of the shed, were two yellow points of light reflecting right back at me.

I whispered, "Mr. Cosmo, I presume?"

The two points of light blinked, and Mr. Silverthorn said, "Is it him?"

"I think so."

I remembered Mrs. Silverthorn saying Cosmo wouldn't answer to anything but his full name, but I had a feeling under these circumstances he might be willing to make an exception. I got down on my hands and knees and moved the light from side to side, but now he had turned his head in toward the corner. "I can't see his face, but I see a lot of fluffy orange fur, and yep, I see a white-tipped tail."

Mr. Silverthorn sighed with relief. "Oh, thank goodness! Mrs. Silverthorn will be so happy."

I moved a little closer and lay down flat on the concrete so I could get a better reach. I knew the ground was probably filthy. Lucky for me I had Ethan's black hoodie to cover my blouse, but my cream-colored capris would probably be ruined. I didn't care. All I wanted to do was get Cosmo out of there as safely and quickly as possible.

Mr. Silverthorn said, "How does he look?"

I held the flashlight steady and reached down into my pocket to get a treat, working my fingers along the top of the plastic bag to pry it open. "He looks pretty well fed, actually, which may make this a little harder." I extracted a cube of cheese between my thumb and forefinger and held it out in front of me, reaching under the Dumpster as far as my arm would go.

I said, "Cosmo . . . uh, I mean Moses Cosmo Thornwall, I know you're probably quite satisfied with all those tasty scraps from Butch's Dumpster, but I was just wondering if I might interest you in a little late-night snack of cheese . . . ?"

For good measure I moved the flashlight over so Cosmo wasn't blinded by the light, and then my jaw fell wide open.

I couldn't believe what I was seeing.

There, right in front of my face, was one of Mr. Hoskins's chocolates, the ones he'd had in the bowl next to the register, the ones wrapped in shiny silver foil with red stripes. I could feel every neuron in my brain shifting into overdrive as I lay there in total silence, trying to explain it . . . trying to come up with some kind of reasonable explanation.

Mr. Silverthorn said, "Is everything alright?"

I blinked a couple of times. To be honest, I wasn't sure. It felt like the entire alley was beginning to slowly spin around me. I guess under normal circumstances it wouldn't have been that unusual to find one of Mr. Hoskins's chocolates on the ground in the alley behind his store, but this was different. This particular chocolate wasn't on the ground.

It was in my hand.

I was holding it between my thumb and forefinger.

I said, "I don't know how this happened, but . . . I thought I had some cubes of cheese in my pocket, but I don't. It's chocolate."

There was a pause. "Did you say chocolate?"

I instantly thought of Baldy . . . *What you do with chocolate?* I had just assumed he'd had a drug-induced dream, but was it possible that he was telling me the truth, that he had actually given me chocolate?

I pulled the plastic bag out of my pocket and pointed the flashlight at it. Sure enough, there were three other chocolates just like it inside. I shook my head. "I must have grabbed the wrong bag or something, but . . . I have no idea how I got them. They're the same chocolates from the bookstore."

I tried to think. I was certain that both times I had visited Baldy at the hospital, I'd left my backpack in the car. In fact, the only time my backpack had been anywhere near him was after the accident, when I'd put it down on the sidewalk next to him. Was it possible he'd secreted these chocolates in my bag when I wasn't looking? And if so, why?

I heard Mr. Silverthorn take a couple of steps forward. "Here, I'll take them. Unless this cat shares your weakness for chocolate, I'm afraid we'll have to try something else."

I was about to agree when I stopped cold.

Mr. Silverthorn had used that very phrase before, my "weakness for chocolate." Now that I thought about it, he'd mentioned chocolate the very first time we met, when we spoke briefly on the steps of the mansion. I specifically remembered him saying that Mrs. Silverthorn and I would get along splendidly, because she "also" loved chocolate.

At the time I hadn't thought much of it, but now, hearing him use that phrase again . . .

I pushed myself up off the concrete and stood there for a few moments with my back to him, trying to get my bearings. Then I turned and raised the light to his face. He looked completely and utterly confused.

"Miss Hemingway, are you alright? What's the matter?"

I could feel my heart beating. I said, "Mr. Silverthorn, the first day we met, you told me your wife *also* liked chocolate. What did you mean by that?"

He frowned slightly and tilted his head to one side. "Pardon me?"

A tiny tremor began bubbling up in my throat, but I forced myself to keep going. "You said she *also* had a weakness for chocolate . . ."

He shook his head and shrugged slightly. "My apologies, Miss Hemingway. I certainly didn't mean to offend you in any way."

"No, it's totally fine, I'm just . . . the thing is . . . how did you know?"

I could feel the chocolate getting soft in the palm of my hand, and I thought of the crumbling Silverthorn Mansion, struggling to hold on to its former glory, smothered in a thick web of rosary pea vine. Then I saw Baldy's panic-stricken face as he turned to me in the hospital room and cried, *I told you don't eat!*

The glow from the flashlight on Mr. Silverthorn's face was dim and flickering now, like a dying candle. I tried shaking the flashlight to try to make it brighter, but that only made it go out completely, and now we were standing there in complete darkness.

He said, "Miss Hemingway, I'm afraid I don't understand. How did I know . . . what?"

I said, "How did you . . ." but my words faded away, because I already knew the answer.

I remembered that first evening, after Baldy's car crash, when I'd gone to Beezy's Bookstore and met Mr. Hoskins. I was standing in front of the old cash register and the bowl of chocolates on the counter-top, and Mr. Hoskins had just returned from the back office, where he'd wrapped my book up in paper and twine. He caught me eyeing the chocolates and offered me one, and I specifically remembered what I said to him.

I said, *I have a weakness for chocolate.*

It was completely quiet now except for a low droning drumbeat coming from some-where far away, and then I realized the drumbeat was me. I could literally hear the blood pumping through my ears. As my eyes slowly adjusted to the darkness, Mr. Silver-thorn gradually came into view, bathed in the pale blue light from the moon overhead. My mind flashed to the old woman in the video, making her way to the bookstore, and then I saw one of Mrs. Silverthorn's gray wigs.

My voice trembling, I said, "Mr. Silver-thorn . . . where were you the night Mr. Hoskins was murdered?"

There was a long pause. He was about ten feet away. He calmly put the cat carrier down on the ground and then reached into his jacket, and then I saw the gleam of something metal in the moonlight as he raised his arm and pointed a pistol directly at me.

He said, "This is a very unfortunate turn of events."

A cold tremor crawled up my spine as I felt my breath catch in my throat. I said, "It was you. It was you in the video. You dressed up in your wife's clothing, and then you put on one of her wigs. You hid somewhere in the store until I left, and then you killed Mr. Hoskins. You killed him for his money."

His face was grim. "You're very smart, aren't you? And yes, you're right about my disguise, but the rest of your theory is incorrect. Mr. Hoskins was already long dead by then."

I shook my head. "You're wrong. He was alive when I left the store."

The vaguest hint of a smile brushed across his face. "Sometimes I wonder that I didn't more seriously pursue a career on the stage."

He held the gun steady as he reached up with his free hand and slowly pulled his long silvery hair forward so that it fell down both sides of his face. Then he hunched his body over and patted his pockets, shuffling toward me and muttering in a creaky voice, "I'm taking a trip very soon, my dear, but I do hope you'll enjoy your book and your chocolate in equal measure."

Then he raised himself back up and smiled wistfully.

It was all I could do to keep from fainting. The only things missing were the red beret and the dark wrap-around glasses.

"I'll admit I was nervous, as evidenced by my failure to lock the door. So very stupid. The fact that you'd never met Mr. Hoskins was a wonderful stroke of luck for me — and I might add, Miss Hemingway, for you as well. Otherwise, I would never have been able to let you leave the store that night, although in retrospect that might have been easier for everyone, easier than" — he waved his hand between us — "all this."

My mind was swimming, but I managed to whisper, "And the woman in the drawing . . ."

"Oh, very good, now you've hit the nail square on the head. Imagine my surprise when Janet informed me you'd found something in that tree and put it in your pocket. What possessed you to poke around in that hole I'll never know."

"The woman in the drawing . . . is Janet."

He frowned. "Oh, dear, no, why would you think that? No, I'm afraid the woman in the drawing is my wife, immortalized, as it were, in a very private moment."

"Mr. Hoskins . . ."

He nodded. "Yes, he's quite a fine artist, isn't he? I found that drawing one day when

I was going through the library, looking for books we might sell to pay off some of the bills. That's somewhat embarrassing to admit to you now, but no matter. You can imagine my surprise. She must have hidden it in that book at some point and then forgotten."

I could see his eyes, floating just above the barrel of the pistol. I said, "Mr. Silverthorn . . . why?"

"Oh, I think you know why, my dear. I'll let no man take away my dignity. I have my good name to protect, after all." His hands started to tremble slightly as his eyes narrowed. "And I'm not a fool, Miss Hemingway. I know very well what you and this entire town think of my family. My fortune may be lost, but when they tell the story of Oliver Silverthorn, it will not include the word 'cuckold.' "

His entire body shuddered at the word, and I thought to myself, *This cannot be the way it ends.*

"Mr. Silverthorn, I think I should tell you that I have a friend. He knows you. He knows you quite well, in fact, and I've told him everything I suspected. It won't do you any good to kill me now. When he finds out, he'll tell the police everything and they'll arrest you. Your only hope is to turn yourself in."

"I believe you're referring to my missing footman, Mr. Vladim?"

"Yes, I am. And I know where he is."

He nodded. "I'm sure it's a lie that you and Mr. Vladim have talked about me at all, but yes, I know where he is, too. And you may be surprised to know that your 'friend' was on his way to the bookstore to help me with Mr. Hoskins when he crashed into that landscaping truck."

I shook my head. "I don't believe you. He may be a criminal, but he's not a murderer."

He smiled. "He doesn't want to go to jail for bank robbery; therefore he does what he's told or I'll report him and his wife to the police. I'm not a violent man, Miss Hemingway, all present appearances to the contrary. I would never have shot Mr. Hoskins if I'd had another option. My plan was to distract him while Vladim replaced those chocolates by his register with others to which I'd added a secret ingredient."

"A rosary pea."

"Oh! I see you've been reading your book. You're quite remarkable, aren't you? Yes, a rosary pea. I knew from my wife that Mr. Hoskins never left the store without finishing off the chocolates in that bowl, so my plan was perfect. However, Mr. Vladim seems to have had a change of heart at the last minute. He apparently decided he'd rather die in a car crash than take part in a murder, and I imagine he thought he had thwarted my plan — for a bank robber, quite an honorable act when you think about it. But he didn't die in that crash, did he?"

I just stared at him, dumbfounded.

"Miss Hemingway, your attention to detail is impressive, so I'm rather surprised you don't remember me. I was there when you saved Mr. Vladim. I was right in front of you . . . in a black Cadillac . . . ?"

As I stood there staring into his steel gray eyes, the barrel of the gun trembling in the space between us, a series of images played through my mind, like a montage in fast motion. The old woman in the Cadillac in front of me, her mannish jaw, her white gloves stretched over her hands, her perfectly coiffed hair like a wig, and that lavender scarf tied around her neck . . .

Mr. Silverthorn seemed to be a man of more than a few disguises.

He shifted the gun from one hand to the other, and even in the low light I could tell it was fitted with a small, cylindrical piece of metal . . . a silencer.

He nodded at the bag of chocolates in my hand. "I assumed those chocolates were destroyed in the fire, but apparently he put them in your bag at some point. He's a smart fellow. I should have known. He probably thought they could be used to incriminate me."

I shook my head and tried to concentrate. "Why drag him into it at all?"

"Culpability, Miss Hemingway. Had everything gone as planned, I knew the police would scan the footage from that webcam across the street, and they would have seen Vladim entering the store. Once I'd turned him in, it would only have been a matter of time before they traced the poisoned chocolate to our kitchen, where Janet prepares our meals. Then they would have found the cash from Mr. Hoskins's register, the cash that I had hidden somewhere in Vladim's bedroom."

I closed my eyes and slowly shook my head. He had probably asked Janet to make the chocolates. Either she'd put the rosary peas in herself or he had added them later. Either way, the whole time Vladim and Janet had been working for Mr. Silverthorn, they'd been afraid he would turn them in to the police, and here he'd planned on doing exactly that, and framing them for the murder of Mr. Hoskins on top of it.

I said, "You've forgotten one thing, Mr. Silverthorn."

"What is that?"

"You have no power over Mr. Vladim now. The police have identified him. When he's well enough he'll go to trial, and I imagine they'll be very happy to give him a lighter sentence in exchange for the story he'll tell about you."

"Yes, I've considered that possibility already. I'll be paying Mr. Vladim a visit as soon as I leave here."

My heart stopped. "No. You'll be caught. They'll figure it out."

"I appreciate your concern, but they won't. I wasn't seen going in or leaving the bookstore, and I didn't touch a thing without gloves on, so there are no fingerprints. And with no one left to testify otherwise, I'll be quite fine."

His words were confident and assured, but I could see he was still trembling, and there was fear in his voice. I was certain he never thought it would come to this, and in spite of myself I felt a momentary pang of sorrow for him.

I shook my head. "Mr. Silverthorn, is this really the story you want to be told about you?"

His eyes softened. "My dear, the story ends here."

I saw the blast more than felt it. A small flash of light. I remember thinking of the brilliant shade of yellow the sun turns as it dips its hazy edge into the sea, and as my head hit the pavement, I thought of Cosmo. It's funny how the mind works. I thought to myself, *Now I'll never catch him.*

I lay there on my back and listened to the clicking of Mr. Silverthorn's footsteps receding in the distance, and then shortly thereafter the low rumble of a car starting up and speeding out of the alley.

I waited.

There wasn't any pain, just a vague and distant ache in the back of my head where it hit the concrete, and then a strange feeling of pressure on my sternum. The pressure shifted slightly, and I opened my eyes. At that point, I was certain it was a dream. There, in the center of my chest, was a big fluffy orange cat, sitting primly and looking down on me with a slightly curious expression in his deep green eyes.

I whispered, "Cosmo?"

He purred gently and his eyes narrowed, as if to say, "Pleased to meet you."

A tiny smile played across my lips. "Likewise."

As slowly as possible, I inched my left hand down along the concrete and eased my cell phone out of my side pocket. When she didn't answer at first, my heart started racing, but luckily, after the third ring, the line clicked and I heard McKenzie's familiar voice. "Dixie?"

I tried to keep myself as calm as possible, but my voice was shaky. I said, "Samantha?"

There was a pause. "Dixie, what's wrong?"

I took a deep breath, "Mr. Silverthorn killed Mr. Hoskins. And he's on his way to the hospital right now to kill Vladim, the bank robber I pulled out of that car crash."

I heard a sharp intake of breath. She said, "Where are you?"

"I'm in the alley behind the bookstore. He just left me. If you go now you'll get to the hospital before him. Sarasota Memorial Hospital. And I think he might be dressed up like an old woman."

"An old woman?"

"Like the old woman in the video."

"Dixie, what —"

I interrupted. "You have to trust me this time."

There was a pause. "I'm sending my men to the hospital now. Are you sure you're okay?"

I said, "I'm sure," and then I just clicked

the phone off. I didn't think there was much more to say.

I lay there and watched the stars overhead pull in and out of focus. It was completely quiet, except I thought I could just make out the gentle hum of the ocean and the rhythmic song of its waves rolling in to shore, the song I've heard my whole life. In a little while I started to shiver slightly, and I could feel my hands and feet beginning to turn cold.

As gently as possible, I eased myself up on my elbows and slowly turned my head over to my left shoulder. In the bunched black fabric of Ethan's big hoodie were two burned, dime-sized holes, one where the bullet went in, and another where it went out.

It had completely missed me.

29

For a long time, longer than I care to admit, I dreamed about Christy every night. I'd dream I was tucking her in at bedtime, or cleaning her Popsicle-stained fingers with a warm washcloth . . . just little things, little moments that either did or didn't actually happen. She was always giggling and happy. She'd tell me not to be sad, because even though she was gone, she was always with me. I'd wake up in the middle of the night and chase after the scattering remnants of those dreams, like dissolving vapor trails from a jet plane.

Most mornings I'd have her clothes for the day neatly laid out on her bed, but she'd paw through all the closets like a wild animal and come downstairs in an outfit of her own making — one of my T-shirts over a sundress with baggy leggings and over-sized sunglasses, or a fluffy pink tutu over faded jeans with one of Todd's ties draped casually around her neck.

As I drove home through the darkened, moonlit streets of Siesta Key with all the windows open and the cool, salty air streaming through the Bronco, I thought about Baldy and Janet, driving across Texas and holding up banks to save their child. I couldn't exactly condone what they'd done, but I certainly understood it. If I'd been given half a chance to save Christy, nothing could have stopped me.

Nothing.

So who was I to judge? When Christy was killed, I had dedicated my entire life to fighting on the side of the law, but I knew down to the soles of my feet that all it would have taken was just the tiniest slip of fate to throw me right to the other side of it. If I'd thought robbing banks would have helped her, I would have robbed banks.

By the time I turned down the driveway, I'd made up my mind. When McKenzie called, I wouldn't say a word about Janet unless she asked me point blank. I wasn't exactly sure what my plan was, and I didn't see how I'd ever get a chance to talk to Janet before the police did, but I was still holding on to the hope that somehow I could convince her not to run.

Then there was Mrs. Silverthorn . . .

When I got to the curve in the lane, I switched off the headlights and rolled the rest of the way down with nothing but the moonlight to guide me. Once inside the carport I cut the ignition and put my seat back. I had a feeling my phone would be ringing any minute, and I didn't want the guys to hear. The thought of having to explain everything tonight made me shudder to the core. So instead I leaned my head against the window frame and stared at the darkened treetops, breathing in and out.

I caught a glimpse of myself in the side mirror and thought, considering everything, I looked okay. I felt okay, too. In fact, except for the gnarly bump on the back of my head and the feeling I'd been whacked in the trunk with a Louisville Slugger, I felt pretty damn good.

I looked over at the passenger seat, where Cosmo was sitting quietly inside his cat carrier and watching me carefully. I whispered, "Moses Cosmo Thornwall, considering everything, you look pretty damn good, too."

He squinted his eyes and said, *"Mrow,"* which I took to mean, "I love you too, but get me out of this stupid box, you foolish woman."

I figured I'd take Cosmo to Dr. Layton

396

for a checkup in the morning. For now, he could stay with me and get a good night's rest. I just hoped Ella Fitzgerald wouldn't be too horrified to have him sleep over. Then, just as I predicted, the phone rang.

McKenzie barely waited for me to say hello. "I just received a report that we had a call earlier tonight from the butcher. He said he heard a pop and then saw a car speed out of the alley. He wasn't sure, but he thought it might have been a gunshot."

I said, "Yeah, that was Mr. Silverthorn."

There was a pause. "Dixie, would you care to expound on that statement?"

"Oh, sorry. Yeah, he shot me . . . but it was dark and he was shaking. He missed."

"And you're just telling me this now?"

"I wanted you to get to Mr. Vladim before he did."

She sighed. "Well, you were right. We arrested Silverthorn in the lobby of the hospital in a white dress, a gray wig, and full makeup. He had a pistol hidden under his arm."

I said, "He was going to kill Mr. Vladim. He knew what Silverthorn had planned. And that nude drawing I found? It was Mrs. Silverthorn. I'm not sure if it's true or not, but he took it to mean she'd had an affair with Mr. Hoskins."

There was a pause. "Dixie, I'm afraid I owe you an apology. You may have been wrong about poison being involved, but you were certainly right about a connection to the Silverthorns."

I said, "Yeah, well . . ." but I stopped myself. I knew if I told her I had four chocolate-covered rosary peas in my pocket she'd be banging on my front door in two seconds flat.

She said, "So the old woman in the video, it was Mr. Silverthorn. He hid in the back and then killed Mr. Hoskins after you left."

I sighed. "No, the man in the store, the man who sold me the book . . . wasn't Mr. Hoskins."

I could almost hear her mind shifting into gear over the phone. She said, "Dixie, I need you to come down to the station. *Now.*"

I thought for a moment. I imagined myself walking into that station again after all these years. I imagined passing through its double glass doors, letting them close behind me with a whispered sweep, walking down the linoleum-floored hallway, the walls lined on either side with framed portraits, color photographs of the head brass and department heroes, and stopping at the front desk to check in . . . a walk of less than twenty feet, a walk that I'd made so many times before, and yet had seemed so impossible for so long.

I said, "Detective, it's late, and I've had a long day. I was in the middle of something important when Silverthorn called me tonight. I'd like to get back to that."

She was quiet for a moment. "Alright. Where would you like to meet?"

I said, "How's nine o'clock at your office?"

There was a pause, and then she said, "Excellent. Are you sure you're okay?"

"I'm fine. Thanks."

"Dixie, I believe it's me who should be saying thanks."

I felt my cheeks turn warm. Whenever I talked to McKenzie, I always had this nagging suspicion that she wondered how in the world I'd managed to become a sheriff's deputy in the first place — that I was just some silly blonde with an overactive imagination. It felt good to know that maybe, just maybe, I was a silly blonde with an overactive imagination that she respected. I pictured a press conference where she thanked me for solving the case, and then the mayor stepped in to present me with the key to the city . . .

She interrupted, "But Dixie, there's one more thing. I'm afraid you may have to testify on this one. Mr. Silverthorn seems to have known what he was doing. There's no sign of him in the bookstore, and without hard evidence that places him at the scene of the crime, I'm afraid it will be your word against his."

I nodded quietly to myself, and then the image of Mr. Hoskins appeared in my head, or, I should say, the man I *thought* was Mr. Hoskins — that sweet, bumbling old man I had instantly liked, the man who had reminded me so much of Mr. Beezy, my old childhood friend, when life was simple and the world was such an innocent place.

I could see Mr. Hoskins's red beret, his funny yellow suspenders and red shirt, and I remembered pointing to his chest and saying, "You forgot a couple of buttons."

McKenzie said, "Dixie, are you there?"

"I'm here."

"Was there something else?"

I said, "Yeah. Those brass buttons on Mr. Hoskins's shirt? You should check them for fingerprints. I think you'll find they match Mr. Silverthorn's."

After we hung up, I tiptoed across the yard and up the steps, carrying Cosmo with me and preparing the story I'd tell Ethan when I got inside, but he wasn't there. I took a couple of bowls down out of the cabinet and filled one of them with some of Ella's kibble — I didn't think she'd mind too much — and then I filled the other bowl with fresh water from the tap. Cosmo didn't seem too interested, though. He was already thoroughly exploring every inch of the apartment, so I left him to get acquainted with his temporary lodgings and went back downstairs.

Michael and Paco were still wrapped in each other's arms and sound asleep in one of the chaise lounges. Sprawled out in the next lounge over was Ethan, perfectly still, his dark, curly hair falling partly across his face and the top button of his pants undone — something he does when he's eaten too much.

I smiled. There was an empty plate on the deck under his chair with some crumbs of key lime pie, and he was holding one arm over his chest, his fingers splayed delicately across his throat, as if to say, "Why, I do declare!"

Luckily for everyone, there were still a couple of slices of pie left on the table. I took one and sat down quietly next to Ethan. I took a bite. It felt like pure, unadulterated joy on my tongue. Like God was petting me.

Ethan stirred and looked up at me with

squinted eyes. "Hey, babe. How'd it go?"

I whispered, "Fine. We found Cosmo. He's gonna spend the night with us."

He said, "Nice job," and then ran his hand up and caressed the back of my head. I felt a jab of pain from the bump there and pulled away.

"Watch the hair! It took me half an hour to get it to look this gorgeous."

He curled tighter around me and smiled sleepily as he laid his head in my lap. "Wow. You are such a girl."

I gazed down at the ocean and watched the moonlight bounce and glitter on the waves as they rolled silently up on the beach. I should probably have been sleepy, too — my body felt like it had been hit by a runaway train, and the bump on the back of my head was pounding away as if it had its own pulse, but I didn't feel the least bit tired. I was wide-awake.

"And also . . . we found out who murdered Mr. Hoskins."

I looked down so I could watch Ethan's reaction, but his eyes were closed and his lips were slightly parted. I could hear his breathing, slow and steady, and every once in a while his eyelids flickered slightly. Michael and Paco were still fast asleep; with their legs and arms all intertwined, it was impossible to tell whose was whose.

I whispered, a little louder now, "Yeah, it was Mr. Silverthorn."

No one stirred.

"He found a naked drawing of Mrs. Silverthorn, and guess who the artist was?"

Michael snorted softly.

"That's right, you guessed it. Mr. Hoskins. Silverthorn decided they'd had an affair, so he made some poisoned chocolates and told his footman he had to plant them or he'd turn him in for robbing banks."

I took a bite of pie and glanced over at Paco. "Yep, his footman was Mr. Vladim, and Silverthorn planned on framing him for the murder, so he dressed up like an old lady and followed Vladim to the bookstore to make sure he did as he was told."

Suddenly there was a quiet *"thrrreeep!"* and Ella Fitzgerald hopped up and gazed longingly into my eyes, purring like an electric razor.

"You heard me, an old lady! But Vladim didn't do what he was told. Instead he crashed into a truck — that's where I came in — so Silverthorn went to the bookstore and knocked Mr. Hoskins out and dressed up in his clothes and sold me that book and then dragged Mr. Hoskins into a crawl space and shot him and then snuck out the back door."

I covered Ella's ears for that last part and then looked around. "Am I going too fast?"

Ethan said, "Unhh."

"Oh, and Mrs. Silverthorn's maid is Vladim's wife. She's the other bank robber they're looking for. Except I'm the only one that knows that. And I'm going over there in the morning to convince her to turn herself in. Either that or tell her to run away. I'm not sure I want to see her go to prison, but I know that would make me an accomplice to a felon. And I've been walking around all week with deadly chocolates in my bag."

Ella yawned.

"Oh, and I almost forgot, Mr. Silverthorn shot me in the alley tonight."

I took one last bite of pie and then raised my fork in the air with a flourish. "But he missed!"

I looked around. Nobody said a word. Ella stretched herself into her best scary-cat pose and then curled up in the nook of Ethan's arm. The rest of them just lay there, snoring quietly.

And that was it. Nobody launched into a lecture about how I'm always getting myself in trouble and how I should be more careful, how I should've known better than to snoop around that bookstore late at night, how I should let the sheriff's department do their job and mind my own business and *blah blah blah* . . .

I figured I could always fill them in on the details later . . . maybe. For now I just wanted to enjoy the moment, the gentle hush of the waves rolling in, the palm trees and pines swaying gently in the breeze, the night-blooming cereus twining overhead and filling the air with its sweet scent, and all my favorite men and furry beasts and Michael's world-class key lime pie.

There was one last piece sitting on the pie plate all by its lonesome in the middle of the table. I stretched my arm out as far as I could, but it was too far away, and with Ethan's head on my lap and Ella curled between us I knew if I got up I'd wake them all and spoil the moment. So instead I just sat there.

My gardening book was at the opposite end of the table, opened halfway and lying facedown at Michael's spot. There was a scratch pad next to it where he had scribbled a couple of notes. Hopefully, with Silverthorn's fingerprints on Mr. Hoskins's buttons, McKenzie wouldn't need the book as evidence. That way Michael could keep it.

As for the chapter on poisonous plants, I

figured maybe I'd keep that for myself — it had definitely turned out to be a pretty good reference tool for solving a mystery — and you never know when something like that might come in handy.

ABOUT THE AUTHORS

John Clement is the son of **Blaize Clement** (1932–2011), who originated the Dixie Hemingway mystery series and collaborated with her son on the plots and characters for forthcoming novels. Blaize is the author of *Curiosity Killed the Cat Sitter, Duplicity Dogged the Dachshund, Even Cat Sitters Get the Blues, Cat Sitter on a Hot Tin Roof, Raining Cat Sitters and Dogs, Cat Sitter Among the Pigeons, The Cat Sitter's Pajamas,* and *The Cat Sitter's Cradle.*

Visit their Web site at
www.DixieHemingway.com.